THE COWBOY'S SURPRISE BABY

MELISSA SENATE

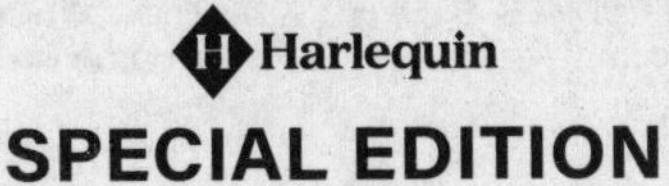

Harlequin
SPECIAL EDITION

PLEASE RECYCLE
THIS PRODUCT IS RECYCLABLE

Recycling programs for this product may not exist in your area.

ISBN-13: 978-1-335-47269-4

The Cowboy's Surprise Baby

For questions and comments about the quality of this book, please contact us at CustomerService@Harlequin.com.

Harlequin Enterprises ULC
22 Adelaide St. West, 41st Floor
Toronto, Ontario M5H 4E3, Canada
www.Harlequin.com

HarperCollins Publishers
Macken House, 39/40 Mayor Street Upper,
Dublin 1, D01 C9W8, Ireland
www.HarperCollins.com

Printed in Lithuania

1 2 3 4 5 6 7 8 9 10 LIT 28 27 26 25

She opened the door, expecting to see her friend, but a man stood there. There was something strangely familiar about him.

“Sarah Dawson?” he asked, tipping his hat.

“That’s me,” she said.

“I’m wondering if you know a Will Riley,” he said, his gaze intent on her.

She couldn’t help it—the gasp escaped her. “I do. Well, sort of. I met him a year ago after a rodeo in town.”

The guy was eyeing her as if trying to figure something out. “This is the Will Riley you met?” he asked, holding up his phone with a photo.

Her hand flew to her mouth as a wave of emotions hit her. She stared at the photo on the little screen.

“That’s him,” she said, her chin lifted. She narrowed her gaze at the man on her doorstep. Maybe the reason he looked kind of familiar was because he was related to Will. They had the same blue eyes now that she looked more closely.

Cody’s eyes.

Dear Reader,

When cowboy Boone Riley finds his late brother's To-Do list, he's determined to complete it. He's particularly curious about #3 on the list: *Apologize to Sarah Dawson at the Dawson Family Guest Ranch*. He knocks on Sarah's door only to meet a woman holding a baby—with the unmistakable Riley blue eyes.

Boone vows to help raise the surprise baby nephew he didn't know existed. But Boone comes from a long line of cowboys who couldn't commit to people or places. Yet the slow-burn attraction between them is undeniable. Can Sarah dare to trust her heart again?

I hope you enjoy Sarah and Boone's story, part of my long-running Dawson Family Ranch series (which can be read in any order). I love to hear from readers. You can reach me at MelissaSenate@yahoo.com or on all social media platforms.

Warmest regards,

Melissa Senate

Melissa Senate has written many novels for Harlequin and other publishers, including her debut, *See Jane Date*, which was made into a TV movie. She also wrote seven books for Harlequin Special Edition under the pen name Meg Maxwell. Her novels have been published in over twenty-five countries. Melissa lives on the coast of Maine with her son and their rescue shepherd mix, Flash.

Books by Melissa Senate

Harlequin Special Edition

Dawson Family Ranch

For the Twins' Sake
Wyoming Special Delivery
A Family for a Week
The Long-Awaited Christmas Wish
Wyoming Cinderella
Wyoming Matchmaker
His Baby No Matter What
Heir to the Ranch
Santa's Twin Surprise
The Cowboy's Mistaken Identity
Seven Birthday Wishes
Snowbound with a Baby
Triplets Under the Tree
The Rancher Hits the Road
The Cowboy's Christmas Redemption
The Rancher's Surprise Deal
The Baby's Christmas Ranch
The Cowboy's Surprise Baby

Visit the Author Profile page
at Harlequin.com for more titles.

In loving memory of my mother and grandmother.

Chapter One

As Boone Riley went through his half brother's apartment, he found himself close to tears one second, then smiling with nostalgia the next. Everything in the small one-bedroom, from the Cheyenne Rodeo poster above the sofa to the closet full of Western-style button-downs to the refrigerator containing five kinds of hot sauce and not much else, reminded him of Will. The brother he barely knew, barely understood. Now Will was gone.

They'd been working on their relationship—or Boone had. He'd been trying to get closer to Will, four years older, his entire life, but the guy had always been a lone wolf. For the past few years since Boone lost his mother, he had only two relatives left: his Uncle Angus and Will. Despite the fact that he rarely saw Will, it meant something that his brother had been out there, albeit raising hell, breaking hearts, and disappointing people. That Will Riley wasn't alive and well on this earth had hit Boone hard. The guy had had his faults, but he'd had his good points too. Like just a week ago, the last time they'd spoken, and Will had said yes to a road trip to see their uncle since Angus's girlfriend had broken up with him and he was down in the dumps. Boone had been looking forward to it—an hour's drive to catch up with Will, some family time with the Riley men.

Now…

Early this morning, Boone had been mucking out a stall in the stables at the ranch where he was a cowboy when his cell phone rang. He'd ignored the unfamiliar number—then gotten knocked upside the head at the voicemail message. The Darlington, Wyoming, sheriff's office. Will had been fatally injured while attempting a daredevil stunt on a dirt bike at midnight. In his jacket pocket was a small flask full of whiskey, his wallet, and keys. Will's landlord had provided the sheriff's office with the name he'd put down as emergency contact on his apartment lease: Boone.

He'd let his boss know what happened, was assured he should take the next few days off, and he'd driven the half hour out to Will's apartment above a hardware store. The landlord met him at the door. Will was two months behind on rent and had apparently gotten fired from his cowboy job at a nearby ranch. Boone had sighed hard around the lump in his throat and promised the man he'd settle up what Will owed him and would clear out the apartment. That had gotten him the key.

Boone dropped down on the edge of Will's bed, his head feeling hollow, his chest raw. As a kid, he'd always been awed by his older and fearless half brother who wouldn't give him the time of day. But the older Boone got, the more he realized that Will had been more reckless than fearless. He just didn't seem to care about anything or anyone, except having his needs met, whatever they were. Will was a good-looking guy, tall and muscular, and he always had pretty women on his arm, none he'd ever committed to. Boone only knew this because he'd insisted on seeing Will every couple of months and twice in the past year when they'd been out together in town, a woman had marched up to Will and yelled at him about how it was his loss. *Probably is*, Will had said at the most recent incident without sarcasm or a smirk.

Boone had always believed his brother had a decent heart but that it would take falling hard in love to finally change his way of living. Their uncle was sure of that, which had surprised Boone given that Angus, like all the Riley men, wasn't exactly a romantic who wore his heart on his sleeve.

Boone got up and went into the kitchen, opening up the cabinet under the sink and hoping he'd find some trash bags. There were two left. Given the size of the place and the lack of stuff, one would cover what needed to be tossed and the other for a donate bag for clothes. The landlord had told him the apartment had come furnished except for kitchen stuff and he could leave any personal items a new tenant might want, like dishes and pots. There was pretty much two of everything—two plates, two forks. He was glad he wouldn't have to deal with getting rid of the love seat and bed and the kitchen table and chairs. He'd clear out the junk, sweep up, pay the landlord, and be on his way with whatever mementos that felt special, that felt like Will. The rodeo poster. A wood figurine of a horse rearing up. The paperback thriller on the bedside table.

Then he'd stop at the sheriff's office for Will's wallet and accompany him to the morgue to ID his brother, which he'd been trying not to think about. He'd call Uncle Angus, and they'd make arrangements based on what

Will had once said in a morbid conversation—he wanted his ashes scattered in the river where he liked to fish as a kid, just Boone and their uncle raising a flask. If Will had friends or was seeing anyone who he should call, Boone didn't know. Will tended to alienate people and burned bridges.

Boone had no doubt he'd break down once he was back home in his cabin and would have to phone Angus with the news. Their uncle had needed a pick-me-up, and this loss would hurt hard. But Angus would immediately drive down and at least they'd be together, have each other.

After cleaning up and filling the trash bag, Boone headed to his pickup for a cardboard box he had in the bed. Back in the apartment, he removed the rodeo poster and rolled it up, then moved into the bedroom and cleared the closet and dresser. Into the box went a belt with Will's favorite buckle, plus the figurine and book. Under the paperback on the bedside table was a piece of paper face down, a pen beside it. Boone picked it up.

STUFF TO DO was scrawled in blue ink across the top of the page.

1. *Do better with Boone*
2. *Apologize to Uncle Angus*
3. *Apologize to Sarah Dawson—works at Dawson Family Guest Ranch*
4. *Pay back Eli Charlson the 50 bucks—with interest if can swing it*
5. *Apologize to Jennifer Parkalini*
6. *Settle up your bar tabs at Drink Up and McDeedles*
7. *Do better, period*

* * *

Number one poked at his heart. So did number seven.

Boone stared at the list, wondering what the apology to their uncle was about. Angus hadn't mentioned any words or rifts. Whatever it was, it would come up today, and surely the notation would make Angus feel better about whatever happened between them.

The names Sarah Dawson and Jennifer Parkalini were unfamiliar. If Will felt the need to apologize to the two women, to actually put their names on a list, he must have done some damage. Broken hearts? Ghosted them?

Boone would pay back Eli Charlson, whoever he was, and settle up the bar tabs.

He dropped back down on the edge of bed, staring at the words, at Will's scrawled handwriting. *Do better with Boone. Do better, period.*

His chest ached, and a lump formed in his throat. *Dammit, Will.*

His brother had been trying, and that was everything.

As Boone sat there, rereading the list, he made a decision.

He was going to take care of items two through six. Will's final wishes were laid out right here, and number seven—*Do better, period*—was proof that his brother would want Boone to fulfill them. Maybe it would help fill the holes deep inside. The one that had always been there where Will had been concerned. And the one left by his loss.

Number two, the apology owed their uncle, he'd take on this afternoon.

Then he'd track down Sarah Dawson. Hopefully he wouldn't get slapped across the face in proxy for whatever his brother had done to merit an *I'm sorry* from the person least likely to ever say those words.

Sarah Dawson pressed a kiss to her fingertip and touched it to the forehead of her baby son, who'd finally closed his eyes and stopped fighting his late-morning nap. Cody had been squawking his head off just two minutes ago, overtired but not wanting to be out of his mama's arms. Now he looked so serene and peaceful, a hand flung up by ear, his little chest rising and falling in his pj's imprinted all over with little cowboys. "Love you, sweet boy," she whispered, then left the small second bedroom she'd turned into a nursery.

She had a good hour and a half before Cody would awaken, and though she could use a nap herself since he'd been up twice during the night, she had few things to take care of. A basketful of clean laundry to fold and another wash to start, the dishwasher to unload, and two matchmaking concerns.

Somehow Sarah had become an unofficial matchmaker for the Dawson Family Guest Ranch staff and anyone in town who could use a little help finding a partner. It started a couple of years ago, when she'd fixed up a few coworker friends, from fellow cowgirls to ranch hands to a cook in the cafeteria, and word had spread that she had a knack for pairing people up. She'd even fixed up the widowed owner of the feed store she lived beside, and now he and his new love were engaged. Unfortunately that meant her landlord had even *less* time to make the few necessary repairs in her apartment. Introducing him to his future wife didn't seem to earn her any bonus points when it came to fixing squeaky door hinges or her wonky air conditioner these warm June days.

She grabbed the load of laundry and lugged it over to the washer and dryer stacked in a utility closet, thinking about how her skills in matchmaking didn't apply to herself and never had. She'd always been a believer in giving people a chance, and she tended to overlook flaws and focus on good points. In her last two relationships, those flaws—yellow flags, nothing major—had taken over, though. Cody's sweet little face floated into her mind, settling her heart whenever she thought about her love life. She couldn't even label Cody's father a "relationship" since he'd disappeared from her bed the minute she'd fallen asleep after he'd gotten what he wanted. She hadn't pegged him for a one-night stand. Not for a second. In fact, she'd been so swept up by their chemistry, her attraction to him that she'd thrown the ole caution to the wind. That he'd slipped away and hadn't called or texted the next day—or ever—had hurt bad.

They'd exchanged numbers when they'd still been flirting at the bar they'd met at after a rodeo. She'd used that number six weeks later when she found out she was pregnant—and had been stung to learn it was phony. An online search of Will Riley hadn't gotten her anywhere. He'd said he was a cowboy at a ranch an hour away, but she had no idea which town, which direction, or where to start. She'd tried anyway, calling around with stupid hope in her heart, but she hadn't tracked him down.

Sarah hadn't been interested in finding him for herself. Cody was the reason she'd been so determined. *You're someone's father, you thoughtless user*, she'd mentally yell into the ether even now after all these months.

He was out there somewhere, no idea about the little guy in the bassinet down the hall. Cody deserved to know his dad—and his paternal family. Sarah had lost her mother as a teenager, and her father had died from an illness just weeks after Cody's birth. She was the only child of only children. And so it was just her and Cody.

Sarah sighed with a hard edge as she always did when thinking about all that and went into the kitchen to make a pot of coffee before starting the wash, overflowing with onesies and pj's. She'd just flipped the On switch to Mr. Coffee when the doorbell rang. She frowned, hoping the sound wouldn't wake Cody, who was a light sleeper. She waited a beat—silence. Good.

She went to the door, figuring it was her friend Annie, a fellow cowgirl at the guest ranch. Sarah had been on maternity leave the past three months, but that was coming to an end in just two weeks on the last day of June. Annie stopped by every day with ranch gossip and to see how she could help, whether with folding laundry or washing baby bottles, and Sarah was so grateful for her. Like the sister or cousin she'd never had.

She opened the door expecting to see her friend, but a man stood there. She'd never seen him before, but there was something strangely familiar about him. He was in his late twenties, with dark hair and blue eyes. Good looking. Tall and muscular like a cowboy—and he did wear a cowboy hat.

"Sarah Dawson?" he asked, tipping the hat. "You work at the Dawson Family Guest Ranch here in Bear Ridge?"

"That's me," she said, wondering who he was. Ah—maybe he'd heard about her matchmaking skills and was here to ask about getting paired up. Sarah liked to conduct her "intake" interviews in person and take notes rather than ask people to fill out forms. She could tell a lot in five minutes with someone, let alone a solid half-hour interview.

"I'm wondering if you know a Will Riley—from Darlington," he said, his gaze intent on her.

She couldn't help it—the gasp escaped her. She'd just been thinking of Will. She didn't know he was from Darlington, which was about a half hour north. "I do. Well, sort of. I met him a year ago after a rodeo in town. But we just—" She bit her lip. "I haven't him seen or heard from him since." She cleared her throat, unsettled by the sudden question and the jumble of words coming out of her mouth.

The guy was eyeing her as if trying to figure something out. "This is the Will Riley you met?" he asked, holding up his phone with a photo.

Her hand flew to her mouth as a wave of emotions hit her. She stared at the photo on the little screen. At the handsome cowboy she'd met at the bar while Annie had been dancing with her boyfriend. The man Sarah had slept with on the first date—heck, first meeting—something she never did. Their amazing night together—romantic, fun, life stories swapped. His parents were long gone. He had a half brother who was always trying to make them closer as a family when Will was ambivalent about that out of long-held spite toward their father. She'd been rapt as he'd told her all that at the bar, mistaking—like a fool—his opening up for something else, like depth or a real interest in her. He'd wanted or needed to talk—and then expend some *physical* energy—and had. Then he was gone, his needs fulfilled. End of story. Old as time.

"That's him," she said, her chin lifted. She narrowed her gaze at the man on her doorstep. Maybe the reason he looked kind of familiar was because he was related to Will—the half brother. They had the same blue eyes now that she looked more closely.

Cody's eyes.

"Why do you ask?" she said, crossing her arms over her chest. What on earth could he be here for?

The guy took off his hat and held it against his chest, something coming over his expression that told her immediately that Will Riley was dead.

She sucked in a breath.

"My name is Boone Riley," he said. "Will was my brother. I'm sorry to tell you that he died—just a week ago. Dirt-bike accident," he added.

"Oh no," she whispered, tears pooling in her eyes, her throat tightening along with her chest. Her son's face filled her mind. He'd never know his father. The hope she'd had that one day she'd find Will, that she could connect father and son was gone. She glanced up into sorrow-filled blue eyes, her heart going out to the stranger on her doorstep. "I'm so sorry," she said. "I don't have any siblings, but I can imagine the pain of losing a brother."

He gave something of a nod.

"Come in," she said. "I just made a pot of coffee."

"I could use a cup."

Okay, she thought. She'd pour them coffee, and she'd have a moment to digest what she'd just heard. Then she'd tell him about Cody. The baby nephew he didn't know about.

That would be a blessing for Boone Riley. An unexpected tie to the brother he'd lost.

And Cody now had an uncle. And surely more family.

Boone stepped in, hanging his hat on one of the hooks by the door. He followed her into the narrow kitchen, which had a small round table by the window. She gestured for him to sit down.

As she filled two mugs and rooted in the fridge for the cream, she suddenly froze, realizing how odd it was that Boone had come with the news in the first place. If she'd meant enough to Will for him to tell his brother about her, he wouldn't have given her a phony telephone number. So why was Boone here? How had he known about her? And what would make his grieving brother pay a personal visit to her to deliver the news?

First things first. "I'd like to see some ID," she said. "So I can be sure you are who you say you are."

"Of course," he said, pulling out his wallet. He handed over his driver's license. Boone Riley. He looked a lot like Will, even in the little photo.

She nodded and handed it back.

As she brought over the coffee, Boone was taking something from the pocket of his shirt. A folded piece of paper. He set it down beside the mug, adding a sugar packet and stirring. She watched him take a sip, then another. He unfolded the paper. Some kind of list, from what she could see.

"When I was clearing out Will's apartment," he said, "I found this list on his bedside table. He flashed it at her, long enough for her to see the heading *Stuff To Do*. Number one is *Do better with Boone*, which really got me. We were never close, despite all my trying. Number three is to apologize to you. That's why I'm here."

Sarah blinked. She found her gaze narrowing again. "I'd rather he'd have gotten in touch with me than put me on some apology list." She shook her head and looked at Boone. "Sorry. I'm being unkind, and I certainly don't mean to be. I'm just surprised."

He nodded, seeming to give her a moment.

Sarah let out a hard sigh. "I had something important to tell him, but I couldn't track him down. I tried—hard."

"Maybe he figured as much and that's why you were on the list?" Boone asked. "There were only three people to apologize to. The others were about paying back money and being a better person."

A better person. That was something, at least. As was knowing she *had* stayed on Will's mind to the point that he'd added her name to the people to apologize to. She was long past caring for herself, but she liked that for Cody.

"He couldn't have known I was—" She stopped, thinking about that night with Will Riley, the sexy smile, the chestnut-colored curly mop, the blue eyes so like Boone's. And Cody's. She started asking herself the same question she had since the night she'd met Will. Had he known the condom had broken—which had to have been the case since they'd used one and she'd gotten pregnant anyway? Was that why he'd slipped away the moment he could? Maybe.

But he'd given her the fake number before they'd even tipsily kissed their way into her bed that beautiful late May night. Either way, he'd never intended to see her again.

Boone sipped his coffee, then set down the mug. “I don’t know what Will did that warranted an apology and it must be weird to get it secondhand, but I hope it helps.”

Sarah stared at him for a moment. “It does.”

“Waah! Waah!” Cody’s cries from the nursery were sharp. Sounded like some sudden gas pains to Sarah.

Boone startled, his eyes widening. He seemed about to say something, but Sarah had already popped up.

“Back in a second,” she said. “There’s someone you’ll want to meet. And he just woke up early from his nap.”

Chapter Two

Surprised, Boone watched Sarah Dawson hurry down a short hallway and through a doorway. A couple of fussy cries came from the room.

"Who woke up early and all cranky from his nap?" he heard her saying.

Sarah had a baby?

She came back into the kitchen holding an infant against her chest and rubbing his back. Or at least Boone assumed it was a "he" due to the blue cowboy pj's, which he thought were very cute.

"I hope I didn't wake him up," he said.

Sarah leaned against the counter, rocking the baby a bit. "Nah. He's a light sleeper, and if the doorbell didn't wake him up, our voices definitely didn't. I think he just had a little tummy ache, but it looks like it settled once I got him vertical." She gave the baby's head, topped with fine blond hair, a kiss. "Isn't that right, sweetums?" she cooed, her gaze soft on the infant.

Boone was transfixed for a second. Love *emanated* from her. He hadn't spent much time—any time, really—around mothers and babies. The look on her face was something to behold.

Confused, Boone stared at the two of them. Will had

been dating a single mother of a baby? And it hadn't worked out for whatever reason? Likely the fact that she was a mother in the first place. Boone couldn't imagine his brother being interested in a woman with a child. Will had flat out said he'd never date a woman with a kid. His brother wasn't one to even acknowledge babies or children were in the same air space. The last time Boone had gotten together with Will, they'd stopped in a coffee shop and there was a mom holding a toddler in front of them. The kiddo was facing them and staring at Will as though his face were fascinating. Boone had been all smiles at the little girl, playing a round of peekaboo. Will didn't pay a lick of attention to the kid, his eyes glazing over that he was subjected to a child in the first place.

But wait—Sarah had mentioned she met Will last year, and given that the baby she held was at most three or four months old, the timing didn't add up for her to have been a mom then.

Whatever Will was apologizing for, it likely had nothing to do with the baby.

"Boone Riley," she said, "meet your nephew, Cody Dawson." She turned slightly so that he could see the baby's face.

His mouth dropped open. For a second he was stunned speechless, frozen in his chair.

Nephew. *What?*

He bolted up, staring at the baby as understanding began to dawn. "My nephew? You're saying—" He looked from the tiny face to Sarah. "This is *Will's baby*?"

She held his gaze and nodded. He looked back to the infant. Suddenly he could see Will's eyes—heck, his own eyes. He stepped back for a moment, then took two steps closer, his heart racing, his collar feeling tight suddenly.

"Will has a child?" he asked—stupidly. *Get it together, man. Your brother had a baby. She just said so.*

"Yes. He's three months old. Came right on his due date too. I'll tell you, I appreciate predictability."

Boone was dumbfounded. "I didn't know," he said, shaking his head slightly, trying to let the news penetrate.

"Will didn't either. Like I said earlier, there was something important I had to tell him but I couldn't track him down. I tried."

There was a story there for sure, but right now, he was totally focused on the baby. He couldn't take his eyes off him. Will's son. Boone's *nephew.* He could hardly believe this was real. He took in the little face, the sort-of scowl, the sleepy eyes. Boone had the sense that the baby was content for the moment but one wrong move and the kiddo would start screeching.

My nephew, he thought. *I have a nephew.*

As some of the shock was wearing off, something just as strong was replacing it. A feeling of actual happiness. Just days ago, when he and his uncle had been scattering Will's ashes in the Darlington River, Boone had held it together until Angus had said, voice cracking, *Just us now.*

But there was a baby, another Riley. His brother's *true* legacy.

"My God," Boone whispered, his gaze on the tiny child. "This is something."

"I'm glad you're having this reaction," Sarah said. "Cody could use more family. It's just me and this little guy. My parents are gone, and I have no other relatives left."

Very little family. Another thing they had in common. She'd gone through so much on her own. The pregnancy, for one. The birth without her own mother—let alone the baby's father. Taking care of a newborn. The past few months couldn't have been easy.

She gently caressed the infant's cheek. "I was so heavy-hearted about not being able to connect Cody with his paternal side. And now here you are." Her expression brightened. She looked so hopeful and happy all of a sudden.

"Cody," he repeated, the name finally registering in his overworked brain. He felt a smile coming. "Will would have liked that name."

She gave him something of a smile, as if touched to know that. "My dad's name was Christopher. That's where I got the *C* from."

Boone almost gasped. "My dad's name was Cal."

"Huh," she said, her eyes suddenly misting. "That's nice, then. Both grandpas represented."

He reached out his pointer finger toward the baby's face, then paused. "Can I touch him?"

"Sure," she said. "You can hold him if you want."

He gnawed his lip for a second, his heart beating fast again, an adrenaline rush mixed with worry—what if he dropped Cody? The urge to hold his nephew was too strong, though. This was his kin, his blood, his brother's son. "You'll have to show me. I've never held a baby before. None of my friends have kids yet."

"It's pretty natural once you have hold of him," she said, and he appreciated the assurance in her voice. "Just make sure his head, bottom and back are supported." She transferred him into Boone's awkwardly outstretched hands.

Goose bumps lit up both arms as he cradled his nephew carefully against his chest and looked down at him. Cody seemed content, the scowl softening. "He likes me," Boone said, hearing the wonder in his voice. He looked up at Sarah, who was smiling.

"Of course he does—you're Uncle Boone."

Uncle Boone. Again, that feeling of happiness spread through his chest. A bit more comfortable now with this precious little weight in his arms, he slightly rocked his arms the way Sarah had earlier, humming a bit of a song his mother used to sing him as a kid.

"Let's go sit on the sofa," she said. "Maybe he'll fall back asleep. He barely got his nap."

Boone followed her into the small living room and carefully sat down, so aware of the baby, whose eyes were definitely drooping. Cody was so cute. Boone could sit here for hours, just holding him. He watched the baby fighting sleep until the eyes closed and stayed shut. "Aww," Boone whispered.

"I can take him," Sarah said, getting up. "Sometimes he transfers easily to his bassinet."

He wasn't ready to hand him over. "I'll hold him—if that's okay."

"Of course," Sarah said. "I couldn't be happier that you're clearly a doting uncle. It's what I always wanted for Cody. *Family.*"

"He's got me now and my Uncle Angus. He lives up in Clover, about an hour away. My dad's brother."

"I remember Will mentioning his uncle. Addicted to cheeseburgers, particularly with hot sauce."

Boone's gaze shot up at Sarah. "Will told you that?" Suddenly he wondered about their relationship, clearly very short-lived. His brother had never been one to easily open up to people.

She nodded. "He said he only had two relatives left and that he shouldn't take them for granted but he was bad at that."

Huh. Will *had* opened up to this woman. That shouldn't be too surprising, given that she'd made his list. "Yeah, he was. That's why the list meant so much to me. That he was trying. That he wanted us to get closer—or at least that's how I read it. That he wanted to pay back people who lent him money. The apologies."

Sarah winced. "Well, I guess I know why I was on the list. He really blindsided me. I thought we had this amazing chemistry—sharing our life stories, really talking. You meet someone, and it's immediately like all those love songs. And then…he just up and left in the middle of the night."

That was typical Will Riley. Between the angry women marching up to Will and the stories he himself told Boone, his brother had been a serial leaver. *Even when I really fell for someone in the moment, I don't know... I'd just wake up and have to get the hell out of there, and then I'd forget all about them.*

Boone had never been able to commit either, but he thought that was more about not falling in love, not finding his person yet. He wasn't really sure. His dad had affairs, his three marriages lasting barely five years each. It had seemed clear Will had taken after their father, but

Boone had always worried he did too, even if slightly. He couldn't imagine treating someone he'd found special, treating *anyone*, the way his father and Will had. Uncle Angus had remained a bachelor till his early thirties, finally succumbing to an ultimatum. But even he was divorced now.

The noncommittal gene was strong in the Riley men.

One thing was for sure, though. Will *hadn't* forgotten about Sarah Dawson—clearly.

Her expression turned a bit stony. "We'd exchanged numbers at the bar where we met. He'd said, 'Gimme me your number in case I have too many beers and forget to ask later.' I thought, *Wow, I'll definitely be seeing him again*. But it must have been a ploy to earn my trust. Because the number he gave me was phony. Turned out to be for Sure-Wheels Rent-a-Car. At first I thought maybe he worked there as a side hustle since he'd said he was a cowboy. But they didn't have a Will Riley on staff. I even called back a second time to make sure."

Huh. That was crappy of Will. And just like him, unfortunately. Boone had passed the car rental place on the highway in and out of Darlington, the easy-to-remember number in blinking neon.

His brother was gone, and Boone hated focusing on the bad. He looked down at the baby—the legacy that mattered. Cody. Definitely a cowboy's name. There were dirtbag cowboys—and Boone would not consider his brother one of those. And then there were those who tried to live by the code of the west—like Boone. Like his uncle, even though he'd been in law enforcement at the sheriff's office, not ranching. Cody would be one of the good guys; Boone would work hard to make sure of it. From what Sarah had said, she'd welcome having him and Angus in Cody's life. Boone intended to be a big part.

"Do you think that's what Will wanted to apologize for?" Boone asked. "Leaving the way he did?"

Boone had no doubt his brother had done that countless times. But there were only two women on the list. He frowned—and swallowed. When it came time to pay Jennifer Parkalini a visit about her name being on the list, would he discover another baby? A similar story? He'd been planning on taking care of the list in order, but maybe he'd better go see Ms. Parkalini sooner than later. He'd asked his uncle if any of the names were familiar to him, but Angus had shaken his head and said Will hadn't talked much about his life. They'd kept the conversation to the rodeo, cars, and Wyoming in general.

"I guess," she said. "I barely knew him, though. What do you think?"

"I can't be sure," he said, "but my gut tells me you made an impact on him and he thought you deserved better than that."

She gave him something of a smile. "Well, that's nice of you to say. All I know for *absolutely* sure is that he gave me the best gift of my life. Cody is the greatest thing that's ever happened to me."

Once again, her eyes were soft on the baby in his arms. He could see, and hear in her voice, just how much she meant those words.

"On the list," Boone said, "Will had written that you work at the Dawson Family Guest Ranch. You're the owner?" Probably not, he realized, or she'd live on-site and certainly not in this tiny apartment beside a feed store. He'd never been to the guest ranch, but he'd heard it attracted visitors from all over the country.

"Ha, I wish," she said. "Second cousins own it—six siblings. I've worked there since high school. I'm a cowgirl. I lead a lot of the horseback riding tours and help out in the stables. I've been on maternity leave the past two and a half months, but that ends in a couple weeks."

"Who will watch Cody when you go back to work?" he asked.

Her expression changed for a moment as if she didn't like the subject. "I'm covered there—the ranch has a daycare for both staff and guests, and it's very well run. I hate the idea of leaving Cody for an hour, let alone all day, but I know he'll be well cared for and I can pop in and see him on my breaks and lunch."

He felt that in his gut. Breaks and lunch. That had to be hard for a new mom just going back to work. "I'm glad you have that for him." He was quiet for a moment, his gaze on his nephew, his little sleeping form in the cowboy pj's. "It would mean a lot to me to be a real part of Cody's life. Not just Uncle Boone who lives a half hour away and sees him on his birthday and holidays."

"That would mean a lot to me too. And him," she added, upping her chin at her son.

Boone felt that in his chest. He was very glad to hear it.

It was Friday. He could spend the whole weekend with Cody. "I don't need to get back home—to my job—till Monday morning. I have the whole weekend to visit, if that's okay with you. I passed a motel and a couple of bed-and-breakfasts on my way here—I'll get a room."

"That sounds great," she said. "When he wakes up, you can give him his bottle."

"I'd love that." His head filled with all sorts of things he could do with his little nephew. Boone could take him out for walks in the stroller and point out all kinds of things, like dogs and trees and cars. He could tell him about his dad and grandfather. In a couple of years, they could play peewee softball and Boone could get Cody his first fishing pole. Will, up there in heaven, would like that.

"I remember hearing that the Dawson Ranch has a petting zoo," Boone said. "Maybe after he eats, we could take him there and show him the animals?" He felt his cheeks burn. "Not to drag you around—you could probably use a break, but I wouldn't feel comfortable taking him out on my own. And I'm sure you wouldn't allow that anyway. I have a lot of ropes to learn."

She smiled. "You'll pick up the basics in unclehood fast."

He loved the idea of babysitting. Once he knew what he was doing—how to change a diaper, for one, how to make a bottle—he'd give Sarah lots of time to rest and relax.

"The petting zoo is one of my favorite places to take Cody—in the stroller and in the chest carrier. That and the duck pond in the park in the center of town. It's a gorgeous day for either."

"Great," he said, gazing down at his nephew as warmth and tenderness wrapped around him.

Before he'd knocked on Sarah Dawson's door, he'd been grieving and feeling off-center and hollow. Now Boone felt like *he'd* been given a gift.

Chapter Three

Fifteen minutes later, Cody began to stir in his uncle's arms. Sarah loved being able to use those words. *His uncle.* She still couldn't get over how life had changed with Boone's arrival. The news about Cody's father, which was very sad. An uncle, who seemed like a good guy and wanted to be part of his life, which was wonderful.

As they'd sat across from each other in the living room, Sarah had given Boone a basic education on all things baby and her baby in particular. The basics of Cody's schedule, from sleep to feedings to his baths. His favorites, like the way his face lit up at the color orange, his big baby laughter when Sarah would hold up his little stuffed lamb and make it appear and disappear behind her back, and how he loved bath time and having shampoo rinsed out of his hair. Boone had taken it all in as though completely delighted with each factoid. He'd repeat things she said as if committing them to memory.

She stood to head into the kitchen to prepare a bottle. "You can settle him in his infant bouncer," she said, gesturing to the seat by the sofa.

"I like holding him," Boone said, looking at Cody. "And I have three months to make up for."

Sarah actually felt her heart warm. “That’s really sweet.”

Boone looked up at her and smiled.

She headed into the kitchen and made a bottle for Cody, then walked to the doorway and called out, “Boone, can I get you something? More coffee or juice or something?”

“I’m all set,” he said. “But thanks.”

She brought in the bottle and sat beside him, showing him how to hold it for Cody, explaining how to know when he was done, even if the bottle wasn’t empty. The baby finished the entire bottle, and Sarah grabbed a burp cloth from the stack in a basket under the coffee table and showed him how to burp Cody.

“Wow, that’s loud coming from such a small body,” Boone said on a chuckle.

“It’s funny how tiny humans make such loud sounds—you should hear him laugh.”

“I’ll work on telling you baby jokes,” he said to Cody, repositioning him in his arms as if he’d been taking care of a baby for a while, not just twenty minutes. He’d gotten more comfortable and he cared, and the combination had worked its magic.

Just as Sarah was bringing the bottle to the kitchen, the doorbell rang. “Twice in one morning,” she said.

She opened the door to find a clearly upset Jeremy Golding on the step. In his early twenties, lanky and blond, Jeremy was usually full of fun stories and big smiles. To see him frowning and troubled was unusual. This had to be about his love life. Sarah had paired him up with someone she was sure was a solid match, and the first date last week had gone great. Last night was date number two. Something must have gone wrong.

"Sarah, I'm sorry to bother you," Jeremy said. "I know you have a little baby. But I've been going out of my mind about my date with Deanna last night. I did something wrong, but I don't know what."

Hmm. Jeremy was such a nice guy—super polite and easygoing. He'd gotten in touch a few weeks ago—he'd been single for over a year and heard about her matchmaking and hoped she might have someone in mind for him. They'd gone for a walk in the park, Sarah pushing Cody in his stroller, and she'd gotten a good sense of him and knew exactly who to pair him up with. Deanna Wooley, a ranch hand in the petting zoo. Deanna had asked Sarah to match her a couple of months ago, but none of the single guys she knew seemed right—until Jeremy came along. They both had the same sweet, kind energy aside from having a lot in common. It was always more the energy, the hopes and dreams than a checklist or ticked boxes, and an overall *feeling* Sarah got that had her connect certain singles.

"Sure, Jeremy, come on in. I do have company, though. We can talk out back."

Jeremy glanced around and spotted Boone on the sofa, baby in his arms. "Oh, I'm sorry." He shook his head. "I'll go."

"It's okay," Sarah assured him, sending Boone an *I hope you don't mind* look. She had the sense he didn't. Boone seemed pretty easygoing himself.

"If you're sure," Jeremy said. "I don't mind talking openly—heck, I wouldn't mind a guy's advice too."

Boone glanced over at that. "I'll help if I can."

Sarah gestured toward the love seat across from the sofa, and Jeremy sat down.

"As you know, last night was my second date with Deanna," Jeremy said. "She mentioned she'd told you we were meeting at the new Italian place since we both live downtown."

Sarah nodded. "And I know you were both looking forward to it."

"I sure was. We had a great time at dinner. And then we had a nightcap at Delaney's, and I must have said something wrong because she got this funny look on her face, and a few minutes later, she said it was getting late even though it was barely nine. She said good-night and hurried out. I was so stunned I just sat there for a while, trying to figure out what happened."

"I can definitely help with that part," Boone said, surprising Sarah.

Jeremy's miserable expression brightened a bit. "Oh good." He faced Boone, eager to hear what the guy in the room had to say. Sarah was too.

Boone glanced down at Cody, whose eyes were open and alert and perfectly content at the moment. "You said you must have said something because she got a funny look on her face and then all of a sudden called it a night."

Jeremy nodded. "Right."

"So, let's narrow down *what* you said that made her uncomfortable," Boone said.

Exactly what Sarah would have suggested. "I agree. What were you talking about at that moment?"

Jeremy gave a frustrated shrug. "That's just it. Nothing I can put my finger on that could have offended her. We were talking about hiking—we're both avid hikers—and about summits. We've hiked many of the same mountains. I said it was a dream to hike in Maine—Katahdin, Cadillac Mountain. And that was it. She couldn't get away from me fast enough. I called her last night and left a voicemail, but no response."

"Huh," Sarah said, perplexed like Jeremy was.

"You sure that was it?" Boone asked.

Jeremy nodded. "We'd been talking about hiking for a good twenty minutes. We'd walked into Delaney's talking about it and continued while sitting at the bar. It was the whole conversation. She'd said she hoped to hike Denali in Alaska one day, and I said me too, then mentioned the Maine mountains."

Cody started to squirm, letting out a fussy little cry.

Boone shifted the baby a bit in his arms. "What's wrong, little buddy? Uncle Boone's got you." He moved him more vertically, and Cody piped down.

Jeremy shot up. "I'm really sorry for interrupting family time. I'll get out of your hair."

Sarah walked him to the door. "It's no trouble at all. I do try to keep out of matches once they're made, but I can try checking in with Deanna."

"I'd appreciate that," Jeremy said. "Even if she never wants to see me again, I'd like to apologize for whatever I said that bothered her. I really like her." He turned back toward the living room. "Thanks for helping," he said to Boone.

Boone nodded. "Sorry I couldn't do more."

Sarah opened the door, and Jeremy left. She headed back to the living room and dropped down across from Boone. "I feel bad about not being able to lighten his mind."

"Doesn't sound like he did anything wrong. More likely whatever he said about Maine was a trigger. You just never know what might suddenly affect someone, make them think of something negative."

Sarah paused. "Yeah, I think so too. You know, you're pretty good at this. I should hire you, but I matchmake out of the goodness in my heart, so there's no pay."

"How many couples have you fixed up?" he asked, gently smoothing Cody's hair.

"Last count, seven that stayed together. Only three that didn't last past a few dates."

"Wow," he said. "That's a great track record."

"Except when it comes to myself," she blurted out. She could feel her cheeks burn. Not only because she'd made such a personal statement but the last guy she'd let into her life was his *late brother*. "Sorry. That was thoughtless of me."

"You're absolutely entitled to your feelings about Will. And I'm sure those feelings are complicated. Besides, the whole reason I'm here is because Will wanted to apologize for his bad behavior. So…" He smiled, immediately making her feel better.

Boone Riley was a nice guy.

"How about we get Cody ready to go and hit the road," she said, eager to get to know Uncle Boone better and truly delighted by the idea of her baby son spending time with him. "The goats always brighten my mood, no matter what."

He stood, holding Cody high in the air, which elicited a big laugh from the baby. Boone, clearly charmed, said, "Oh, you like that, do you?" And lifted him again, two more times, getting more baby laughter. It was infectious, of course, and they were both laughing now.

As she got Cody's diaper bag together to attach to the stroller, she had the good feeling that Boone would be a real blessing in their lives.

Boone thought the Dawson Family Guest Ranch was spectacular. Twenty minutes from downtown Bear Ridge, the place managed to be both rustic and modern at the same time and very inviting. The dude ranch was totally different from the cattle-breeding operation where Boone worked. It was guest-focused, of course, which infused the atmosphere with a welcoming spirit. There was the very popular petting zoo, horseback riding, hiking on Clover Mountain at the far end of the property, fishing in the adjacent river, cowpoke classes for kids and adults, educational workshops, wilderness training and tours, crafts, a lodge for indoor recreation, and a cafeteria. The ranch had guest cabins, from small to luxe, and offered day passes for those who not planning to stay overnight.

Sarah showed Boone around, often waving at fellow employees and stopping to chat for a moment. They both seemed to get the same happy kick out of hearing her introduce him as Cody's uncle. As they strolled around, Sarah had yawned a couple of times, and again he felt bad for dragging her out when she could probably use a nap. Maybe by tomorrow, when he was more comfortable with his new role and Sarah had some trust in him, he could watch Cody while she napped or took a break. He'd even offer to stay inside the apartment like a mother's helper if she'd prefer until they knew each other better. He'd supply her with references for his character too, if that would help ease her mind.

After weaving around the crowded petting zoo, they decided to sit down at a bench across the path. From this angle, Cody would still be able to see the goats jumping up on their logs and little playhouse too.

For a few moments, Sarah was quiet and seemed lost in thought. Boone didn't try to fill the silence. He had the feeling she needed a little time to gather her thoughts. He had a feeling she was still thinking about what they'd talked about before they'd left.

"I'm trying to come to terms with the fact that Cody will never know his father," she said, her gaze on the goats. "All these months, I always had this hope that I'd somehow track Will down."

He'd been right about the subject weighing on her. "I can understand that. I'm glad I'll at least be able to answer any questions he might have when he's older. What his father was like, that kind of thing."

Sarah nodded. "Was there a funeral?"

The question brought back the recent memories of that day and a poke at his heart. He himself was still coming to terms with the fact that he'd never see Will again, never hear his voice, never get that close brotherly relationship he'd always been after. He had the list, though, the black-and-white handwritten surprise that all his efforts had meant something to Will, that he wanted to do better by Boone.

"Will had said a few times that when it was his time, he liked the idea of his ashes scattered in the river he fished in as a kid. I never knew him to go fishing as an adult, but the memories must have been special to him."

Sarah gave him a gentle smile. "My dad always said he wanted his last meal to be a sardine sandwich even though he hated sardines because his mom made them for lunch once a week when he was a kid. It was the memory, the love that stuck with him."

"Did he have a sardine sandwich in his final days?" he asked, hoping he wasn't poking at her own tender feelings about someone close to her she'd lost.

Her eyes misted and she nodded. "A few days before he passed. I made it just the way he told me his mom did, with a side of chips. He was only able to take one bite, but the look on his face… It gave me such peace."

"I'm really glad to hear that," he said, squeezing her hand for a moment. He was quiet for a few seconds. "Since until today I didn't know Will had another relative in the world and he never talked about friends and was a bridge-burner, it was just me and Uncle Angus for Will's memorial. We took a rowboat out on the Darlington River and talked about what we loved most about Will. Shed some tears, managed to laugh at some funny stories." He gave a nod, remembering how raw he'd felt on the boat, grateful for his uncle's steady presence.

"The Darlington River," she repeated. "I'm sure one day Cody will want to visit, maybe even go fishing there himself as a tribute."

He nodded, a lump back in his throat, and went quiet again, watching the goats, glad for the distraction. "My uncle was on Will's list—for an apology. I showed Angus the list and asked about it, but he got a little emotional and said it was nothing and changed the subject. I tried to bring it up a couple of times, but he wouldn't talk about it. I'm even more curious now."

"Maybe he just needs some time," Sarah said. "When my dad died, I couldn't talk about him at all."

"You must miss him a lot."

"I do. I talk to him all the time. Randomly too. Sometimes I'll be standing in my kitchen trying to decide what I want for breakfast, and I'll say, *Dad, which should I have, Apple Cinnamon Cheerios or oatmeal?* And I'll imagine him telling me that oatmeal will fill me up longer. I feel comforted."

"I get that," he said, suddenly picturing a table laden with her cereal and her dad's sardine sandwich, chips on the side. His heart went out to her. She'd lost her last relative. "It must mean a lot to you that your dad got to meet Cody."

Her eyes lit up. "You should have seen how happy my dad was, holding his grandson. I'll forever cherish that. He was sick for a while and went downhill so fast." Her expression changed then, and he could see the grief etched in her pretty face. He realized in that moment that her sorrow was also for Cody, who'd lost his grandfather.

He reached out his hand to hold hers again, and she glanced at him in surprise, then squeezed quickly and pulled it away.

"I'm okay," she said. "But thank you."

He nodded and adjusted his hat to shield his eyes from the June sun. He noted the visor of the stroller protecting Cody from the bright sunshine, plus his little tan boater's hat. Boone made a lot of mental notes about the way Sarah had parked the stroller close beside her, facing away so he'd have a view but his profile still visible so she could keep an eye on him. She lifted a hand to move a swatch of her blond hair behind her ear, and he was struck by how pretty she was. Not that he hadn't noticed when she'd opened the door this morning, but then it was more in a general taking-in. Mid- to late twenties. Tall. Long wavy blond hair. Pale brown doe eyes the color of driftwood. Sarah was lovely.

He felt funny for thinking so. For noticing. He cleared his throat. "Can I hold Cody? I can sit him down on my lap."

Her face brightened again. "Sure. Why don't you do the honors of taking him out of his stroller so you get used to unclicking and clicking the harness."

He stood and bent over the stroller, clicking the latch and picking up his nephew. He settled Cody against his chest, just taking him in for a moment. "Hey there, little guy. It's your Uncle Boone."

Sarah chuckled. "He's staring so hard at you."

He was indeed, the big blue eyes fixed on Boone's face. He sat back down, carefully settling the baby on his lap and facing the goats. One jumped up just then, and huge baby laughter came out of the tiny body.

Boone and Sarah cracked up in unison.

"Ooh, it's my favorite three-month-old!" came a female voice.

They both turned. A tall redhead was coming toward them with a smile.

"Hi, Deanna," Sarah said. "Meet Cody's uncle, Boone Riley. Boone, my friend and coworker Deanna Wooley."

Deanna. Likely Jeremy's date last night, Boone realized.

They made a little small talk, then Sarah asked if she could talk to Deanna for a minute.

Deanna definitely hesitated but nodded.

"You've got Cody?" Sarah asked him.

"Sure," he said, puffing up a bit that she clearly trusted him to watch over the baby. Solely responsible, even for a minute, he tightened his grip a bit on Cody. *Precious cargo*, he thought, running a finger down the baby's soft cheek.

The two women walked a few feet away. In just a few seconds, Deanna's expression changed, and then she hurried away. Sarah came back over, looking concerned. Uh-oh.

"Is that the Deanna who suddenly called short the date last night?" Boone asked, though he had no doubt it was, especially after their interaction.

"Yup. I mentioned that Jeremy had stopped by earlier worried that he'd offended her in some way. She looked upset and told me he was a nice guy but not for her. Then she said she had to run and took off." She bit her lip. "I felt bad prying in the first place, and now I feel worse."

"I always think it's better to talk about a problem than ignore it," Boone said. "It's indirectly your business, so you weren't prying so much as trying to help. And I'm sure you did."

"Help? How? She got upset and couldn't get away from me fast enough."

"Like I said, talking about an issue is always better than ignoring it. Deanna clearly doesn't want to talk about or think about what was bothering her. But poking at an issue—or a person—usually gets it out."

She scrunched up her face a bit. "You think so?"

He nodded. "It forces the hand, the mind, a little—that's all. I didn't say it's comfortable."

She seemed to be considering that. "Well, I feel for both of them. I guess we'll see how it shakes out."

He shifted Cody on his lap. "I won't be surprised to hear that Deanna has some negative associations with the great state of Maine. The Pine Tree State is on my list of places I'd love to see someday."

"Same here. And I definitely think you're onto something—with everything you said. You just never know what the most innocent of comments can trigger in someone. I have a feeling they'll end up talking through it."

A hoot of baby laughter came from Cody, and they turned their focus to him and watched the goats together, Boone suggesting they get closer to the pen. Holding his nephew, they moved over to the fence, Boone telling Cody everything he knew about his goats—which was a lot, actually, and probably a little boring to a three-month-old.

"You're so good with him," Sarah said, giving her son's hair a gentle caress.

Touched—and surprised—he turned toward her with a smile. "I appreciate hearing that. Like I said, I want to be a real part of his life, so that matters to me."

Cody started rubbing his eyes, and Boone cuddled him closer.

"I might not know much about babies," he said to the baby, "but even I know that means you're tired."

"It's a bit past his nap, and he only got half his morning one. I should get him home. I'd love to get an iced coffee for the road, though. The cafeteria is right down that path," she added, pointing toward a hunter-green building with a steeply pitched roof. Lots of people were milling around, the picnic tables on the side full.

"I could use one myself," he said. A cold drink and some additional caffeine would hit the spot that this morning's many surprises—from Cody himself to how much he'd opened up—had poked at.

They turned for the cafeteria. After they got their drinks and headed for the exit door, Boone noticed a big bulletin board on the wall by the door. One large post listed job openings at the ranch. A cook here in the caf. Grounds maintenance. Daycare sitter. And an experienced cowboy/cowgirl.

Huh. If he got a job here, he'd be right in town, able to develop a close relationship with his nephew. With his mom gone, there was no real reason to stay in his hometown anymore. If he moved to Bear Ridge, he'd be a half hour closer to Angus too. Boone would think on it. But a baby nephew was a good reason to move to the same town. He could be of real help to Sarah too.

She seemed like a good person and was clearly a loving, doting mother. She'd done so much on her own. He could really step in, step up. He'd mention it to her later and see what she thought. She'd said she liked the idea of Cody having more family, but having an uncle suddenly horning in might feel overwhelming.

"Ah," she said, taking a long sip of her iced mocha. "Perfection."

"Same," he said, practically done with his already.

Cody rubbed his eyes again, letting out a big yawn.

Time to get the little guy back home. "I'll drop you two at your apartment," Boone said, "then I'll go get myself a room in town. I hope we can meet tomorrow." Even he heard the hope in his voice that she'd say yes. He might find Sarah Dawson very attractive and easy to be around, but it was his baby nephew who had him wrapped around his tiny pinky. Boone couldn't get enough of Cody.

"Of course," she said with a smile. "We can take Cody to the park and duck pond."

He smiled too. "Sounds great. I know babies and cowboys are on the same *early to rise* schedule. I can meet you at your place at eight if that works."

"Perfect," she said, and they turned to head toward the parking lot.

"Oh—will you take a picture of me and Cody so I can show my uncle?" he asked.

Sarah touched a hand to the region of her heart. "How sweet." She pulled her phone from her tote bag.

He kneeled down beside the stroller, leaning close to Cody.

Sarah snapped the photo. "Give me your number, and I'll text it to you. That way you'll have mine too."

A few seconds later, the ping alerted him he'd received the photo. He opened it, and for a moment he was so moved by the sight of himself with his three-month-old nephew, this miraculous connection to his late brother, that he felt a lump in his throat. He quickly added Sarah's name to the contact info.

On the drive back to her apartment, he decided to bring up the post he saw for the cowboy job. "There's nothing holding me to the town I live in besides my current job," he added, "but there's a huge reason for me to move to Bear Ridge."

A thoughtful expression came over her face. "Wow, you're really committed to being Cody's uncle if you're thinking of moving. That's really nice, Boone."

Good. He was relieved she didn't think he was jumping the ole gun. But Cody was his nephew for *life*, so moving for him seemed perfectly reasonable to Boone. "Plus, I like the idea of working at a dude ranch. And since Cody's a Dawson, I like having a connection to the ranch that bears his name. Second cousin once or twice removed or not."

Sarah laughed. "There are so many Dawsons in Bear Ridge that I barely know how I'm related to most of them."

The connection made the town and the dude ranch special to Boone. Icing on the cake was that Sarah worked there and they could easily coordinate him spending time with Cody.

She poked around her tote bag and pulled out her wallet, then took out a card and set it in the console holder. "This is the ranch foreman, my boss. Send him your résumé. I'll let him know to expect it."

That could give him a leg up on other applicants. "I really appreciate that. Thanks, Sarah."

"Of course," she said, sending him a warm smile.

Huh. Boone glanced in the rearview mirror; Cody's car seat was rear-facing, so he couldn't see his little nephew, but he'd managed to get attached in just a few hours and the more he thought about moving to Bear Ridge, the more he was sure of it.

He wasn't able to be the brother he'd wanted to be, but he'd definitely be the uncle Cody deserved.

Chapter Four

An hour later, Sarah sat at her kitchen table across from her best friend, Annie, and Annie's mom, Doreen, who'd always been like a dear aunt to Sarah. The two Cartwell women, twenty-seven years apart, looked so alike with their shoulder-length light brown hair and hazel eyes. They even dressed similarly, in jeans and slim-fitting Western shirts, though Annie liked to wear a lot of jewelry, mostly turquoise. They all had coffee in front of them, Doreen slicing the cinnamon coffee cake she'd brought. The baby monitor was in the center of the table, Cody catching up on his cut-short morning nap by sleeping hard.

Sarah hadn't even called them to tell them she had big news. The big-hearted Cartwell women often popped by, texting to make sure it was a good time, with meals or little gifts for Cody. She honestly didn't know where she'd be without them. And they'd arrived today at the perfect time. After Boone had dropped her off, she'd had a good twenty minutes to herself to think about all that had happened this morning—and to start processing. And now she had the two women closest to her to talk it all over with. She couldn't wait to tell them all about Uncle Boone.

But Annie seemed like she was bursting to say something. "Okay, full disclosure," Annie said, pausing to pop a bit of the cake into her mouth. "I got a text from my cousin Tara, who was filling in at the Dawson Family Ranch gift shop today. She said you were walking around the ranch with a man earlier. A very *good-looking* man. She said he was even holding Cody." Her eyes twinkled. "You're dating someone and didn't tell me? We've been best friends since second grade!"

"And he must be pretty special if you'd let him anywhere near that precious boy," Doreen added. "So tell us everything."

They both sat with eager faces, waiting to hear all about the new man in her life. She smiled at how off track they were.

"Not dating anyone," Sarah said, taking a sip of her coffee. "But turns out that Cody has an *uncle*."

They both leaned forward with wide, surprised eyes, mouths dropping open.

"What?" Annie said. "An uncle?"

Sarah took another sip of her coffee, grabbed her phone, and held up the photo she'd taken of Boone beside the stroller, his warm, bright smile and Cody's cranky little face, then filled them in—from when her doorbell rang this morning to Boone accompanying her and Cody to the ranch to stroll around.

"Wow!" Annie said. "Let me see the pic again."

Sarah held up her phone so they could both get a better look.

"He *is* good looking," Annie said. "And Cody looks so much like him. Same eyes."

Sarah nodded. "Apparently the Riley eyes." She felt

her own mist up. "It means a lot to know that. I knew Cody's dad for all of five or six hours. Now I have some family history. Not to mention easy access via Boone to medical history."

Doreen gave a firm nod. "That's definitely good to have."

They all took one last gaze at the photo, then Sarah put her phone back in her pocket.

"It's so poignant," Annie said. "The list and Boone deciding to carry out his brother's last thoughts and wishes."

Sarah nodded. She agreed one hundred percent. She thought about what Will Riley had briefly told her about his relationship with his half brother when they'd been at the bar. He'd rolled his eyes a bit when he'd talked about how Boone kept trying to make them closer, but Sarah had gotten the feeling that it meant something to Will, even if he found it intrusive for whatever reason. Maybe once she knew Boone better, she'd tell him about that—highlighting her take on it. Or maybe she'd keep it to herself since that part of the conversation had lasted less than thirty seconds over gin and tonics. She'd see. "It says a lot about Boone that he'd take on something like that."

Doreen added a slice of cake to her plate. "Yes, but *what* does it say? I mean, I agree it's nice that he's taking on his brother's to-do list. But who knows what it's rooted in? Guilt?"

Doreen Cartwell wasn't one to mince words or hold back from her thoughts and opinions. She told the truth as she saw it and didn't sugarcoat. Sarah had always appreciated knowing she'd always hear Doreen's honest opinion, no matter what.

Annie stared at her mom. "Guilt? What would Boone have to feel guilty about? From what Sarah told us, he'd been working on his relationship with Will since they were very young and it was Will keeping Boone at arm's length."

"True," said Doreen, "but if they weren't particularly close, why would Boone feel the need to visit total strangers to let them know Will wanted to apologize for something? Or that he intended to pay back those he'd borrowed money from?"

Sarah sipped her coffee, taking in Doreen's words. "He told me he was deeply moved by the fact that Will made that list at all, that he was trying to be a better person. And he was very touched that he himself was on the list too, that Will intended to do better by him as a brother."

"I hear you, I really do," Doreen said. "I just think Boone is working through something by taking on the list. People get very wrapped up in stuff like that. It fulfills something in them. And then when they feel better, they move on, back to their lives."

Annie tilted her head. "Huh."

Sarah understood exactly what Doreen was talking about. And it quite possibly could apply to Boone if not for one very important detail. "But the list—and my name on it—introduced Boone to his baby *nephew*. There's no moving on from that." She told them that he'd taken note of the cowboy job posting and planned to apply just so he could be closer to Cody and be a big part of his life. "And if you saw Boone in action today—

not just words—you'd likely have the same good feeling about him that I do."

"Well, that he's interested in moving to Bear Ridge for Cody's sake does speak volumes," Doreen said. "I'll withhold judgment until I meet him myself." She smiled and ate another bite of cake. "It's just that if anyone hurts you or that baby boy, they'll answer to me." She jabbed her spoon at herself for good measure.

"Oh, I know it," Sarah said with a smile.

"Sounds to me like Boone formed an instant bond with his baby nephew," Annie said. "That's lovely."

Doreen nodded. "It is. To discover a nephew right after losing his brother—that's quite a blessing." Her expression softened. "I can certainly understand why he's one hundred percent in. But...like I said, we don't know him and once a need is met, sometimes the novelty wears off and they're suddenly not around as much. I just don't want you to get hurt." She eyed Sarah for a moment, and suddenly Sarah realized she was talking about something else entirely too. That Sarah might see Boone as some kind of hero, riding into her and Cody's life.

That she might start falling for him.

Well, he might be very good-looking and kind, but Sarah was done with falling for anyone. Let alone someone so important in her son's life. If they got involved and broke up, like every relationship Sarah had had so far, how would that affect Cody and his own relationship with Boone—his brand-new uncle?

Good thing she was off men for the time being. Her most recent relationship, which had lasted almost a year, had come to a painful end, the guy being unable to commit and then meeting someone immediately who he'd proposed to after three weeks. That had hurt. It wasn't about him being unable to commit; she just hadn't been The One.

Then she'd let herself get sweet-talked by Will Riley, thinking maybe she should just focus on chemistry, that special feeling that someone *could* be The One and forget about ticking boxes before she got to know someone anyway. Instead of listening closely to what he'd said to determine his dependability and trustworthiness, she'd let herself be pulled by how she'd *felt*.

She let out a hard inward sigh. Until she could better set her own good matching skills on herself, she wasn't going to date. Or even notice Boone's sex appeal. If he did move to town, he'd get snatched up in a hot minute, and that would probably be for the best. She could find him someone wonderful herself, not that he'd need any help meeting women.

"I'm not trying to be negative about a very positive thing," Doreen adding, wrapping her hands around her mug. "Maybe I'm just playing devil's advocate."

"I get it," Sarah said. Several times in her life she'd experienced people coming in hot only to eventually back away—and not only in romantic situations. Everyone at the table had been through that in some form or another. "But I do think a baby relative is a whole different thing. Cody is special to Boone. I can see it. You will too when you meet him."

"Perhaps we can all go the park together sometime soon," Doreen said. "I definitely want to meet this man."

"Me too!" Annie said. She shook her head in wonder as she wrapped her hands around her mug. "I'm still getting over Cody suddenly having an uncle—and a great-uncle. I'm so happy for him."

Sarah felt herself beaming. Cody having paternal family meant the world to her. "Same. Two more people to love him." She thought about the tender way Boone had held his nephew, her heart flooding with warmth. "We're getting together tomorrow, so I'll arrange something for the four of us in the coming days."

"Just remember," Doreen said, "if you ever need to call in the cavalry, we're here. And we'll show him what's what."

Sarah smiled and lifted her mug to clink with Annie's and Doreen's. She had a very good feeling about Boone Riley. "To Cody, to family—and to *chosen* family," she said.

"I'll clink to that," Doreen said, reaching across the table to squeeze Sarah's hand.

Bear Ridge had its share of accommodations since aside from a nearby rodeo, the Dawson Family Guest Ranch's cabins were pricey and some folks preferred to stay elsewhere while just buying day passes. Boone chose a bed-and-breakfast on Main Street instead of one of the cheaper motels along the highway. "Nicer" was important in case he'd have the opportunity for a longer visit with his nephew. He had a suite with a sitting room and also a private balcony, the property bursting with flower boxes and stone walkways. Sarah would certainly like it. She probably even knew the proprietors.

After dropping off Sarah and Cody, he'd driven back to his cabin and packed a suitcase, some basics, his one suit and nice shoes, just in case he'd need them. By the time he got to the inn he was starving and stopped at the diner a couple of blocks away, opting to sit at the counter for a turkey club and fries.

Between the drive home and back, the solid dinner, and a long, hot shower, Boone was in a good place to call his uncle with the big news. He'd almost called Angus the moment he'd dropped off Sarah and Cody, but he'd still felt so mystified and stunned and thought it best to be in the frame of mind to answer his uncle's questions instead of saying *I really don't know* over and over.

It was such a nice night—low seventies, the sun setting—that Boone wanted to sit out on his deck and call Angus, but this was a small town and he certainly didn't want anyone overhearing his conversation. He sat on the love seat in the living room and opted to video call Angus.

His uncle's face, showing the grief from losing Will and the heartache over his girlfriend ending their relationship a couple of weeks ago, appeared on the small screen. Angus's salt-and-pepper hair was still thick and on the longer side, the Riley blue eyes sparkleless. "Hey, Boone. Holding up okay?"

"About that—you know how we thought the silver lining about Will was the list he left behind? Both of us being on it? Well, wait till you hear this."

"If it's nice news, I'm all ears," Angus said.

Boone could see from the background that Angus was on his sofa, what looked like a frozen dinner on a plate on the coffee table beside a bottle of beer. "I told you I was going down Will's list and that I'd be knocking on a Sarah Dawson's door this morning."

"Right. The list said she worked at that popular dude ranch."

Boone nodded. "Well, the reason Will wanted to apologize to Sarah Dawson was because he turned their… meeting into a one-night stand and then ghosted her. He even gave her a phony number."

Angus let out a sigh. "He must have thought highly of her to want to apologize, though," he pointed out. "I mean, that was pretty much his MO with women."

"Yeah, I figured Sarah Dawson must have made an impact. And I'm glad she did because her being on that list led me to discover that I have a baby nephew and you have a great-nephew."

He watched his uncle's face change, the mouth dropping open, surprise lighting his features. "A nephew? *What?*"

"A three-month-old boy. Name's Cody. Little cowboy."

"You're telling me Will has a child out there?" Angus asked, clearly as unable to process the information as Boone had been hours ago.

"Not 'out there.' Right here in Bear Ridge. I spent a good part of the day with Sarah and our nephew. I got myself a room at a B and B in town. I'm going to stick around, let Sarah get to know me so she feels comfortable. My showing up was a big surprise." He filled his uncle in on everything up to this point.

"My God, that's a lot to process. A nephew! And you're planning on moving to Bear Ridge—that's big."

"The connection I felt to that baby was instant, Uncle Angus. I've never experienced anything like that before. He's my flesh and blood. He's my brother's child."

Angus nodded, his eyes misty with emotion. "Like you're mine. I know the feeling well."

A warmth spread through Boone's chest. Boone's dad and Will had been two peas in the ole pod, whereas Boone and Angus had always felt more alike.

"Sarah's very happy that Cody has paternal family," Boone said. "Once the shock of discovering each other settles, I'll suggest we get together with you so can meet your grandnephew."

"A nephew! Three months old," Angus said, letting out a whistle in wonder. "This is beautiful news, Boone."

"Right? Hang on a second—I'm gonna send you a photo Sarah took of me and Cody." He quickly texted the photo, then tapped the video screen. "Take a look at that when we disconnect. I'll be in touch very soon, Uncle Angus. You take care, okay?"

"I haven't felt this spark of happiness in weeks," Angus said, his blue eyes making that evident. "Bye for now."

They disconnected, and Boone clicked on the photo app, studying the tired little face of his nephew, easily able to see his brother in Cody. And Sarah too. The rest of the baby's face was hers. But Cody had his father's dark blond hair; Sarah's was lighter. He wished she'd been in the photo, which felt like it was missing her.

He realized right then that he was looking forward to seeing Sarah as much as he was his nephew. She'd made everything about today—from the shocking news to letting Boone spend hold and feed Cody to the trip to the dude ranch—easy. She could have been bitter about Will's treatment of her and closed the door in Boone's face. But knowing she had Will's child, she let him in.

And suddenly he'd gone from being bereft about his brother to holding the baby nephew he hadn't known existed.

Sarah was a good person—kind and generous, no doubt about it. And a doting mother. *Beautiful* also came to mind to describe her, but once again, Boone blinked that thought out of his head.

If ever a woman was off-limits, it was Sarah Dawson.

Chapter Five

The next morning, Boone had breakfast in the B and B's screened-in dining room beside the flower-filled yard. Nothing like a Western omelet, excellent home fries, and strong coffee. He glanced at the time on his phone—just past 7:00 a.m., which he knew was a fine time to email the foreman at the Dawson Family Guest Ranch to apply for the cowboy job. He typed out a cover letter, noted that his nephew's mother, Sarah Dawson, had given him the man's name and contact info, attached his résumé, and hit Send.

At 7:50 he was on his way to Sarah's apartment, revved up about seeing Cody, about being proactive with the job posting when his phone pinged with a text. Boone pulled over. The foreman. *That* was fast. Within two minutes, Boone had an interview today at 4:00 p.m. He had a good feeling about this—all of it. Things were falling into place, and when did that ever happen? *Meant to be*, he told himself.

Last night, he'd barely been able to fall asleep with his excitement at how his life had changed with the ring of a doorbell. A baby nephew. Possible new job. New town. A new life and new Boone. He'd been forced to be an absentee brother, but he wouldn't be an absentee uncle, sending birthday cards every year and being surprised by how big Cody had gotten. Boone would see his nephew *regularly*. He'd be at Cody's preschool graduation in a few years. He'd be at every school event. He'd teach Cody how to ride a bike. Take him fishing. Show him how to shave when the time came.

You would have liked doing that, Will, he thought with a twinge of sadness taking over his good spirits. He could just see his brother standing before the bathroom mirror, teenaged Cody beside him, razors and shaving cream at the ready, Will explaining to his son that some women liked clean-shaven men, some serious five-o'clock shadow, some light beards, and still others full beards, so you couldn't go wrong.

He smiled, suddenly missing Will and all they'd miss together. The chance to see his brother grow with being a father. The chance for the four Riley boys to do things together—camping, taking a boat out, hitting balls, taking turns pitching, batting, and chasing down the impressive ones.

He sat with the feeling, letting it be, letting himself grieve. Cody's sweet face, the big blue eyes, his fine blond hair floated into his mind, and Boone felt himself brighten.

"I'll do everything a dad would do," he said into the air. He chuckled at the thought of himself sitting down with Cody to talk about the birds and the bees.

Slow down, there, partner, he told himself. *The kid is three months old.* But it seemed okay for Boone to get ahead of himself when it came to a magical nephew.

When he arrived in the feed store's parking lot, he texted Sarah to let her know just in case the doorbell would wake up Cody from a nap. Boone knew the basics of the baby's schedule from his conversation with Sarah yesterday, but today he'd learn the nitty gritty. As he approached her apartment on the side of the feed store, she opened the door, Cody in her arms.

He swallowed for a second, caught off guard by his reaction to her. She wore jeans and a long-sleeved pale blue T-shirt, her hair in a long ponytail. Not a stitch of makeup. Granted, she *was* beautiful, as he'd acknowledged last night, but he wondered why he was so struck by her now. If Boone was in a bar with his cowboy friends, the women who usually turned his head were the opposite of Sarah. Tight, skimpy clothes. High heels. Glossy lips. Done-up hair.

But as he stood there on her doorstep, he could barely drag his eyes off her.

Maybe it really was nothing more than that she was the link to this brand-new world he found himself in. That she was holding his new nephew. Boone *was* still reeling from the huge surprise.

"Come on in," she said. "I just made some coffee. Are you hungry? I have bagels and cream cheese. Or eggs and sausage if you want something heartier."

"I had a great breakfast at my B and B," he said, taking off his hat as he followed her to the kitchen. "I could definitely do with another cup of coffee, though." He smiled at Cody. "Hey there, little guy. It's me, Uncle Boone."

Her driftwood-brown eyes lit up. "That will never get old," she said, "even years from now. I feel like the words *Uncle Boone* will always give me a happy jolt."

"Same," he said, glancing at her. He could see the

wonder on her face, same moony expression he'd noticed every time he caught himself in a mirror in his suite yesterday. They were both gobsmacked. "Our lives changed—all three of our lives."

She nodded. "From no family but each other to an uncle and great-uncle."

"To no family but a great-uncle to a baby nephew and his very kind mother." He looked at Sarah. "I mean that." And he did. *Of course* he was struck by her—it was the kindness, her generous nature *and* the link to Cody—not attraction. He felt instant relief at realizing that. "I appreciate how you're letting me into your lives. Someone else might have been more…"

"Mistrustful," she finished for him.

He winced a bit at that, though it had been the very word in his head. She didn't know him at all and had no reason to trust him yet, but he'd earn it soon. "Yeah." He looked at Cody, who was staring at him with those big blue eyes. "Can I hold him?"

"Sure," she said, handing Cody over.

Except this time, Cody clearly wasn't feeling it. During the transfer and the moment Boone had him against his chest, Cody's face scrunched up and he let out a *waah*, batting a bit at the air.

"Aww, what's wrong?" Boone said gently. "I'm your Uncle Boone. From yesterday."

"He's probably just a little cranky from being shifted," Sarah said, heading for the coffee maker on the counter. "I'm sure he'll settle down."

Cody started bawling. Full-out crying and clearly wanting to be back in his mother's arms.

"You can try some of the tricks I showed you yesterday to get him to calm down," she said. "He'll get used to you. No worries."

Boone *was* worried—well, a little. He wanted Cody to take to him. To have instant feelings like Boone had for him.

He's a baby. Welcome to the unpredictable.

"How about if I sing you an old cowboy ditty and sway you a bit?" Boone asked, gently rocking back and forth. "*Oh, give me a home where the buffalo roam, where the deer and the antelope play,*" Boone sang.

He glanced at Sarah, who'd stopped in her tracks and was smiling at him.

"Well, that seems to be working," she said on a chuckle.

Cody had stopped crying and was staring at Boone. He quickly sang some of the second verse, Cody's eyes, now bright again, laser-focused on his face. "*Where never is heard a discouraging word and the sky is not clouded all day.*" He added a little *ooh-woo* at the end, and Cody giggled. "*Ooh-woo,*" he trilled—to the baby's delight.

Boone was quite happy. "Huh. Look at that. I see I'll have to learn as I go with this one."

"Yup," Sarah agreed. "Just as I did." Her smile lit up her whole face, and again he couldn't look away. "You can put him in his infant seat while we have our coffee," she added, gesturing at the bouncer in the corner. "He loves the mobile and lullaby player."

He kneeled down and settled Cody on the seat, latching the harness as Sarah squatted beside him to press the buttons. He was so aware of her suddenly, catching the scent of vanilla. She moved her hair behind her ears, and again he noticed how pretty she was.

What was with him this morning? He must have been so focused on Cody yesterday that nothing else had gotten through his brain. Like the fact that he was attracted to Sarah—which felt very inappropriate for a number of reasons.

She stood and headed back to the coffee maker, and he was glad for a moment to shake off his wayward thoughts.

Sarah's off-limits. He was here for his nephew and to make Sarah's life easier. Not to complicate things, to confuse things by being attracted to her.

And attraction was a complicated thing in itself, multilayered. He was drawn to her for obvious reasons—that was all this was. She was his nephew's mother. And a warm, kind person. She'd welcomed Boone immediately. Of course he felt a strong pull to Sarah Dawson.

It was nothing to worry about.

She's pretty. She's nice. She's important in your life. You're just having an outsize reaction to all that. In a few hours, things will settle down and you'll get that platonic feeling where Sarah's concerned.

He turned his full attention to his nephew. Cody was content to suckle on his pacifier and stare up at his mobile, which was slightly circling around, the little carousel horses dipping up and down. Sarah brought the mugs of coffee to the table and then filled a little tray with cream and sugar, and they both sat down.

He added cream and sugar to his and took a sip, noticing she took her coffee black. "I got so caught up in seeing my little nephew again that I forgot to tell you my other big news—I have an interview with the foreman of the Dawson Family Guest Ranch today at four p.m.

Mentioning that you gave me his contact info clearly got me a fast response."

"That's great, Boone. I'm glad I could help." She eyed him for a moment, and he wondered what she was thinking. Was she surprised he'd followed through? "So after sleeping on it, you're still full speed ahead on the idea of moving here?"

Now it was his turn to eye her. She did seem surprised—and maybe a little wary? "Definitely. Does that seem a little nuts to you? I know it's sudden, but it's not like I'd say, 'Well, I've gotten to know my nephew and I'm not feeling it, so I'll be moving along now...'" He smiled. "It's not like being impulsive over a woman or chasing a pipe dream. This is *family*."

She seemed to like that answer because she instantly relaxed, her shoulders actually unbunching before his eyes. But then she seemed to be considering something because her expression changed again. "Well, finding out your brother has a child, a baby, is huge. I can see you wanting to jump in whole hog. But in a few weeks, when it's not so new..."

Boone frowned, then found himself relaxing a bit with a thought. "This is clearly a case of you not knowing me well. Cody isn't a novelty. I don't follow the wind. I'm about responsibility and commitment and honor."

Again she seemed to be taking that in, her gaze assessing on him. "The cowboy code," she finally said with a hint of a smile. "Good enough for me to take you at your word, then." *Until you show me otherwise*, her expression seemed to add.

"My actions will back them up. You'll see." He downed the rest of his coffee. She *would* see. Boone would be a contender for uncle of the year. Cody—the idea of him, the *reality* of him—was very important to Boone.

She took a long sip of her coffee. She was processing; he could tell. It suddenly occurred to him that she might have gotten some feedback on the situation from those close to her. As though someone had told her to be on guard or something. Which was good advice. She *didn't* know him.

Boone finished his coffee and set down the mug. "I grew up close to my mom, not close to my dad, not close to my brother, and reasonably close to my uncle, who always tried his best with me and Will but had that Riley distance in him too. I'm the one who didn't inherit it."

Except when it came to women, maybe. He could still hear his ex-girlfriend, Laurene, using the stories he'd tell about his family against him, saying that he was just like his dad and brother but maybe even worse because he'd make it seem like he'd commit, then never would. *At least Will and your dad came flat out and said, Don't expect much from me.*

He inwardly sighed. He was twenty-eight years old and hadn't been able to commit to any of his girlfriends, but he did believe it was because he hadn't met his person. He'd had quite a few girlfriends too. A female friend, a cowgirl at the ranch he worked at, had told him there was a disconnect between the women he was attracted to and what he claimed he was looking for. He'd told her she was judging books by their covers. Just because he went for flashy didn't mean there wasn't substance underneath. *Then why haven't you connected with any of them?* she'd asked. *Why haven't you fallen in love?*

If you want to know what I think—and he hadn't been sure he did—*I think you go for a certain type to avoid real intimacy.*

Boone didn't know what to think about that. Maybe she'd been right. He wasn't even sure what real intimacy was. Talking in depth? Opening up about stuff that sometimes kept him up at night? If that was the case, maybe she had been right about him. Boone *did* like to talk about what was on his mind, but only to a point before he'd start feeling uncomfortable. Usually because he didn't have answers.

Surely having a baby nephew, new family would change Boone in big and small ways. Maybe he'd finally find a woman—a flashy woman—who he *did* want to have those big and serious conversations with. Maybe he'd finally feel that pull to propose marriage. Have a baby himself. Give Cody a cousin.

"Sounds like you were the glue of the family," Sarah said thoughtfully. "I'm curious about something," she added, her gaze on Cody in his baby seat. "What kind of dad you do think Will would have been? If he knew about Cody, of course."

Good question. And one he hadn't had time to think about. "I really don't know. On the drive here, I actually imagined Will teaching his son how to shave." He smiled for a second, then felt it fade. "I wish I could say for sure that he'd have stepped up, that having a baby would become the most important thing in his life. But I'm not sure. Would he have run scared? I do believe he would have stepped up financially. He might have even gotten a second job if he knew he had a child." Yeah, the guy with the unpaid bar tabs? Boone really wasn't sure of anything. Then again, he had to give Will credit for wanting to pay his debts. He instantly felt better being back to thinking that his brother *would* have been there financially for his son.

She tilted her head. "I'm trying to figure out if you knew him well enough to not to be sure or if you didn't know him very well at all."

"I go back and forth myself on that question," he admitted. "But I think it's the former. When I was a kid and a teenager, my TV, my version of video games was trying to figure out my older brother. It was my mission in life. To crack the code. Never quite did, but I do feel like I knew him."

"I'm glad to hear that. For Cody. He'll know his father through you."

Boone felt that like a punch to his gut. Of course he wanted Cody to know his father through him. But Will had been both complicated and very simple, leaving him difficult to understand, to explain to others. He and Uncle Angus had tried for years. All Boone was certain about was that he'd never say an unkind word about Will to his child. But he'd have to answer. Help Cody feel like he knew his father, that he could *feel* him in his bones, his heart.

So, Uncle Boone, what was my dad like?

Boone would focus on Will's good traits. That he was up for anything. That he'd try anything. They'd have a laugh over Will Riley's love of hot dogs piled with the works, that he was scared of spiders since getting bitten once as a kid right in his own home, that he always talked about having his own huge ranch one day and going to the local animal shelters to adopt all the mutts that had been there for a long time, the seniors, the not-so-cute ones, the dogs that needed training.

Maybe one day Will would have settled down and had a family of his own. Surely if he'd known about Cody, he'd have fallen so hard for the little guy, his own baby, that he'd become a good dad. That was what Boone decided in the moment. And when it would come time to talk about Will with his son, he'd have a good overall answer.

That settled something in his own heart for the moment.

"I think Cody would have Will Riley wrapped around his little pinky in two seconds," Boone said, liking the assurance in his voice.

Once again, Sarah's warm, pleased smile lit up her face. He liked that he could do that, make her happy. She'd been on her own for a long time with a lot on her plate.

The lullaby on the bouncer stopped, the sudden silence catching his attention.

"Darn thing goes in and out," Sarah said. "It's secondhand. I'm lucky to have it all."

He raised an eyebrow. Secondhand. Like probably everything in her small apartment, he thought, glancing around. The place was spotless and smelled nice, but the furnishings were definitely thrift store.

"Must be very hard taking care of an infant on one salary," he said.

She nodded, looking away for a moment. "I get by. No extras, but I can pay my bills. My dad's medical bills took my savings. But it was money well spent. No regrets. I'll build up my emergency fund again. Then a rainy-day fund."

He felt a punch to the gut before? That was nothing compared to this one wrecking his midsection. No savings. No emergency fund. A bouncer seat that constantly stopped working.

"Sarah, I really do believe Will would have financially contributed to Cody's well-being. And especially given that you meant a lot to him to be on his apology list, I know he'd want me to take over that part for him. Even if that weren't the case, I'd want to as Cody's uncle. One new bouncer seat that plays lullabies with a spinning mobile coming up. And whatever else you need."

She sat stock-still for a second, not looking at him, then she burst into tears and covered her face with her hands.

He shot up and went over to her, scooching in front of her. "Hey, what's wrong? What did I say?"

She sniffled and wiped at her eyes, then shook her head. "You just have no idea how nice it is to hear you say that, Boone. That Cody's uncle, who didn't exist before yesterday morning, wants him to have a working bouncer. It means a lot to me."

He took her hand in both his. "It's long overdue. And it's my pleasure."

She stood then and went to the counter to grab a tissue. She dabbed at her eyes and caught her breath. He stood up, and she suddenly walked over to him, her arms extended.

They embraced, a short thank-you hug that had him wrapped up in the scent of vanilla again before she pulled back, dabbing more at her eyes.

"Thank you, Boone. For coming here. For caring. Believe me, I knew how much I needed that, but to have it happen…it's like a dream come true."

She gave him something of a smile, and he could see she was feeling a little exposed. A chunk of his heart was lost to her right then.

This woman was important to him, and he'd do right by her. He'd do it in Will's name and in his own.

Chapter Six

As Sarah sat in the passenger seat of Boone's pickup for the trip to the baby store, Cody nestled in his rear-facing infant car seat in the back, she bit her lip at how emotional she'd gotten earlier. One nice gesture, a kind word, and she was hugging the man. Kindness and generosity toward Cody, she reminded herself. From his kin who hadn't existed in their world until yesterday. Of course she was emotional. Boone certainly hadn't seem put off by her display, something else she liked about the guy. He was compassionate.

Still, she kept thinking about Doreen's worry that Boone was so focused on the to-do list because he was caught up in grief over his brother and that once things settled down for him emotionally, he'd be ready to move on. She certainly didn't want to get caught up herself in expectations of a doting uncle, a friend she could lean on in Boone Riley if he wasn't one to count on.

He has an interview in town at four p.m., she reminded herself. *And he said himself: He believes in the cowboy code.*

And if he wasn't? If Doreen was right? Well, at least Cody was a baby who wouldn't get too attached to Uncle Boone. And she wouldn't let herself either.

Stop thinking about that, she ordered herself. *Focus on what's great—which is that Cody's uncle is sitting beside you and cares about him so much already that you're headed to Brewer to pick out what you need for him.* Brewer was a bigger town about a half hour away with the big-box stores and specialty stores. Boone had said he liked the idea of going to Baby Bonanza since it was all things baby and he owed his nephew a few missed gifts. Which led to him asking all sorts of questions about the birth—the time, how it went, if Cody cried, how much he weighed.

"Of course he was born in the wee hours—just after one a.m.," Sarah said as Boone merged onto the highway. "I was both exhausted and full of excited energy."

"Who was with you in the delivery room?" he asked.

She glanced at him in surprise. Interesting question. She liked that he was curious about everything concerning Cody—from the big things to the smallest details.

She'd never forget the Cartwells in the birthing room at the hospital, Annie holding her hand and telling her to *breathe*, *breathe*, *breathe*, and Doreen over by the OB and nurse, calling out what was happening. *I see the head! Sarah, the head!* "My best friend, Annie, and her mom. Annie's been my bestie since elementary school, and her mom has always been like an aunt. They've always rallied around me."

"I'm glad you have them," he said, glancing at her. "It's so important to have people you can count on."

"Who's that for you?" she asked, suddenly very curious herself. "Your uncle?"

"Angus's always been something of a loner, but if I needed anything, I know he'd drop everything in a heartbeat. I have some good friends too. From childhood, like you. And my cowboy buddies at work."

"No girlfriend?" she heard herself ask before she could stop herself.

Again he slid a glance her way before giving the road his full attention. "Nah. I was seeing someone a couple months ago, but…"

"But what?" Sarah pressed, feeling her cheeks flush. She was being nosy, but she was *very* curious. About Boone and what made him tick.

"After we went out a few times she told me she wouldn't keep dating me unless we were exclusive. I told her I didn't date more than one person at a time, but I guess she took that to mean I was—" He gnawed his lip for a second, his gaze fixed straight ahead at the windshield. It was clear he did *not* want to be having this conversation.

"Serious about her?" she prompted.

"I misread her and she misread me. I never want to hurt anybody."

No one ever does. But when it came to romantic relationships, someone always seemed to end up with a busted-up heart. No matter how transparent and upfront. It had been that way for Sarah and, from what Boone was saying, for him too.

"If I'd known about Cody's birth," Boone said, clearly changing the subject back to what they'd been talking about a minute ago, "I would have been pacing the waiting room, holding my giant stuffed panda or giraffe and balloon bouquet." He took in a breath, and she felt him glancing at her again. "I wish I'd been there. But I'm here now. And I'll *be* here. You can count on that, Sarah."

She could hear the conviction in his voice. "I wasn't fishing," she said, thought she might have been. She wasn't even sure herself. She did want to know him better. "Look, this situation we're in—this sudden family connection and all it brings. It's brand new for us both. We'll just have to take it day by day, get to know each other, understand each other. It's been, what, twenty-four hours?"

He smiled then and looked relieved, his hand loosening on the steering wheel. "A wild twenty-four hours, huh?"

She smiled. "From not knowing the other—and that little guy in the back seat—existed to going to Baby Bonanza to pick out a new bouncer." She shook her head with a smile, marveling over it all.

"And anything else you need, Sarah. I'm serious about that. I noticed that Cody doesn't have a crib, only the bassinet, and he's probably going to outgrow that now that he's three months, right?"

She'd been thinking about that the past few weeks. Three months had gone by so quickly. She probably had another month, another five to eight pounds before Cody would need to transition to a crib. "I can get a good one secondhand," she said. "Cribs are very expensive."

"I'd like to get him his crib. It seems like an uncle thing to do." He flashed her such a warm smile that she could see he really meant it. "And it's not just about making amends for Will. No matter what, I *am* Cody's uncle."

She was so touched that she reached out a hand to his forearm on the steering wheel, and he glanced at her, a nice camaraderie between them. "Thanks, Boone." The words didn't convey what she was feeling—the burst of happiness in her heart, what his generosity meant to her.

With his left hand he touched hers on his arm for a moment, and she felt so connected to him in that second that she froze up.

Don't get attached, she reminded herself. *Don't have expectations, no matter what he says. You don't know him yet. Heed Doreen's words to be on guard.*

Trusting too quickly had worked against her before.

Baby Bonanza was huge. The store had everything from the basic items, like cribs and strollers and clothing, to newborn-sized leather jackets, bottle sterilizers, and some very high-tech trash bins for dirty diapers. There were rows of toys by age range, and Boone had his eye on a very cute black-and-white stuffed goat that reminded him of a real one at the Dawson Family Ranch petting zoo.

He had hold of Cody's stroller while Sarah, their cart beside her, was looking at stacks of pajamas on a table. She seemed transfixed by the footie ones with little bulldogs and another with Siamese cats. She held one up with the cats and touched a hand to her heart.

"How adorable are these?" she said, then laid it back down and began looking at the stack marked twenty-five-percent off.

"Well, let's get one of each—a bulldog and a Siamese. And any others you like. Are those little lassos on that one?" he asked, leaning closer. "Well, look at that." He laughed. "Can't you see Cody in that? It'd go great with the cowboy pj's."

"They're twenty-four dollars each," she said, eyeing

the price tag. "I mean, fine, they're soft and well-made, but come on, store." She shook her head and picked up one of the pj's on sale.

"Hey, didn't I say the Riley name has a lot of catching up to do when it comes to Cody?" He smiled. "He needs at least those three great ones—the lassos, the cats, and the bulldogs."

"I've never spent more than five dollars on pj's," she said, biting her lip. "There's a nice thrift store in Brewer called Little Savers. We can see what they have. Heck, they might even have one of these. Babies grow out of clothes fast, so I always find treasures there."

Boone had nothing against secondhand stuff. But he had quite a bit of savings because he'd been working since he was sixteen and had always drawn a salary on top of room and board at the big ranches he worked at. He reached a hand to hers, and she looked at him. "Sarah, you don't have to carry the weight alone anymore. So no need to look for bargains. Cody *needs* those lasso pj's."

She bit her lip, then her expression softened. She picked up the lasso pj's, then kneeled down in front of the stroller and held it up for the baby to see. "What do you think, Mr. Cody? Is it you?"

Cody stared at the pj's so hard it was clear he liked them.

"Cody has spoken," Boone said. "They're a must get."

She smiled and put the three pj's in her cart. "Thanks, Boone. I'll be saying that a lot."

Except she didn't need to. It was a Riley's turn to support Cody and then some.

They continued through the store, Boone keeping an eye on Sarah's gaze and expression. Every time he could tell she wanted something but would pass it up in the name of saving money, he insisted she get it. Soon enough the cart was filling up.

"Looks like we have the same age baby," a male voice said, and both he and Sarah turned around. A young man smiled at them, a baby in a carrier on his chest. A woman a few feet away and deep in study of the playpen display glanced at them and smiled. "Three months, am I right?" he asked.

Boone nodded. "You got it." He played a quick round of peekaboo with the baby staring at him, the little girl not the least bit interested. Hey, at least she wasn't bawling.

"Let me guess," the guy said, eyeing Boone, tilting his head left and right. "You're the uncle."

Boone felt himself wince, though he wasn't quite sure why. "I *am* the uncle."

"Ha!" the guy said with a literal snap of his fingers. "I knew it. Ages, family relations—it's my gift."

Boone could feel a frown pulling at the awkward smile on his face. "Just curious—how? What's the giveaway that I'm the uncle?"

The guy looked Boone over, tilting his head again, practically rubbing his chin in thought. "It's the overall vibe—doesn't say *daddy*." The woman at the playpen display called him over, and he smiled at them and hurried to her.

Boone narrowed his eyes at the guy's back. "Why did that guy get to me?" he whispered to Sarah.

Now she was eyeing him. "Why *did* he?"

Boone shrugged, not sure what was going on with him. Why would anything about Boone Riley say *I'm someone's father*? Of course he didn't give that vibe. And of course everything about him said *uncle*. That was who he was. Uncle Boone.

Except there is no daddy when it comes to Cody. His father was gone.

Unsettled, he felt compelled at that moment to spring Cody from his harness in the stroller. He picked him up and cuddled him against his chest.

I'll fill in—don't you worry, he silently told Cody.

He could feel Sarah's gaze on him and wanted to change the subject, move along. "There's the crib section," he said, upping his chin toward the back of the store. "Let's see what they have." He settled Cody back into his stroller and started moving in that direction, Sarah pushing the cart beside him. He turned his attention to the cribs lined up on platforms, all colors and styles imaginable. "This is nice," he said, appreciating the craftsmanship of the acacia-wood spindle crib.

"Oh, Boone, it's a beauty," Sarah said, her gaze soft on that very crib. "I just love it."

"We have the same taste." He gave a chuckle as a memory hit him. "Four years ago, when my Uncle Angus's wife divorced him and he moved into a small two-bedroom rental house, I took him furniture shopping. Him and me—not the same taste in the slightest." Boone mock-shivered. "He actually bought a *camo* sofa. And a deer head to mount on the living room wall. He even bought a camo bedding set for both his bedroom *and* the guest room."

Sarah laughed. "Was he replacing what he lost in the divorce, or was he finally able to decorate to his own heart's desire?"

"Definitely the latter. My ex-aunt was all about cottage chic, not hunter's paradise." He chuckled again. "I remember telling him that he might want to tone down the 'guy-heavy' décor for when he's ready to date, and he said any woman he'd be interested in would like camo bedsheets."

"You know, he has a point. As long as the basics are covered that all women want in a man—like manners, honesty, and respect, to name a few—I say go for niche if that'll make you happier. The little things can go a long way in building closeness and intimacy. Finding a woman who appreciates a camo sofa while curling up together to watch a movie…"

Boone grinned. "I see why you're the matchmaker and I've never fixed up anyone in my life."

A Baby Bonanza salesperson came up to them. "Looks like you folks have a completely full cart. I can take that to the register if you want to continue shopping without pushing this mammoth thing."

Sarah smiled. "That would be great."

"And we'll take this crib," Boone told the woman.

Sarah's gaze shot to him, then to the price tag. "I don't know—it's very expensive."

"Fifteen percent off all cribs this week," the woman said, pointing to the banner hanging above the cribs.

"You love it, right?" Boone asked. "And I can see Cody napping away in his little lasso pj's."

Sarah bit her lip. "You're sure?"

"Very," Boone said. He turned to the salesclerk. "We'll take the crib."

The woman smiled. "Excellent. I'll bring a slip up with the rest of your items."

"Onto crib mattresses and sheets," Boone said, gesturing at the aisle across.

"You made of money, or what?" she asked, hands on hips.

"I have a nice savings account. I earn a decent living and believe in socking money away. My mother instilled that in me. Save, invest, plan for the future. Thanks to that way of thinking, I'm able to outfit my new nephew with a nice nursery, so I'm—"

He shut up fast when he noticed Sarah's eyes were welling with tears. She swiped the back of her hand under her eyes, turning away as if she didn't want him to see that she'd gotten upset.

"Sarah?"

She shook her head. "I'm okay. Sometimes I just feel like a flop, you know? *I* haven't been able to make a nice nursery for my son."

He kept one hand on the stroller handle and reached out for hers with the other, giving it a squeeze. "First of all, you absolutely did. And on your own. That's *amazing*. Cody has everything he needs. He's so well taken care of in every regard. I'm so impressed by you, Sarah."

Her chin lifted slightly then, the tears stopping. "Well, I'm impressed by you."

The compliment went straight into his chest. "Honestly, I just met you yesterday, and I already know that Cody is the luckiest baby in the world to have you as a mom."

She looked into his eyes with such a touched expression that it stole his breath for a moment. "That's truly the nicest thing anyone has ever said to me. *Could* ever say to me."

The saleswoman was suddenly back, looking at both at them expectantly. "Did you want some help in choosing a crib mattress? We have six different models, including ones that have dual sides—one side firmer for infants and the other softer for toddlers not quite ready for big-kid beds."

The moment had felt so…charged with something he couldn't define that he was glad for the interruption, the talk of mattresses and their intricacies.

"That would be great—thanks," Sarah said fast, focusing on the saleswoman.

And Boone realized she'd felt it too.

Chapter Seven

Sarah was feeding Cody on the sofa while Boone put together the beautiful new spindle crib in the nursery. She was pretty good with a tool kit but had no patience for a million little nuts and screws and labeled parts, so she was glad when Boone had said he was a whiz at assembling furniture.

No doubt. The man seemed good at a lot of things.

She winced at how emotional she kept being around him, tears flowing a little too often, a little too easily. With the exception of the Cartwells, she never let herself be so vulnerable around people. And his response every time was so compassionate and kind. He wasn't uncomfortable around a teary woman the way some men could be.

Hopefully not because he made his girlfriends cry, she thought with a frown. From what he'd told her, he'd broken a few hearts due to his inability to commit, though he'd explained that dating only one woman at a time had been misconstrued for something more serious. She wondered how many of his exes had been hoping for an engagement ring and gotten broken up with instead and an *I'm really sorry we misunderstood each other.*

She shifted Cody in her arms, wondering about his exes, his type.

You might be a matchmaker, but his love life is not your concern or business, she reminded herself. Once he was done with the crib, he'd be heading back to his B and B to prep for his interview this afternoon. She was relieved that she'd have a little space from him. Boone was having some kind of effect on her. An outsized effect.

"By the way," he called out from the nursery, "I can take care of the nursery door's lock mechanism. The door doesn't stay closed."

See, this is why he's having that effect. He's very nice to have around. Handy. Helpful. You could use someone like Boone Riley in your life. That's all.

That she noticed how attractive he was was perfectly normal. The man was objectively good-looking. Tall and muscular but lean. The thick dark hair and warm blue eyes. Add all that together with how kind he was…

Snap yourself out of it, Sarah ordered herself.

"That would be great," she called back. And it was. She'd meant to fix that stupid door mechanism for weeks, but since she usually kept the door ajar and had no free time, it had stayed wonky.

So accept his helpful ways and keep your focus where it needs to be: Raising Cody. Taking care of business.

Ever since Will Riley she'd promised herself, for Cody's sake especially, that she'd be very careful with who she handed her heart to. Boone Riley was already earning pieces of her heart as a friend, as her son's uncle. And it had to stay just that. She could rattle off ten reasons off the top of her head. Another hundred if she were making a list.

She was in no danger of her growing awareness of Boone going anywhere.

Her phone pinged. The feed store owner—letting her know that tomorrow afternoon he was painting his back room, which shared a wall with her apartment. It could get a little fumy, and I know you have the little one, so a heads-up if you can stay at a friend's for the day and overnight.

Sarah frowned.

"Everything okay?"

She glanced up to find Boone standing in the doorway of the nursery, a little Allen wrench in his hand. She explained about the landlord's text. "I can stay with Annic or Doreen, but I hate intruding on them. Doreen's husband has a bad back that's acting up, and Annie lives with her fiancé and they're very much in the pre-honeymoon phase."

"Well, I have a two-part idea, then," Boone said. "The first is that we could go visit great-uncle Angus and stay with him for the day. He'd love to meet you and his grandnephew. He's texted me a couple of times to ask when he might get to see Cody. And to be honest, he could use a happy visit. He was down about a breakup right before we lost Will, so things have been extra hard for him."

She loved the idea of visiting Cody's great-uncle for the day. "Let's do that," she said. "I can't wait for Cody to meet more of his paternal family. And if meeting his great-nephew will put a smile on Angus's face, all the better." She tilted her head. "What's the second part?"

"That involves staying the night at my suite at the B and B. It has a bedroom and a separate sitting room that has a pullout sofa. You and Cody are welcome to the bedroom, and I'll take the sofa bed."

She swallowed. Spend the night in Boone's hotel suite? Even in separate rooms it seemed a little…intimate.

Only because you were just thinking how hot he is, she told herself. *So cut it out.*

"That sounds great too. Thanks, Boone. Let's plan on the visit, and then we'll stay the night at your B and B."

Boone nodded. "Perfect. I'll let him know. We could head there around noon tomorrow."

"Sounds good," she said. She looked down at Cody, who'd just finished his bottle. "Ready for a burp?" she asked, scooching him up to her shoulder and patting his back. "Oops," she added, grabbing a burp cloth from the basket under the coffee table and quickly sliding it between Cody's mouth and her tank top. "Nick of time," she said as a loud sound came from the baby.

"Hey, Cody, now that you're fed and burped," Boone said, "maybe you'd like to see your new crib."

Sarah's mouth dropped open. "You're done? That was fast."

He chuckled. "If you call an hour and a half fast."

"It would have taken me all day and night," she said, getting up and shifting Cody in her arms. She followed Boone into the room and gasped at the sight of the crib by the rocking chair. He'd even attached the mobile they'd bought and put on the new sheets. She'd have to wash them first, but how thoughtful was that?

"Do you love it, Cody?" she asked, giving her baby son a kiss on his cheek. "I sure do."

"It does look great," Boone said. "And I checked everything to make sure it's sturdy for this guy." He walked over to Cody and gently gave his soft hair a caress.

He was standing so close. Her heart quickened for a moment, surprising her. She was just grateful—that was all. *Stop reading into every little thing*, she told herself.

"I'll get the door taken care of," he said, gesturing behind her, "And then I'll take off."

Suddenly she wished he could stay longer. "Thank you so much," she said, trying to keep her voice neutral and even. "For everything."

His smile was so warm, so heartfelt that she was speechless for a second. For so long she'd been on her own, and now here was someone on her team, on her side. She'd had no idea just how much she needed this. Whatever this was, this…attraction and awareness of Boone, it was just that. *Appreciation.* The man was a blessing.

"Anything," he said. "Anytime."

And she absolutely believed he meant it. Which meant she had to be careful with herself. With Cody. She could *not* fall for this man.

Heed that, Sarah Joy Dawson. He's off-limits. Just remember that, and all will be not only well but great. Don't heed it, and you'll be making trouble for yourself.

Luckily Cody was generally a predictable napper, and Sarah had been able to schedule a new matchmaking hopeful during his afternoon snooze. Boone had left a couple of hours ago to prepare for and then go to his job interview, and Sarah had spent a good twenty minutes doing a few breathing exercises she'd learned in her maternity yoga class, which helped her get her equilibrium back. She felt like herself again. In control, ready to take on her day.

Thirty-three-year-old and divorced Lindy McDonaugh sat across from Sarah on the love seat, an iced coffee from Dunkin' Donuts in front of her. The tall, fit brunette looked a little cynical, like she was not expecting much. Sarah well understood that. Lindy's mom had pestered her to give the matchmaking she'd heard so much about a try, and she'd worn her daughter down. Lindy had gone through two not-so-great short-term relationships since her divorce last year. She wanted to find her soulmate. And her mom kept reminding her about her biological clock, which was making Lindy more anxious than she already was. Lindy had shared that her ex-husband had admitted to being on the fence about having children but that he was pretty sure he'd change his mind. By the time he'd flat out told her he didn't want kids, they had a bunch of other problems that had done a number on their marriage.

Sarah did believe in soulmates—and that there was more than one out there for every person. Lindy's soulmate at twenty-two, when she'd gotten married, and now at thirty-three were likely very different people. There were those couples who'd found each other young and grown together, like Sarah's parents had. Anything and everything was possible when it came to love. She believed that. Aside from considering herself pretty good at reading people—most of the time—she thought that optimism about romance was what made her see possibilities in connections that others might shake their heads at. *How'd you ever think to put those two together?* was a question she was often asked at an engagement party.

"Thing is," Lindy said, taking a sip of her coffee and setting it back down, "my mom was able to get me to reach out to you because I *do* want to find my life partner." Her eyes welled with tears. "Ugh, I'm so emotional. Maybe I'm not ready to date."

"Or maybe it's just hard, from putting yourself out there after all you've been through to wishing and hoping and keeping the faith."

Lindy brightened a bit. "It *is* hard. But everyone says you're the relationship whisperer. So I'm putting myself in your capable hands."

Sarah inwardly winced. She was pretty darn good at matchmaking. But her last match, Jeremy and Deanna, had run into that speed bump. Hopefully Deanna would open up about whatever had turned her off to him and they'd have another date.

"Okay," Sarah said, taking out her red leather journal book, which she used for notes. "Tell me what you want in a relationship. Everything that means something to you. Then we'll talk about absolute nos, the deal breakers."

Lindy took another sip of her coffee. "I want to get married to my Mr. Right and have a baby within the next couple of years. So someone who not only wants that but is *ready.* Given my history, with basically being lied to and strung along, I can't fool around with that."

Sarah nodded and jotted that down. Lindy hadn't gone into great detail about her divorce, but the pain etched on her face, in her eyes as she'd talked about it said a lot.

"Aside from that," Lindy added, "the most important thing to me is to *matter.* I don't care if he's six feet. I don't care if he's particularly funny. He doesn't have to look like Chris Hemsworth. I just want to matter. I want someone to care how I am, how I'm feeling, if I'm sick, if I'm sad, if I'm late coming home. I want someone to care that it's my birthday. Or that I'm worried about my dad's heart issues. Does such a man even exist?" Her shoulders slumped. "Actually, dumb question. Of course he does. I have friends and family with great husbands and boyfriends. My dad is super caring. It's just *my* picker that's off."

And mine when it comes to myself, Sarah thought, with a lot of compassion for Lindy.

"I wonder if being a caring person is an actual personality trait or if it's chemistry based," Lindy said, picking up her coffee. "Or will a guy who doesn't *seem* so caring on the surface be a great partner because he falls in love? You know that saying—if he wanted to, he *would*."

Yes, Sarah knew it well. "That's an interesting question." Sometimes, though, when the honeymoon phase ended, a partner who love-bombed in the beginning did a complete turnaround. "If a caring guy is your top thing, then go for the guy whose family and friends would describe him that way if I asked for the top five traits that best described him."

"Definitely," she said. "Got anyone who fits the bill?"

Boone Riley immediately came to mind on the caring issue. A younger man at twenty-eight to Lindy's thirty-three, which was certainly no big deal if the maturity level was a match. But though he might've been full speed ahead as Uncle Boone, she had no idea if he wanted a baby of his own, let alone to get married. She only knew he hadn't found his own life partner yet. But was it because he *wasn't* ready? Hadn't really been looking?

Suddenly she recalled his reaction to the guy in Baby Bonanza who'd correctly pegged him as the uncle and not the dad. He seemed affronted, like it was some kind of an insult. That had been interesting. It wasn't as if the guy had been wrong. And Boone with his stylish and carefree cowboy look did give off "fun uncle hanging out for the day" vibes instead of dependable ole dad.

Not that Boone wasn't dependable. In fact, knowing him the short period of time she did, Sarah would list caring and dependable in his top five traits.

He was not a match for Lindy. She knew that right away because Lindy's top ask was for someone who wanted marriage and family right away, and if Boone wanted that, it would have been clear from their conversations.

And anyway, it wasn't like he asked her to put him on any matchmaking lists.

A funny feeling came over her, a prickle of awareness that she was relieved he wouldn't make the list of possible matches for Lindy McDonaugh. But what about another woman who'd come to her for a fix-up and was looking for an all-around great guy, someone who wanted marriage and family in the abstract but not now. Then what?

She swallowed as she realized she didn't like the idea of putting Boone on anyone's list.

Maybe because she was feeling selfish; she liked having his full attention for Cody. And yes, in all honesty, for herself. The man was helpful, compassionate, someone solid to talk to, to lean on. Someone who cared about her son and, by extension, *her*.

And maybe because she was attracted to Boone Riley.

But as she'd already settled with herself—she couldn't

go there. There was no way she and Boone could get romantically involved without jeopardizing a lot. They were working on something important together, building a strong friendship so that he could be a big part of her son's life.

You are attracted to him, though, a small voice whispered. *Attracted and interested. Because he* is *an all-around great guy.*

The thought made her so nervous that she realized she'd *better* consider him for fix-ups. If he was even interested in that. She'd simply ask him—that would at least put some emotional distance between them. They'd both know they would never end up on a date with each other.

As Lindy took a bite of the lemon cookies that Sarah had set out on the coffee table, she was beginning to understand that she wasn't comfortable with either idea. Dating Boone herself—or him dating anyone else.

She forced her mind off her own love life—or lack thereof—and onto Lindy's. Two guys did come to mind for her. Sweethearts. Caring. Dependable. One was divorced like Lindy, with a four-year-old son of whom he shared joint custody. The other was single and thirty-five and looking to settle down.

"I have two great possibilities," Sarah said.

Lindy's face lit up, and Sarah was reminded why she gave so much of her time to matchmaking.

But the little blast of relief that Boone's name would *not* come up left her unsettled.

At just after 8:00 p.m., Boone sat out on his private deck at the B and B with the takeout he'd gotten from the Bear Ridge Diner: a turkey club, fries, and a slice of peach pie for dessert. He was on the final quarter of the sandwich when his phone rang. He glanced at the number on the screen and then grabbed it.

Dean Sheffield, foreman at the Dawson Family Guest Ranch. And quite possibly his new boss. He'd thought the interview had gone great earlier this afternoon. He'd left feeling so positive about the job, the ranch, and the potential boss.

Two minutes later, Boone disconnected with a huge smile on his face, his entire body buzzing with excitement. The cowboy job was his—at quite a salary jump too, given his experience, willingness to work weekends, and his interest in dealing with the "public," meaning leading trail rides for guests and giving cowpoke workshops for kids. He'd start in four days. There were often small cabins available for staff, but all were taken at the moment, which was no problem at all. Boone wanted to make a home in Bear Ridge.

A nice place, his first two-bedroom apartment, so that he'd have a room for his little nephew. Maybe he'd even look into buying a small ranch where he could have a horse of his own. A pony for Cody in several years. He'd think long-term, not just what his basic needs were right now.

He popped a french fry laden with ketchup into his mouth, leaning back on his chaise and enjoying the weather, the moment, and all the future had in store for him. A few hours ago, his current boss had called him to let him know he'd gotten a reference call from Sheffield, and his boss had sung his praises. The man had said he'd be sorry to see Boone go but understood his personal life was taking him in this new direction. There were cowboys and cowgirls hankering for extra hours, so Boone didn't even need to give notice. Which meant he had the next few days to devote to finding a home and spending time with Cody.

And Sarah.

Earlier today, after he'd put together the crib and she'd come in to see it with Cody, for a moment there they'd stood so close that he could have easily kissed her. The thought had flitted through his mind—what it would be like, if it would lead to more. He'd reminded himself he couldn't go there and tried to fill his head with boring or unpleasant images, but Sarah's pretty face and her lush figure kept popping in.

Tomorrow would be easier; the visit with his uncle would be family focused, a very good reminder that keeping things platonic between him and Sarah was necessary so that everything between them would remain on an even keel for Cody's sake. He'd called his uncle right after leaving Sarah's place to make arrangements, Angus very happy about the visit.

And *happy* was the name of the game when it came to all things Cody. Boone would do well to remember that, no matter how attracted he was to Sarah Dawson.

Chapter Eight

In the morning, Sarah emailed Lindy with the basics of the two men she had in mind for her, excited to hear back on who Lindy would choose. Sarah was firm on setting up introductions one at a time. Like how Boone dated, she thought, recalling what he'd said.

Why was the man always on her mind?

Anyway, if it wasn't meant to be with date number one, she'd pass on the contact info for the next person.

That done, she then packed a bag with all Cody's essentials to get him through the day at his Great-Uncle Angus's house in Culpepper, thirty minutes northwest of Bear Ridge. Cody was sitting contentedly in his stroller by the door, watching his mother slick on some raspberry-scented lip balm at the hallway mirror.

"I'm so excited for you to meet your great-uncle!" she said. "I have a feeling he'll be as doting as his nephew Boone."

She was sure Cody was smiling at the news.

The doorbell rang, 12:00 on the dot, and there was Boone, looking even more handsome in a dark green Henley shirt, jeans, cowboy boots, and a tan cowboy hat. Her reaction to him intensified when he took Cody from the stroller and gave him the sweetest hug as if he hadn't seen him in days, hoisting him high the way uncles and grandpas did, absolute delight on both their faces.

Pure attraction. A jolt to the system.

The kind that felt electric at first, then uncomfortable because it wasn't…right.

Once they were in the car and pulling out of the lot, Sarah vowed to ask Boone about fixing him up. And when he slid a glance her way at the traffic light out of town, their eyes meeting in a moment that felt charged to her like that moment yesterday in the nursery, she decided there was no time like now.

"So Boone, I wanted to talk to you about my matchmaking services."

He glanced at her. "There's news about the date that went south—about hiking?"

Jeremy and Deanna, and the mountains of Maine causing trouble somehow. "Not yet. Maybe it's the kind of thing a few days letting it settle will resolve. I'm hoping Deanna will give Jeremy a call to talk about it at least. Gosh, I was so sure about them. Something just felt right."

"Is that your main way of matching people?" he asked. "A feeling?"

"Well, that and listening. I've found that really hearing what someone wants—and doesn't want—is the key. And then using my instincts."

"What kind of woman would you think would be good for me?" he asked.

She froze for a second, surprised by the question. He'd brought up the topic himself. *Was* he interested in meeting someone? Why wouldn't he be? Of course he was. He was single.

"Let's see," she said, stalling for a moment to collect herself. "I'd say someone family oriented. A few days ago, that might not have even been on my list of musts for you. Now it's top. Having a baby nephew you didn't know about has completely changed your life."

"That's true. Now someone who'd be annoyed that I couldn't get together because I was spending time with Cody wouldn't be right for me."

She nodded. "Exactly. So top of the list."

Boone chuckled. "Everyone's picky in their own way, I guess. A coworker told me I have a definite type and she thinks it's the reason why I'm single."

Sarah's ears perked up. "Oh? What type is that?"

"'Dolled up,' she called it. Big hair, lots of makeup, little dresses. High heels."

She gaped at him. "Really? I wouldn't have pegged you for that." She was certainly the complete opposite of that look. Anyone would describe Sarah as natural, a cowgirl-type with the short, unpolished nails necessary for the job, hair in a ponytail. Lip balm. When was the last time she'd worn heels? Cowboy boots were as high as she went.

"The coworker thinks I go for that type of woman because I'm not looking to get serious. Do you think that rings true?"

Not necessarily, she instantly thought. "Well, 'dolled-up' women want love too. My friend Annie loves makeup and high heels. She doesn't leave the house without her false eyelashes. I've never met anyone with more depth and insight than Annie. And she's engaged to a great guy. Outward appearance and what's in the heart, mind, and soul aren't always connected."

"Huh." He seemed to be mulling that over. "I absolutely agree. So then what my coworker said isn't true. I'm relieved because it made me sound like really shallow."

She smiled at that. Of course that mattered to him. "*Were* you looking to get serious when you first started dating any of your exes?"

He gnawed his lower lip for a second. "If I'm being honest…"

She was practically holding her breath. *Say something awful*, she thought. *Something that will definitely turn me off to you.* That would be helpful. Then she could definitely pair him up with someone else who was also looking to just date and expand their social circle, not necessarily for marriage.

"I worry that I might have the Riley blood running through my veins," he said with a frown. "I mean, of course I do—I'm a Riley. But I mean the problem *committing*. Maybe it's why my relationships don't last."

"You've never felt strongly for anyone?" Sarah asked.

"A few times I have. I was crazy about a girl I dated in high school, but she moved away across the country. Before that I thought I was different than my brother, who'd sometimes have two dates on the same *night*."

"And after her? She moved and made you less apt to give your heart to someone again?"

He gnawed the lip again, staring out the windshield. "Probably."

"Afraid of getting hurt?" she asked. "First love is powerful stuff."

"I guess. But then in my early twenties I did have strong feelings for someone else. Mandy was her name.

I told her I wanted us to be exclusive, and she seemed happy. But it turned out she was using me to get her ex jealous, and she dumped me when it worked. They ended up married at least."

Aww. She felt for him. "Bittersweet ending, for sure."

"For me," he said ruefully, then chuckled.

"Okay, so your first romance broke your heart through no one's fault, and your second was a betrayal of trust. I can see why you'd get protective of yourself. Let me ask you this. Those two women—were they the dolled-up types?" She was pretty sure she knew the answer.

"Not at all. They were…more like you," he said, and she felt his gaze on her for a moment. "You know, girl next door."

Her heart sped up. She'd been right about the answer—but hadn't expected him to take it where he went. To noticing *she* was that type herself.

She cleared her throat. "So I guess you go against what used to draw you in order to protect yourself. Does *that* ring true?"

He didn't answer for a moment. "I suppose. Hey, how'd this turn into a therapy session?" He gave a chuckle, but there was something uneasy in it. She'd gotten a little too personal for his comfort.

"Well, if you're interested in a fix-up," she said, "I happen to know a pretty good matchmaker here in Bear Ridge. I can think of one cowgirl, one barrel racer, and a chef at Manelli's Italian Restaurant who would be a good pairing for you."

"Thanks but no thanks," he said, staring straight ahead. "I'm all set."

She was a little too relieved to hear that. And curious. "Meaning you're not interested in dating right now?"

He didn't answer right away. "I'd like to focus on all the changes in my life. My baby nephew. My new job. My new town."

"Ah," she said, pleased by the answer. She would just have to be honest with herself that she didn't want to fix him up, didn't want him to date anyone. Unfortunately, he'd be available for her drool over.

If he *was* dating, he'd be that much more hands-off than he should've been already. But he was saying loud and clear that he *wasn't* available—also good for her and what seemed to be a harmless crush. She knew where he stood, and certainly that little crush would eventually fade away. They'd end up wonderful friends, practically family. "That makes good sense."

He nodded. "What about you?"

"Me?" she repeated.

"What's your type?"

"I've always been all over the place," she said. "Buttoned-up accountants. Too-charming cowboys—like your brother. Soulful-eyed philosophers who love to debate ethical dilemmas."

He raised an eyebrow. "Really?"

"Well, that one didn't last too long," she said with a smile. "But I've never had a type. I like a warm smile, warm eyes. And I trust my instincts, though they don't always serve me well."

He slid a glance at her, and she felt bad at adding that part, since it was clear she was talking about misjudging the man who gave her Cody. "Do you fix yourself up?" he asked.

"I'm taking a break right now. I haven't dated since the news I was going to be a mother. *Single and pregnant* was a tough draw."

He smiled. "Two years ago, a buddy of mine fell madly in love with a single woman who was six months pregnant. They added a baby of their own to their family last year. So you never know."

Leave it to Boone Riley to kindly point out an exception. "That's my motto," she said. "You really do never know."

She felt his gaze on her again, but she kept hers out the windshield. She was dying to know what he was thinking right now.

"And now that Cody is three months old?" he asked. "Are you thinking about dating?"

"Nah. I'm like you—I want to focus on the changes in my life. Motherhood is still very new. And constantly changing with milestones. Things are nice right now, and I'd like to keep them that way. Dating can bring issues I'd rather not bring home with me."

There it all was. Exactly how she felt. It was good they were talking about this. Letting each other know what was what.

"Like disappointments," he said.

"Exactly. I mean, I know it's life. But my twenty-four/seven time with Cody is coming to an end in a couple of weeks. Once I have less time with him, I certainly don't want to take even *more* time away by dating. So, for now, it's just me and him."

She glanced at him then, and he seemed to be taking all that in. She *was* curious if he was attracted to her at all. She couldn't tell, and she could usually peg that in a heartbeat. What she did figure was that Boone Riley was too polite, too rooted in the cowboy code to show any hint of attraction for the mother of his late brother's baby.

She found herself gnawing away at her lower lip. It was the case and came with complications. It was one of the big reasons they should both be off-limits to each other.

"We've been talking so much the time sped by," he said. "We're just five minutes from my uncle's place."

Good. She needed a little space from Boone, even if it was across a room or simply her attention taken by her baby or by conversation with Angus.

But something told her she'd be constantly aware of Boone no matter where he was or who she was talking to.

"Oh my goodness," Angus Riley said, wonder in his voice as he beheld his great-nephew. Boone, with Cody in his arms and Sarah beside him, stood on the porch of the small two-bedroom cape. "He really does look like a Riley—Boone, you weren't exaggerating."

"He sure does," Boone said. "Uncle Angus, meet Sarah Dawson and Cody Dawson. And Cody, this is your great-uncle, Angus, a retired sheriff's deputy for Culpepper County. Anything you want to know about Wyoming state law or history—Great-Uncle Angus is your man."

"How interesting," Sarah said, extending her hand with a warm smile. "It's so nice to meet you."

"Likewise," Angus said, taking both her hands in his. "I was bowled over by the news about little Cody here. I couldn't be happier."

Boone was glad to hear that and the man was all

smiles for the new family member, but he could see Angus was still subdued. At sixty-six, his uncle was in good physical shape, with a head full of thick salt-and-pepper hair, but he had some deep lines etched into his tanned face and serious crow's feet at the sides of his blue eyes. A frown from Angus, his usual expression the past few weeks and more so the last seven days, always looked exaggerated. He was hurting over the loss of Will and his girlfriend, who had given him an ultimatum. They'd been dating for two years, but Angus kept saying he wasn't ready to think about getting married again. The breakup had done a number on him, though. Boone wasn't sure if his uncle hadn't realized how much Ingrid meant to him or if he was more upset that he couldn't have what he wanted—which was to see Ingrid without that ultimate commitment.

They headed inside. Angus's house was pretty nice. Ingrid had been over often, and despite the camo sofa and mounted deer head, the place managed to have a woman's touch about it. Still did, despite the breakup. Angus was keeping the house tidy, hoping she'd come back.

After a quick pointing out of the rooms—kitchen, living room, half bath downstairs with two bedrooms and a full bath upstairs—Angus started setting out lunch: sourdough bread, sliced roast beef and turkey, provolone cheese, lettuce and tomato, and mayo and mustard. They sat down at the round table in the kitchen, Cody content in his stroller and staring at his mother at the moment. Boone was touched by his uncle making a fuss over the three of them coming to visit; in addition to the lunch and a box of pastries, he had a bag full of gifts for his grandnephew.

"Aww, adorable," Sarah said as she pulled a soft teddy bear from the bag. Inside were some baby books with teething edges, two pacifiers, and a soft rattle that Cody seemed to love. He shook it, a delayed burst of laughter making them all laugh.

As they ate, Angus took great interest in his grand-nephew, asking all kinds of questions, from whether he was a good sleeper to his quirks. Sarah made both Angus and Boone laugh when she told them that Cody seemed to hate the color yellow to the point that if Sarah used the yellow towel with the monkey ears after bath time or peeled a banana near him, he'd scrunch up his face and get fussy.

Their sandwiches now crumbs, Boone brought Cody over to the table and settled him in his arms for his bottle, Angus commenting on how natural he was as a doting uncle. Once the bottle was empty, Angus suggested a walk to show Cody the neighborhood, and when Boone caught Sarah yawn, he said she should take a nap and let the uncles give Cody a tour around town. Sarah said she'd love a solid nap. She showed Boone how to use the baby carrier on his chest and slipped Cody inside, and Boone felt his heart racing. There was something so special, so powerful about having the little guy right there.

Not to mention Sarah standing so close to him, clicking the harness. He could smell her shampoo. And raspberry on her lips.

Which had him staring at her mouth for a moment before he blinked himself out of it.

"Thanks for the break," Sarah said to him. "Cody was up three times last night, and a nap will seriously rejuvenate me."

"My pleasure," he said, suddenly aware that his uncle was watching him. Paying a little too much attention. Boone hoped his attraction to Sarah wasn't obvious. He moved away quickly, collecting the lunch plates with a running commentary to Cody on how good sandwiches were and when he had teeth, Boone would make him a great Italian sub. The distraction wasn't quite working; he kept glancing over at Sarah, who stood at the top of the stairs with Angus in front of the guest room door.

"Hope you don't mind camo too much," Angus said as she opened the door.

Sarah chuckled. "I'm not a hunter myself, but hey, my eyes will be closed in two seconds." Five minutes later, with her settled in the guest room, Boone, Angus, and Cody went on their way.

It was a beautiful June afternoon, with temps in the mid-seventies, sunny and breezy with blue skies and fluffy white clouds floating by overhead. Perfect for a walk with the baby.

"I'm as wowed as I was when you called me with the news," Angus said, his gaze on Cody in the carrier as they headed down the sidewalk. "Seems like a miracle."

"I know," Boone said, reaching a hand to the top of Cody's head. "Exactly how I feel."

Angus was eyeing him. "And you and his mother seem to get along very well. That's good."

His uncle had definitely noticed the attraction.

Boone nodded. "Sarah's a really nice person. And a great mom. She's so happy that Cody has paternal family now. I do sense a little wariness from her when it comes to me, but that's natural, I think."

"Yeah. Especially with how Will just disappeared on her."

Boone hated that. He stopped walking, more unsettled than he'd been a minute ago. "What am I going to say to Cody when he asks about his dad? Every time I think I have that handled, focusing on Will's good points, his adventurous spirit, I'm back to square one. How am I supposed to explain the reason he didn't even know he had a child?"

Angus seemed to be considering that, quiet for a few moments. "I think there are ways to tell the truth about someone in a kind way. Will *was* an adventurer. Lived by his heart. If he'd known he had a child—" He stopped talking.

Boone looked at his uncle. "So you're not sure either."

Angus shook his head, and they resumed walking. "Would he have stepped up? I don't know whole hog, but I do believe he'd have sent money when he could. Whether twenty-five bucks from his biweekly pay to a thousand if he won on a horse or something." Angus bit his lip and shrugged. "I want to say he would have made his son a priority in his life, but I don't know."

Boone's shoulders sagged, a weight settling in his chest. Again he put a hand to Cody's head and felt himself brighten. "Maybe he would have surprised us. Maybe knowing he had a son would have changed him—instantly."

"It's possible," Angus said. "Like anything. I'd like to believe that, so I will."

Boone nodded. "Me too."

"Anyway, we'll have some nice stories for Cody about his dad." They neared the corner and turned left, where a playground attached to an elementary school was full of kids racing around and happy chatter. They walked up to the fence and watched the kids, some on tire swings, some on the slides, some playing hide and seek or tag.

"This is gonna be my life now," Boone said, shaking his head in wonder. "In a couple of years, I mean. Taking Cody to the playground, watching him come down the slide."

"I'll tell you, Boone. I'm not surprised with how *you've* stepped up for this baby. But I'm impressed." He glanced at him, then back at the kids. "You're changing your whole life. Moving to Bear Ridge, getting yourself a new job—and with a big connection to Sarah."

"What I feel for this little guy," Boone said, looking down at the baby nestled against his chest, "I've never felt before ever. Maybe it's different because he's a part of Will?"

"I'm sure. And maybe you're just ready for this—settling down."

Boone wasn't sure moving to Bear Ridge to be a good uncle meant he was necessarily settling down. But he hoped it meant he *was* getting serious about his future. At the least, he was looking to put down roots.

"Weird thing happened yesterday," Boone said, his gaze on a boy climbing up the ladder to the curving slide. "I took Sarah to a baby store to buy some new things, and a guy with a baby the same age stopped to chat and he said he could tell I was the uncle, not the dad." He paused for a second, wondering again why this had bugged him—and was clearly still on his mind. "What does *that* mean?"

Angus tilted his head as he eyed him. "Probably nothing. Maybe dads look more buttoned up or something? I'm sure *I'd* get pegged as the great-uncle and not the grandfather."

Boone's gaze shot to his uncle. Angus had never wanted kids. One of the reasons he'd agreed to the blind date with his ex-wife thirty years ago was because he'd been told she didn't want to have kids. Since his retirement from the sheriff's department, Angus had let his hair grow longer and he'd stopped tucking in his shirts the way he'd had to for his uniform. He did give off that semi-fun uncle vibe.

"Speaking of fathers, it'll be weird if Sarah marries and suddenly Cody has a dad," Angus said.

Boone swallowed and felt a frown pull at his mouth. He hadn't thought about that. And now that it was in his head, he didn't like it one bit. Cody with a new father? Some stranger doing all the things Boone was learning? Some new guy singing Cody lullabies and feeding him? Taking him to the park to see the ducks, Cody nestled in the chest carrier on his new daddy's chest?

His stomach gave a churn, the frown deepening. "She's not interested in dating right now."

"Well, she just had a baby three months ago. But what about in, say, six months? Or a year? And what if her new husband isn't comfortable with the bio dad's brother constantly hanging around?"

Boone felt himself bristle. "Sarah wouldn't marry a guy like that. Family is very important to her. She's alone except for good friends and distant family in the relatives who own the Dawson Family Guest Ranch. Like I said, that Cody has paternal family means a lot to her."

Angus took in a breath and put a hand on his shoulder. "I shouldn't have said anything. Forget it. Just thinking my anxious thoughts aloud and looking for trouble when there's none."

Except now that it was out there hovering in the air above Boone's head like a raincloud he couldn't forget it. *Quit thinking about it*, he told himself. Sarah *wouldn't* marry someone who'd be uncomfortable about her son's devoted uncle.

He suddenly pictured Sarah in a white dress, walking down the aisle to some faceless guy in a tux—and holding Cody at the altar.

Boone's collar tightened and his skin felt prickly. Now *he* was looking for trouble where there was none. Sarah wasn't even dating, wasn't looking to date. She'd said she wanted to focus on Cody—like Boone was. The changes in their lives.

"You like Sarah—that way?" Angus asked, leveling a look at Boone. "I noticed…some chemistry between you two."

"She's very pretty," Boone said. "Very nice too. She's a great mom. And she's really wonderful to me—so welcoming, like I said. It's impossible not to be drawn to her, you know? But I couldn't go there. Way too complicated for a lot of reasons."

"I don't know," Angus said. "Might *simplify* a lot. But," he added, narrowing his eyes a bit as if deep in thought, "you might be so drawn to Sarah, so committed to making sure she and Cody have everything they need because you want to do right by Will's memory. Either way, don't mistake caring about them for…something more. She gets hurt, you could get shut out of Cody's life."

Boone shivered despite the beautiful weather. And despite the fact that he'd thought about this already. Somehow, having his uncle say it aloud…

He had to be careful about messing up his and Sarah's relationship.

Just one of the many reasons that he and Sarah couldn't get romantically involved, despite how drawn he was, despite how attracted.

Anyway, they'd both said they weren't interested in romance right now.

Change the subject, Boone thought. Fast. "Speaking of all that, how are you holding up? Have you talked to Ingrid?"

Angus frowned. "I texted her two days ago to ask if she wanted to come over for dinner, and she texted back that unless there was a ring and a question involved, she had groceries in her own house."

Ingrid, who Boone had met a few times and thought was great for Angus, was *not* playing. *Good for her*, he thought. His uncle was set in his ways—but had been since he was a kid, according to family lore. The man could use the pushback. "And how are you feeling about that?"

Angus frowned harder, the lines around his mouth deepening. "I have one failed marriage under my belt. I thought that would last forever, especially with everything we had in common. Decades later she up and leaves me for some guy she just met?"

Angus's ex-wife, a former barrel racer, had fallen in love with a coworker at the bank where she worked as a mortgage loan officer. Apparently Angus had always made her feel alone and she'd decided she wanted more from life than a companion who rarely talked to her and found it annoying to answer questions. He'd refused marital counseling, and she'd decided enough was enough.

Angus hadn't planned on getting married at all, but after two years of dating his ex-wife in his late thirties, he'd succumbed to an ultimatum and didn't intend to do it again. But Boone had never seen his uncle like *this*, even during the divorce. It seemed to Boone that Ingrid had Angus's heart in a very different way that had even taken his uncle by surprise.

"Will told me I was an idiot," Angus said suddenly, taking Boone by surprise. His uncle's gaze was on the kids now lining up to go back into the school. "A couple of weeks ago. I told him what was going on with Ingrid, that she said if I couldn't marry her, she had to accept that I couldn't meet her needs. Will told me it was clear that I was deeply in love and should propose, and I told him that was exactly why I shouldn't. Because nothing lasts anyway. He said I was being an idiot, and I told him he was one to talk, that he should stop breaking hearts all over Wyoming." He paused, looking down. "I might have put it a little more vulgarly than that." Tears welled in Angus's eyes. "He changed the subject fast. That was the last time we spoke."

Boone put an arm around his uncle's shoulder. "Damn. So that must have been why you were on the list. Why he wanted to apologize."

"Maybe I am an idiot," Angus said, tears streaming down his cheeks.

Boone tightened his arm around his uncle's shoulder. "You're just working through stuff, Angus. And maybe

Will's helping from above by having you all torn up about your conversation with him."

Boone was curious if Angus had hit a nerve with Will with that comment about breaking hearts all over the state—especially in the more vulgar version. Given the list he'd made, it sure sounded like it. Maybe had even been the catalyst for the list. *Changing* had been on Will Riley's mind, and Uncle Angus had been a part of that.

Boone shared his theory, and Angus brightened some.

"Huh," Angus said. "I hadn't considered that I might have had something to do with Will making up that list. That's nice, Boone."

Boone felt that in his chest. Good. "So maybe you'll consider what he said about you and Ingrid?"

The frown was back on his uncle's face. "I don't want to talk about this anymore," Angus said, his gaze on the baby. "It's probably time for Cody's nap or something." He bent over a bit toward the baby. "Tired, little guy?"

Boone squeezed his uncle's hand. He knew when his uncle had reached his limit for personal talk. "Okay. Let's head back." They started walking, Boone's hand gentle on Cody's head for a moment. "No matter what, everything will work out as it should, Angus. I believe that."

"That's because you have faith in people and always did," Angus said. "I don't, though. Never did. Maybe except for you. So in my case, either you think I'm going to change my mind about proposing, which I won't, or that Ingrid will come back and forget about marriage. I don't see either happening."

Uncle Angus was a tough one. "Didn't you say a little while ago that Cody is a miracle? A sign that anything is possible?"

Angus seemed to brighten again, but then his whole body sagged. "Think Sarah is napping?" he asked, clearly changing the subject. "Must be rough waking up all night long to feed an infant."

An image of Sarah's beautiful face floated into Boone's mind. So many thoughts were running through it. Sarah exhausted at 3:00 a.m., feeding Cody, then raising him all by herself. Sarah at the altar marrying some guy who didn't want a paternal uncle in the picture.

Sarah and her warm smile.

Now it was Boone who wanted to change the subject, to anything other than how *he* was feeling or what he was thinking. He just wasn't sure about anything.

Except when it came to Cody. As Uncle Boone, he wasn't going anywhere.

Chapter Nine

Sarah had woken up from her nap to the delightful sound of chirping birds and a lawn mower in the distance. She'd popped out of the bed in Angus's guest room and just finished freshening up in the bathroom when she heard the front door open and voices.

The boys were back.

Her heart leapt at knowing she'd see Cody in a few seconds. He'd been away for barely an hour, and she'd missed him, even though she'd fallen asleep quite easily.

Because you trust Boone, she realized with a start. She'd known her baby was in good hands. And with an equally doting great-uncle too, who seemed to adore his great-nephew.

That she'd missed Cody, despite knowing he was safe and sound, made her worry about her maternity leave ending. Her last day as a full-time mom was coming right up, and then she'd be working eight-hour days, visiting Cody on breaks at the ranch daycare. She frowned, then sighed. *You've got him for several more days all to yourself, so make the most of it instead of being sad about what's to come. And you should thank your lucky stars for your good situation with childcare.*

The voices in the living room were hushed, and she

smiled, knowing that Boone and Angus were whispering on her account. Nice folks. She headed into the living room to show them she was awake.

Boone and Angus were sitting at the kitchen table, Cody on Boone's lap. They were debating the weather, if it was better to be hot or cold. They stopped and smiled at her when they noticed her coming down the stairs. Angus offered her something to drink, and Sarah opted for sweet iced tea.

Angus had just set the glass down at the table when his phone rang. He lunged for it in the center of the table, grabbing it like it was some kind of lifeline. He stared at the screen, then scowled hard and set it down, clearly sending the call to voicemail. He crossed his arms over his chest.

"Waiting for an important call?" Sarah asked, taking a sip of her tea to make her question seem more casual. She had a feeling this had to do with his ex-girlfriend and the breakup.

Angus didn't respond for a second, then his entire body sagged. "I was hoping it was Ingrid. That we could at least talk. But I guess she figures she said what she had to say—and that I did too." He sighed, staring out the window.

Aww. Sarah felt for the man.

"Does Ingrid know about Cody?" Boone asked.

Angus nodded. "I left a rambling message on her voicemail the day I found out myself. She didn't respond. And I told you about the text I sent her two days ago inviting her to dinner to talk. Unless I'm planning to propose, she's not coming."

Boone seemed to be considering something; Sarah could see the wheels turning.

"Call her right now. Tell her that your grandnephew is over for a visit and you'd love for her to meet him. It's a nice gesture, and it just might get you both in the same room, leave the door open to talk."

"But talk about what?" Angus asked. "Neither of us is going to change our minds. We're in a stalemate."

Boone seemed to be considering that. "Right, but at least you're trying again. You're showing her you care. That you want to share such a major development in your life with her."

"I guess," Angus said. "I mean, I do."

Boone nodded. "If she says no to coming over, well, then you'll have to accept that your actions are definitely having consequences. She wants a marriage proposal, and until she gets one, the relationship is over."

Angus heaved a sigh. "I could give it a try. She does like babies. She always used to stop at every stroller in town to comment on how cute the baby was."

Sarah smiled. "Give her a call. Like Boone said, it's a nice gesture—to want to introduce your grandnephew." If Ingrid was closed to that without the words—or *question*—she wanted to hear, Angus would find out.

"Here goes everything," Angus said and pressed some buttons on his phone, then headed down the hall for privacy.

Sarah looked at Boone and crossed her fingers. "I'm hopeful."

He nodded, moving over to the playpen and kneeling down to look at Cody, fast asleep. "Same. To be honest," he said, lowering his voice, "I think she just might *run* over to meet Cody. A sudden grandnephew—the son of the nephew he just lost—that's big. She might even think that such a special addition to Angus's life will change his way of thinking. More family focused. And maybe that'll be the case."

"It's definitely possible," Sarah said with a nod.

A phone rang in the direction Angus had gone. Boone gently ran his hand over Cody's fine hair, then stood.

They both turned at the sound of footsteps coming from down the hall. "Guess what?" Angus called as he approached. His expression alone told Sarah that the call had gone the way he'd hoped. "She let the call go to voicemail, so I left a message. But she called me right after listening. She said she'd love to meet my grand-nephew and to expect her in a half hour."

Boone smiled. "Great. A possible start."

Angus's smile faded. He paced for a bit, then froze. "Yeah, but I'm worried we'll just have the same conversation, same argument. She'll leave in tears like last time. Playing with a baby for an hour won't make Ingrid *less* interested in marriage. Babies make people think family and forever."

"Honestly, Uncle Angus," Boone said, tilting his head and putting a hand on the man's shoulder, "maybe it'll work its magic on *you*."

Sarah actually saw Angus visibly swallow.

"Do you think that's the sole reason she said yes to coming over to meet Cody?" Angus asked. "Because she thinks I'll change my mind? I won't. And I don't feel right about misleading her. Maybe I should call her back and tell her that."

Oh, Angus, Sarah thought. He was in a tizzy over the

subject of marriage. Sarah was getting the feeling that Angus's aversion to marriage—remarriage—was less about the commitment itself and more about his fear, his bad prior experience. If baby Cody could bring these two together even for an hour, so they could once again be reminded—in person—how they truly felt about each other, it was worth it. Angus might not get down on one knee, but maybe he'd soften enough so that he assure Ingrid he might just need a little more time to get comfortable with the idea. And maybe that would be all right with Ingrid—to a point. Perhaps she'd consider a time frame that she could accept.

"Uncle Angus," Boone said, "let's just see how things go. Give her—give yourself—a chance to be around each other again. A little time has passed since that argument." He paused, looking thoughtfully at his uncle. "You love this woman. That's all you need to know right at this exact minute."

Angus dropped down onto the sofa. He looked over at Cody in the portable playpen. "I do love her. But why can't Ingrid and I be a happy committed couple without the legal crud and all the pomp and formality? Why can't we just *be*?"

"Because the ultimate commitment is important to her," Boone said. "She's made that clear."

Angus scowled. "I've been married. So has she. We're both divorced. Who'd want to do that again? Not having that paper—maybe it's *freeing*. We'd be together because we want to be, not because a document binds us. *Love* should be the binder. Not a marriage certificate."

"The legal crud is important too, though," Boone said.

"Visiting you in the hospital. Making decisions for you, if need be. Rights to marital assets, etcetera."

Good for you, Boone, for bringing up those important points. From this conversation, it was clear to her that Boone Riley was pro-marriage—just something she found herself tucking away. If she ever did fix him up with someone in town, she'd have a good sense of how he felt. Just because he hadn't been able to commit to previous girlfriends didn't mean he wouldn't jump to propose to the right woman—to the love of his life.

Angus scowled harder. "See, you're already talking disaster!"

That snapped Sarah out of her thoughts.

Boone shook his head. "I'm just saying that there are solid reasons for marriage."

Angus sighed and waved his hand dismissively. "I thought the whole point of inviting her over was so that she'd see me in a new light."

Sarah glanced at Boone and could tell he was trying to figure out what light that would be. That Angus was a loving, doting great-uncle? That she'd feel more assured, somehow that he might change his mind?

"What light?" Sarah asked gently. Boone glanced over at her, and she could see he appreciated her question. Angus might be more apt to answer out of politeness than ignore it if it had come from his nephew.

Angus crossed his arms over his chest. "I just mean maybe she'll realize she loves me more than a piece of paper." He lifted his chin and seemed to brighten a little as if he'd found something to focus on. A mantra that could help see himself as right, a line he could toss out.

Except it wasn't just *a piece of paper.* Sarah didn't

have to be a matchmaker in the business of love and couples and happily-ever-after to know that.

In any case, Sarah was very interested in meeting Ingrid. She was pretty good at reading couples, and she was pretty sure she'd know if there was hope there, how Angus and Ingrid interacted, what their expressions said.

But she'd bank on Ingrid hoping a visiting baby grandnephew, a baby he could hold and feel in his arms against his heart, would loosen Angus's closed mind on the subject of marriage. At this point, Sarah wasn't sure of that. But as she'd been learning the past several days, anything really *was* possible.

Had Boone ever seen his uncle so nervous? The man was pacing, constantly peering out the window for Ingrid's car to see if she'd arrived, and Boone had caught Angus checking himself out in the hallway mirror, smoothing his hair and picking lint off his navy Henley shirt.

The man was so clearly *deeply* in love. Boone had a good feeling about Ingrid agreeing to come over. And surely having a successful matchmaker in the mix—someone who could help with any awkwardness or even lead the conversation if need be, just until the ex-lovebirds found their bearings—was a plus.

Finally the doorbell rang, but Angus seemed to freeze. Then he collected himself and went to the door. He ushered in Ingrid, who was holding a small bag from Bear Ridge General Store.

Boone and Sarah, who'd both been sitting on the sofa with Cody on his mother's lap, got up and walked over. As always when he was around his uncle and Ingrid, he couldn't help but notice what a nice couple they made. They just had a similar look—tall and fit, Ingrid in her early sixties with similar salt-and-pepper hair but shoulder length and wildly curly. She wore a long floral sundress with a mesh cardigan and lots of turquoise jewelry, including a few on her toes.

Angus was making the introductions. "And this handsome little fella is my grandnephew, Cody Dawson. He's got the Riley blue eyes."

"It's a pleasure to meet you, Mr. Cody," Ingrid said, smiling at the baby. "I got you a little something." She handed the bag to Sarah.

"How thoughtful," Sarah said, reaching into the bag. She pulled out a little stuffed giraffe rattle and grinned. "Aww, it's adorable. Thank you so much, Ingrid." She turned to Cody and shook the rattle near him.

Baby laughter exploded in the foyer.

Sarah shook it again. More laughter.

Talk about an icebreaker, Boone thought. This was great.

"Can I try that?" Angus asked.

Boone noticed that Ingrid looked quite pleased at that. Sarah handed over the rattle, and Angus gave it a shake. Cody laughed again, making them all laugh.

"What a little darling," Ingrid said. "I don't have kids—just wasn't in the cards for me—but I just adore babies!"

From there they settled into the living room, Angus setting out pastries and coffee. Boone was now holding Cody, who had dozed off.

"You two make such a lovely couple," Ingrid said to Boone and Sarah, her smile warm as she looked at both of them. "And what a story of how you came together. Really beautiful."

Boone swallowed. "We're, uh, not together," he said—awkwardly.

"We're building family bonds," Sarah said quickly, and Boone could have kissed her.

Wrong phrasing, he thought. But he appreciated the comment. That was exactly what they were doing. Building family bonds.

"Oh, sorry for assuming," Ingrid said, her cheeks a bit reddened. "You seem like such a couple." She turned her attention to the baby. "How wonderful to get two new relatives with a knock on the door. What a story," she added. "I'm so sorry about your brother, Boone."

Boone nodded. "I appreciate that. He left behind quite a legacy."

"Just when a person stops believing in much," Angus said, "a baby joins the family. I didn't think much could shock me—especially in a good way."

Boone noted Ingrid's eyes brighten at that.

"Sometimes a shock to the system is just what the doctor ordered," Ingrid said, then picked up her coffee mug.

"You look very nice, Ingrid," Angus said fast, clearly hoping to change the subject.

"Thank you, Angus. You do too."

The two of them held each other's gaze, and it was so clear they were both miserable without each other.

"I'm hoping we can get back together," Angus said suddenly. "I mean, it's obvious we miss each other, right? I've sure missed you, Ingrid."

Ingrid's expression softened, but then she lifted her chin. "Of course I miss you, Angus. I love you. Very much. But I want to get married. That ultimate commitment is very important to me. And I know it's not to you. So…"

"But surely how we feel about each other is more important that some piece of paper with legal mumbo jumbo," Angus said.

There it was, Boone thought. The line he knew Angus thought had weight.

"It's not a piece of paper," Ingrid said. "It's, yes, a legal document, but it tells me that I'm your beloved, your person, the woman you intend to grow even grayer with." She gave something of a sad-tinged smile. "Now that I'm retiring, I want to sit out on the porch with my *husband*—not my boyfriend. Marriage means we're *family*."

Angus seemed a bit deflated, as if he couldn't talk his way out of all that. "Well, look at Boone and Sarah here. They're building family bonds, just like Sarah said. And they're not even a couple."

Oh boy. That wasn't going to score his uncle any points. In fact, from Ingrid's face, he could see she didn't like that one bit.

"Their situation is quite different," Ingrid said. "And forgive me—I know I just met you two ten minutes ago—but you do *seem* like a couple. Honestly, I give it days until you're holding hands as you take little Cody out for a walk in his stroller."

Boone gaped at her.

Sarah did too, her eyes wide. She seemed to have frozen in place on the sofa.

Ingrid bit her lip. "I'm sorry. I'm just…" She took in a deep breath. "I'm just not myself these days. Blurting things out. Bursting into tears. It's what happens when the man you love is being so stubborn and nothing you say seems to matter."

Sarah leaned across the coffee table and took Ingrid's hands. "It's okay. I can understand why you'd think we were together. We've become good friends and we're both very focused on Cody, so we probably present a very united front." She smiled a bit awkwardly, then eyed Angus as if willing him to say something.

Angus seemed frozen himself, but then he turned to Ingrid. "You know how much I love you. Why can't that be enough? Why does marriage have to be the be-all and end-all? The divorce rate is nuts. Why can't we just be *together*?"

Ingrid stood. "We've had this conversation. It was painful then and it hurts worse now because this is the first time I've seen you in two weeks. I wanted to be there for you when your nephew died. I wanted to be there for you when you found out about Cody. But refusing to propose just tells me I'm not important enough to you. That you'll only go so far with me. That hurts, Angus." With that she stood. "It was lovely to meet you, Sarah," she said. With that, she hurried toward the door.

"Ingrid, honey, please wait," Angus called, getting up and running after her.

"I want a marriage proposal. I want you to be my husband. I won't settle for less, Angus Riley." She pulled open the door and left.

Angus hung his head and let out a hard sigh. It took him a minute to turn around. "Dammit," he said, then his cheeks reddened. "Sorry. I didn't mean to curse in front of the baby."

"It's okay, Angus," Sarah said. "I know you're hurting."

Hurting was the key word. Hurting himself. Being his own worst enemy.

"Angus, I know you're sick of me taking Ingrid's side, but I do think you two belong together. And I think you're letting fear control you. It's not marriage you have a problem with. It's the fear that it won't work out, that she'll leave you like Christy did. But she's not Christy. And the two of you are an entirely different couple. Thirty years have passed since you were that loner bachelor who gave into an ultimatum. You're not him anymore, Angus."

Angus was staring at him as if all he'd said had penetrated his thick skull, but then he scowled and looked away.

Sarah was looking at Boone as if she thought he deserved some kind of medal for that little speech, which he appreciated. "Your nephew made some really good points, Angus," she said gently. "Worth thinking about, right?"

Angus made something of a *harrumph* sound and went into the kitchen. "Anyone want more coffee?" he called out in a warmer tone as though he intended for the previous subject to be closed.

Boone said no thanks since they should probably hit the road since it was getting late and that Angus had a lot of thinking to do.

"I'm all thought out," Angus said with a frown as he came back into the living room.

Boone smiled at his uncle. "Well, we'll see when you're tossing and turning tonight. What Ingrid said, what I said might shake something loose in that head of yours."

Angus walked over to Sarah and bent down to run a finger along Cody's cheek. He was still sleeping. "Don't ever let anyone tell you how you feel, Cody. Remember those words." He straightened up and gave Boone something of a glare, then turned his attention to Sarah. "Thank you for bringing him over," he said to Sarah. "It made my day—heck, my *year*—to meet him and you."

"I'm sure there'll be lots more visits," Sarah said with a warm smile.

Angus opened his arms for a hug, and Boone could see Sarah was touched. They embraced with the baby between them, his uncle careful not to squish the little guy. "You take good care of my grandnephew. I already love him to pieces."

"I promise I will," she said.

Boone hugged Angus next. "And no one's telling you how to feel. Just to think about what's most important to you."

"Argh," Angus said like a pirate, waving his hand dismissively. As Sarah shifted Cody in her arms for the walk out to the pickup, he gave the baby a kiss on his head.

His uncle could squawk all he wanted, but Boone believed in his heart that a life with the woman he loved should win over the alternative, which was to lose her. He also believed in his uncle enough to be pretty sure Angus would come around.

And he figured such a belief boded well for himself and his own future, that he'd chose love over whatever the Riley curse was that had kept them from giving one hundred percent of themselves.

Chapter Ten

As they neared Bear Ridge, Sarah sat in the passenger seat beside Boone, thinking about how special the day had been. Cody had two wonderful new relatives. For a man who didn't have children—and never wanted kids—Great-Uncle Angus was a natural around Cody and had taken to him immediately, the baby bringing out a side of him that might have never existed, despite being there for his two nephews all their childhoods. The "granddaddy" element to his relationship with Cody—since he alone could fulfill that role—seemed very meaningful to Angus.

As they'd driven away from his house, she and Boone had talked about just that—and how once Angus sat with his feelings, uncomfortable as they were—he'd see that he wasn't the same man he used to be. Ingrid had surely had a hand in the changes Angus had gone through the past year, and now a baby relative would too.

Sarah watched the scenery go by, the beautiful trees and mountains in the distance, her heart full. Today was everything Sarah had always wanted for her son. Family to love Cody like she did. People she could share worries with, big and small. Her excitement over milestones. Someone to say *Go take a nap—I'll watch the baby.*

She'd had a glorious nap.

And she was extra wide awake right now. Because Boone wouldn't be dropping Sarah and Cody off at her apartment; they'd all be going to his B and B, where they'd spend the night…together. She'd pushed that to the back of her mind all day, having enough to think about. But now it was forefront.

You two make such a lovely couple…

She couldn't stop thinking about Ingrid's assumption that they were a couple, even though Angus wouldn't have described them that way. Ingrid thought so because they came across that way, acted that way. Naturally.

Interesting.

"What a day," she said as Boone turned onto Main Street. "Your uncle hosting us, him meeting Cody, Ingrid coming over, us possibly helping reunite them. I do hope they get back together. As a matchmaker, I definitely think those two belong together. You could *feel* the love between them."

Boone nodded. "I've always thought they were great for each other. Maybe they'll end up compromising. Enough to get back together and go from there."

"What would the compromise be on Ingrid's end?" she asked.

"Maybe giving Angus a time frame," Boone said. "Three months, something like?"

Sarah considered that. "I think with all the big changes in his life so suddenly—the breakup, losing Will, gaining a grandnephew—he actually might really benefit from that extra time. Not forever…three months does sound right. She'd be giving him a chance to get comfortable with what she wants while in the relationship. She just might go for that."

He nodded. "And three months would give Angus some breathing room. I couldn't imagine he'd let her walk away after that. But I don't know. He's a toughie. And were we too hard on him? Getting in his business like we know him better than he knows himself?"

She smiled. "We were definitely on love's side."

He glanced at her and smiled. "That makes me feel better. Thanks for putting it that way. I've been thinking about it the whole drive. What he said to Cody about not letting anyone tell him how to feel. I don't want to strong-arm him into doing something he really might not want to do."

He paused, and she could see he was conflicted.

"I can't see that man doing anything he doesn't want to do," she said.

"That's true. And I really do think it's fear—the shock of his ex-wife leaving him, feeling blindsided, how awful the divorce felt—that has the grip on him. So I feel like I'm doing right by him by pushing a little. A lot, maybe." He slid a rueful smile at her, and she touched his arm in solidarity.

"I'm curious," she said. "Do you know the story of how he came around with his ex-wife? She gave him an ultimatum? How long did it take for him to give in?"

"From stories I've heard over the years, it was just one week. He always said he married the first time around because during their week apart, he missed her enough to realize that it would be nice to have a 'permanent companion.'"

"'Permanent companion'?" she repeated. That was some phrasing.

"He's not exactly a romantic. He's really in love with Ingrid, though. And I have no doubt the depth of his feelings for her are very scary." He glanced over at her. "I was telling him when we went for our walk with Cody that I've never felt about anyone the way I feel about my nephew. That it's powerful stuff."

Sarah's heart jumped in her chest. What a wonderful thing to say. To *feel*. "Really? Is that true?"

He nodded, glancing at her again. "I mean, I loved my parents. My uncle. My brother. I love my friends. But what's going on in this thing," he said, slapping a hand on his heart, "over that little guy back there? Never experienced that before. Must be a baby thing. A baby-relative thing."

She was so moved that she couldn't speak for a second. "I certainly feel that way about Cody. A depth of emotion I can't even put into words. I'm so touched that he means so much to you."

He looked at her and smiled, and something gave way inside her, that gate she kept around the softest parts of herself. *Each hour you're making me trust you more and more, Boone Riley*, she thought—again half nervous, half excited.

Before she could stop herself, she touched her hand to his on the steering wheel, skin-to-skin contact, and he smiled so warmly at her that another little piece of her melted. The part that had been covered in ice.

She kept her gaze out the side window, equal parts worried about herself and in wonder about her developing feelings for this man.

Suddenly, that she'd be staying in his hotel suite was very much in the forefront of her mind.

Boone was practically tripping over his own feet and words as he pulled into the small parking lot of the B and B just past 7:00 p.m. Sarah and the baby would be staying with him for the night. As she got Cody from her car seat while he grabbed her bag, he was so aware of every little move Sarah made. The way she pushed her long blond hair behind her ear as the gorgeous June evening breeze blew a strand in her face. How her sundress skimmed over her body, highlighting her curves. Her pink toenails in her sandals.

"The B and B is so pretty," she said, glancing around as they headed up the stone walkway to the front door.

You're *so pretty*, he thought. He blinked to clear his brain, trying to focus on the building. "It's a nice change from my tiny cabin. I think my suite is actually bigger."

The proprietor greeted them, and Boone led them to his suite on the second floor.

"Wow, nice," Sarah said as they walked inside the large room. "And a view of the town green and park."

Boone showed her the bedroom, which housekeeping had made pristine. He'd be bunking on the sofa bed. He went back outside to get Cody's bassinet and changing pad from the truck, returning to find the baby fussing. Not quite crying, but far from content. Boone set up the bassinet on the side of the bed near the window, covered by gauzy curtains with heavier ones on the sides.

"Let's try bicycle pumps," she said, laying Cody down on the bed and cycling his little legs. He seemed to like that. Then she picked him up and held him vertically against her, patting his back. A big burp emerged. "Success."

But when Sarah put him down in the bassinet, he started crying. Boone sang the baby's favorite Western song, but he fussed harder. He tried picking up Cody and walking him around the suite, and that seemed to calm down the cranky guy. But the moment his body would touch the bottom of the bassinet, Cody's eyes would pop open, his face would scrunch up, and he'd screech.

"Maybe he misses his new swanky crib," Boone said with a smile. "He barely got to use it."

"Probably. And his new sheets with all the cute baby animals. He's always liked his bassinet, though. He's just being a fussbudget. He's usually pretty easy, but he has his moments."

Boone tried singing a new song, a more current one about lost love, and Cody's eyes started drooping. "Hey, he likes soft rock." He kept singing, voice low, and the eyes closed. And stayed closed.

Sarah chuckled. "You're so good with him."

He smiled, then said, "Well, let's see if he screams bloody murder as I lay him down." Boone carefully lowered him, hovering above the mattress, then finally setting him on top. Not a peep.

"Yes!" he whispered on a chuckle. "I've definitely learned more about babies in two days than I ever knew in all my twenty-eight years. Bicycle pumping baby legs is a new one, though. I'll add that to soft rock being his jam." He glanced at Sarah, trying to figure out if she wanted some space. They'd been together since noon and a lot the day before. "I can pick up dinner if you're getting hungry." He liked the idea of eating out on the balcony.

"I have such a craving for pasta," she said, giving Cody's hair a caress before moving away from the bassinet. They went into the sitting room, Sarah dropping down onto the armchair. "I thought my cravings would disappear once I gave birth, but nope."

"What's that place Jeremy and Deanna had their first date—an Italian restaurant he'd said?"

"Manelli's. It's just a few doors down. What I would give for their spaghetti carbonara."

"Done," he said with a smile. "See you in a bit."

Her warm, happy smile made his heart flip over, which sent him out the door in record time. He liked this woman too much. Was too affected by that smile. By wanting to make her happy. And this one was very easy to make happen.

He was back in a half hour with their dinners—her carbonara, Milanese chicken for him, and some garlic knots to share. Cody was sleeping peacefully, so they took the baby monitor out to the table on the balcony.

"Thanks for all this, Boone," she said, munching on a garlic knot. "My craving will definitely be satisfied and then some."

They clinked fizzy water, then dug into their entrees, talking about Bear Ridge and how Sarah had lived there her entire life and never once found the small, sleepy town boring. Boone liked the town a lot. The main street had a general store, a few restaurants, the great diner he'd eaten at the other day, and some shops. The park and town green in the center of downtown was welcoming. He could see himself here, which was a good thing since he'd be calling Bear Ridge home.

"You won't miss your hometown?" she asked, twirling pasta around her fork.

"With such good Italian food in Bear Ridge?" he asked with a grin. "Honestly, I'll always be nostalgic for my hometown since I grew up there. But it's never been the same since my mom died. I don't have family there anymore. Until I found out about my nephew, I'd been thinking of moving to Culpepper to be near Angus, but he might have found that a little *too* close."

She smiled. "I know what you mean. He clearly loves you, but he likes his privacy. So you mentioned at lunch that you'll be heading back home tomorrow to clear out your cabin?"

He ate the last of his excellent chicken Milanese. "What I own can fit in a duffel bag. The cabin came furnished, so it's just my personal stuff. I'll be in and out in under an hour."

Sarah tilted her head as if thinking about something. "What about—" She stopped and twirled her final bite of pasta.

"What about what?" he asked, curious.

"Well, I was just wondering about your childhood things."

His chest got a little tight, as it did whenever he thought about his mother. He missed her and always would. He missed his dad too, of course, but Cal Riley had left his mother when Boone was still in elementary school and he'd rarely come around to visit. Every few months he'd pop in unannounced as if he'd found himself in town and figured he'd stop by.

If Boone had thought that would bring him and Will closer, since his older brother had had the same experience, he'd been wrong. *Listen to your big brother*, Will had said. *You can't count on anyone. Not even yourself.*

That had not made Boone feel better. And unfortunately, it had seemed like Will Riley's mantra. But the list—that beautiful piece of paper in his brother's scrawl—had told Boone that Will had rethought that, that he'd realized he *could* count on himself to be the person he wanted, the brother he wanted to be.

Which was why Boone would believe that had Will known about Cody, he would have been the father he wished he'd had.

He could feel his heart shifting in his chest and swallowed around the lump in his throat. From one bittersweet memory to the next. "My mother would have adored Cody and treated him like an honorary grandson," Boone said. "She was sick for almost a year before she passed. Treatment wasn't working and was just making her sicker, so she opted to just be home with me and a visiting nurse. After she passed, I took a few things from our house that she loved—a couple of mugs, a small painting she'd bought on a trip to Utah—a red wool scarf I use every winter. But the furniture just reminds me of those months. The beds and the area rugs. The kitchen table she struggled to get to to sit down for herbal tea. I donated it all." He sucked in a breath. "I kept a few things from Will's apartment too. His favorite belt buckle, a little horse statue. I'll give them to Cody when he's a little older." He closed his eyes for a second and again had to swallow around the lump in his throat.

Suddenly, it was all too much.

He stood and walked to the railing on the far end,

looking out at the woods. He could feel Sarah moving over to him, her soft hand on his elbow.

"I know just how all that feels," she whispered. "I miss my parents so much. Loss is so hard."

He turned around, and without thinking, he leaned toward her. She kept her gaze on him, her expression full of compassion, of curiosity, of something else he wasn't quite sure of. He leaned even closer, and then so did she, their mouths meeting. Her lips were soft. She pressed a bit closer, deepening the kiss, a hand on the side of his face.

He needed this—exactly this—right now. And apparently so did she.

She pulled away, still looking at him, and he could see the worry in her beautiful face. Just like he was sure was all over his. This wasn't just a friendly kiss. It was much more. It had held desire and understanding, a dangerous combination.

"I think I hear Cody," she said fast, pressing her lips together—rubbing them together like an exorcism or to feel the imprint of the kiss, he wasn't sure. She hurried into the suite, disappearing into the bedroom.

Boone's thoughts traveled to the sofa bed. Where he'd spend the night. Suddenly he imagined Sarah beside him. Naked.

No, no, no. He couldn't be fantasizing about her. Couldn't be *kissing* her, let alone thinking about making love to her.

But he had kissed her. And she'd kissed him back.

They could easily end up in bed next.

Unease settled in his stomach. He quickly packed up

their takeout containers in the bag, then turned to look out at the woods again.

"Still fast asleep," Sarah said in too bright a voice.

He turned to find her in the doorway of the balcony, expression unreadable and clearly as caught off guard as he was. "I… We… I mean…"

She clutched the monitor to her chest. He stared at it, a solid reminder of why they couldn't get involved. They couldn't do anything that would eventually tear them apart, the way dating always did. Relationships didn't last. He and Sarah needed to be solid for Cody's sake.

"I shouldn't have kissed you," he said.

She lifted her chin. "But you did. And I kissed you back," she added. She bit her lip, quiet for a moment. "Look, the kiss made me nervous too. To the point that I pretended to hear Cody stirring to get away from the reality of what's happening between us. But what I realized as I walked away was that maybe trying to ignore what's between us will only make things worse. *More* awkward."

That was true. "But starting something between us… things could go south. Like they always do. And then we'll find out what awkward *really* is."

She seemed to be thinking about that. "Why are you so sure things would go bad? I mean, I don't know why I'm asking since none of my relationships have worked out either." She sighed hard and turned away.

"I guess I worry that I'm more like the Rileys than I realize. My dad, my uncle, my brother—all notorious for having issues with commitment. Maybe that cowgirl was right about me. That none of my relationship have gone anywhere because I didn't *want* them to—because

I really don't want to get serious. Maybe it's just in my blood to be noncommittal. If I start something with you and then end up disappointing you…"

Part of his brain was fighting for them. The list Will made floated into his brain. Apologies. Reparation. Vows to be better. Will wasn't just one thing. Neither was his dad. His uncle certainly was multifaceted. He tried to remember all he'd said to Angus today about love and romance and marriage, but everything was a jumble.

One of the last things his mother said to him flitted through his head: *Don't ever give up on yourself.* The way she hadn't when she got sick. She fought to the end.

They'd often talked about Will and that mantra of his. His mother had been adamant that Boone not think that way. That he try to work on Will too.

His heart twisted. Boone *had* tried. And it had worked, right? The list existed.

He dropped his head back with a hard inward sigh. This wasn't about him—or even Sarah. It was about making sure that nothing came between him and his nephew. His dead brother's son. Boone's future.

He could feel something in his chest tighten. Harden.

"Well, then," she said, eyeing him. Clearly she could see that something in the air, in him, had changed. She'd said she was a good reader of people and definitely was. "Let's just forget it. It was only a kiss. It doesn't have to mean anything. We were just…caught up in an emotional moment. It was a big day. A big couple of days. And big days take their toll."

"Caught up in the moment," he repeated with a firm nod, appreciating the phrase, which felt exactly right.

"Yeah," he said, nodding again. "It's been quite a couple of days."

She gave him an awkward smile, but he could still see the warmth there, and relief trickled into his brain. "In fact, I'm really zonked. I think I'll turn in." As he spoke, his stomach twisted more. That earlier unease was spreading. And he wasn't entirely sure what it all meant. What he was reacting to. Was it just about his relationship with Cody?

Or was he himself gripped by the same fear he accused his uncle of?

Heck if I know, he told himself, aware that he was trying to get out of thinking about this right now. It was all too much. Overwhelming.

He looked at her. She looked at him. And it was clear to see she needed some space too.

But the moment she was on the other side of the bedroom door, his heart beating a mile a minute, he missed her.

Chapter Eleven

Sarah woke up for good at just after 6:30 a.m., Cody still sleeping. He'd been up twice in the middle of the night, and she'd actually been grateful to get out of bed and tend to him. She'd been tossing and turning anyway. Thinking about that kiss and all the reasons why she and Boone Riley couldn't go any further. Taking care of Cody in the wee hours had served as a reminder that she and Boone should be platonic.

Everything Boone had said last night rang true to her. That things could get more awkward. That things could go very south. And suddenly the beautiful relationship between Boone and Cody could be negatively affected.

Let's say you and Boone do get more involved. Because you both want to protect his relationship with Cody, that will always be hovering in the air above the relationship, kind of controlling it. Boone afraid to acknowledge he's not actually falling in love and wants to break up. You reacting. Suddenly you're having arguments. He's storming off. You're frustrated. He wants to see Cody, of course, but that would mean seeing you and you're in a fight. That's how it starts to end both you and Boone—and Uncle Boone's great relationship with his nephew.

Sarah closed her eyes.

But at the same time, what the heck were they supposed to do with how they felt about each other? She'd wondered if he was attracted to her, and she'd gotten her answer in the form of that sweet, sensual, five-second burst of desire and connection. As she'd rocked Cody in the middle of the night, finding herself humming that Western song Boone liked to sing to him, she'd also thought about how Boone had been equally as affected—both by the kiss itself and how wrong it was. At least they were on the same page, she realized with a sigh. They felt exactly the same way.

She'd stayed in her room the entire night after retreating from him, thankful for the attached bathroom and that there was another full bath in the main room of the suite. She and Boone hadn't had to cross paths, allowing them both some time and space to process what had happened between them.

Caught up in the moment? She'd say it was more like many moments that had led to what felt inevitable. Now, as she brushed her teeth in the bathroom, looking at herself in the mirror and staring at her lips, *that* was what worried her. That the kiss had felt like it had been days in the making. A building of trust and closeness, of a shared interest.

She paused at that thought—a shared interest. Cody. She was reminded of what Doreen had said about how Boone might be ensnared by taking care of his brother's unfinished business and when he was more at peace, he wouldn't have the burning need to be such a devoted uncle.

Not that Doreen had put it quite like that, but that was

the gist. Talk about something not ringing true, though. That wasn't the Boone Riley she was coming to know.

People could change on a dime, though, when it came to dating. They thought they felt this way but woke up one day just not feeling it anymore. So they pulled away. Made excuses. And suddenly, a heart was broken.

Age-old story. It happened all the time. It was why both she and Boone were still single.

Any way she looked at it, she and Boone couldn't get together. No more kissing. They'd come to that last night, and she just needed her squishy, hopeful heart to accept it. Her head was there.

That settled, she felt ready to finally open the door separating their rooms.

Boone was sitting on the balcony, a big bag from the Bear Ridge Diner on the table. He was sipping an iced coffee.

"Morning," she called out. "Cody's still asleep."

He turned, his expression capturing the awkwardness they'd both been worried about. She could only imagine what her face looked like.

"Morning," he said, standing. He gave her a warm smile, but she'd gotten to know him enough to see the strain he was trying to hide. "I got a bunch of stuff for us for breakfast," he added, pointing at the bag on the table. "Bagels and cream cheese, fruit salad. If you're in the mood for eggs and bacon or pancakes, I can go back."

Of course he would, she thought with an inward sigh. Boone was a dream man. And had to be off-limits to her.

"Bagels and fruit sounds great," she said. She sat down and rummaged through the bag, pulling out a sesame bagel and a little container of cream cheese. She popped a red grape into her mouth, refreshing, tart and sweet. "Thanks for this."

"I got you a mocha iced coffee, no cream, no sugar," he said, gesturing at the cup. "I remembered that's how you ordered it at the guest ranch cafeteria."

Why are you the perfect man? she wanted to scream. Her last boyfriend, who she'd dated for months, had brought her back a coffee with cream and sugar, the way he took his, when she always drank hers black. It was a small thing, but it added up to him not really *seeing* her, not paying attention. Lindy McDonaugh's top requirement for what she wanted in a relationship came back to her. To matter. Sarah hadn't *mattered* to that guy.

Her phone pinged, and she lunged for it, glad for the distraction from her gloomy thoughts—and from Boone, so tall and strong and handsome in the chair next to her. It was her landlord, letting her know he was in the back room right now at the feed store and there were no paint fumes.

Perfect. She could go home right now. Get away from the scene of the crime.

"My landlord," she said, popping up. "I'm all set to go home. I'll take breakfast to go."

"Sarah," he said but then didn't say anything else. He sucked in a breath. "That awkwardness I was talking about—it's *vibrating*."

She bit her lip. "I know."

This was good. That he'd brought it up. That they'd address it. She'd found herself unable to start the conversation.

Because you like him more than you want to admit to yourself, she understood with sudden clarity.

Any budding romance between them had to be shut down in the morning light—and it was better for her that he do it. She might go back on her own dictums, but if he was the one slamming on the brakes…

"Obviously, I'm very attracted to you, Sarah Dawson. But we both know how complicated things could get. And *complicated* will definitely interfere with the kind of uncle I want to be. The kind of uncle you want me to be."

She nodded despite the churning in her stomach, her heart trying to catch up with her head, which knew he was right. "I feel exactly the same way."

He looked at her for a moment, and what was also obvious was that his own head and heart were in conflict too. "So from here on in, *friends*," he said, extending his hand.

"Friends," she said, shaking it. But the moment their skin touched, she felt it in her toes. Goose bumps raced up her spine, along her arms.

And she knew it was the same for him because he didn't immediately let go of her hand, and he was looking intently at her, as if trying to make himself believe something. Make a vow. Of keeping his lips to himself.

That was how it had to be. And not just to protect his relationship with Cody.

To protect her *heart*, which had been kicked around enough.

Boone hadn't been exaggerating about needing under an hour to pack up his cabin. But since that had gone so quickly, he had hours to fill and the two people he wanted to spend time with were not available. Because of what had happened last night.

A very good reminder of what could happen in the future. The awkwardness between him and Sarah meant they needed to give each other some space. And despite having the whole day to himself and wanting to see his nephew—missing the little guy already—he had to make himself scarce from the Dawsons. For the next bunch of hours anyway.

Maybe tonight things would be back to normal and they could both just forget the kiss and move along.

That was dumb. He wouldn't forget it. How much he'd wanted to kiss her. The yearning. The meeting of their mouths. How soft and warm her lips had been. How right it had felt in the moment. They'd both just have to ignore their attraction.

Except it was more than just attraction. This wasn't a case of lust. He liked Sarah—a lot. He felt so connected to her. When was the last time he'd felt anything like this for a woman?

A long time ago. When he'd gotten his heart handed to him. Once because his first love, albeit puppy love in high school, had moved away. The second time because he'd been betrayed—used.

Another good reminder. Feeling the way he did led to raw, unbearable heartache. And why would he welcome that into his life, which was going so well right now despite the gnawing grief that continuously poked at him? He had a new baby nephew. A new very good friend in Sarah. A new job and new town. He was helping—or trying—to get his uncle back with his ex. Things were good, and he had to keep them that way.

He'd text Sarah later and suggest a walk in the park, to the duck pond she'd mentioned. That would put the focus back on Cody—where it belonged. And set things right between them.

It *would* take some doing on his part to forget the kiss, though. It had lasted all of seconds and yet had been extremely potent. Making him want more—not just sexually, but more of Sarah the person.

He shook his head to clear it, set the box of his stuff in the bed of his pickup, said his goodbyes to his former boss and friends, who were all happy for him—the news about his nephew and the new job at the dude ranch. He'd been asked at least five times—with a big grin—if that meant discounts for them on the day rate and guest rate at the Dawson Family Guest Ranch, and he said sorry, probably not. His cowgirl friend, the one who'd told him his "type" was keeping him single, gave him a hug goodbye and said she was wrong about him, that he clearly *could* commit, and that committing to being an uncle was the most beautiful thing she'd heard in months.

He'd take that. It left him with a good feeling—that he was doing right, including by Sarah and Cody. When it came to being an uncle. A good support system for Sarah. And by making the vow to be platonic.

He sat in his truck, about to hit the road, when he realized how he could fill the day. He could knock off a couple of names on Will's list—the folks he owed money to. He pulled the list from his glove compartment.

STUFF TO DO
1. Do better with Boone
2. Apologize to Uncle Angus
3. Apologize to Sarah Dawson—works at Dawson Family Guest Ranch

4. *Pay back Eli Charlson the 50 bucks—with interest if can swing it*
5. *Apologize to Jennifer Parkalini*
6. *Settle up your bar tabs at Drink Up and McDeedles*
7. *Do better, period*

He paused at number five. Jennifer Parkalini. He'd avoided thinking about the name since meeting Sarah because he hadn't been ready for another shock to the system. But it had been a few days now. Ignoring and hiding his head in the sand had never gotten him anywhere. It was time to deal with who this other woman on the list had been to his brother.

He entered the name into the search engine on his phone. There appeared to be only one Jennifer Parkalini in Wyoming. There were three entries with her name associated. She'd written a letter to the editor of *Whitley Township Free Weekly*, and he clicked on it. An appeal to the community that pet cats should be kept indoors for their sake and the bird population. He went back to the search hits, zeroing in on one that noted age, address, telephone number, and even voter affiliation. It was crazy how much information was right there in a simple web search. Apparently, Jennifer Parkalini was *sixty-four years old.* Huh. She lived in Whitley, which was two towns over from Darlington.

Boone let out a long-held breath on the subject of Jennifer Parkalini and her connection to his late brother. Not a former girlfriend or one-night stand—he assumed because of the age. Will had always preferred his dates to be younger than him since *women mature faster and I'm pretty immature.*

Okay, Jennifer Parkalini was not the mother of another nephew—or niece. So who had she been to Will and what did he have to apologize to her about? Will Riley had never had a cat to let roam free.

Whatever his brother had done to warrant the apology, it had to be big. Maybe he'd cheated her in some way. Disparaged her. Gotten into a bad fight with someone close to her—a son, maybe. Could be anything.

Find out, he told himself. He punched in the telephone number listed in the search details. He instantly got voicemail. *Hiya, you've reached Jennifer. I'll be out of town for two weeks, taking my new RV for a spin.* She gave some details about the RV and the date she'd return. *Leave a message, and I'll call you back when I'm home. Toodles.*

Toodles? Boone couldn't see his brother knowing anyone who went around saying that.

She'd noted the day she'd be back, just under a week from now. He'd try again then. Boone stared out the windshield of his pickup, this new information swirling around his brain. *Who are you, Jennifer Parkalini?*

He punched in his uncle's number. When Angus picked up, he explained what he'd found out.

"Sixty-four?" Angus said. "Interesting."

"Right? What could he have done for this woman to be on the list of folks to apologize to?"

"I'll be curious to find out, that's for sure," Angus said.

"The name Jennifer Parkalini doesn't ring a bell?" Boone asked.

"No. And it's pretty memorable, so not one I'd easily forget."

Angus asked about Cody and if he'd sprouted any teeth or hit any new milestones, which Boone thought was funny given that it had been one day since Angus had seen the baby, but then again, babies changed so fast.

"I kissed Sarah last night," he blurted out. He hadn't intended to even tell his uncle about that. But Boone clearly needed to talk about it.

"I'm not surprised, Boone," Angus said. "It was obvious there's something between you two. Just hovers in the air around you both. Electricity. Even Ingrid saw that within ten minutes."

You two make such a lovely couple...

We're not together...

We're building family bonds...

He swallowed, a lead lump settling in his gut. "We talked about it, and it's not going to happen again. For Cody's sake. Things get ugly between me and Sarah, like you said, it'll affect my relationship with my nephew. Maybe I wouldn't be able to see him as often as I'd like."

"I can't see Sarah being petty," Angus said. "And I barely know the woman. Just a feeling I got from her."

"Yeah, I know. But awkwardness gets in the way. And it's better to just avoid it."

"So you two are just going to avoid how you feel about each other?" Angus asked. "That sounds dumb."

"*Dumb* is risking it ending badly and causing problems." Hadn't he just said that?

"Who says it'll end at all?" Angus asked. "Maybe you two were meant to find each other. Maybe it's meant to be."

Meant to be? Was he kidding with this stuff? "Angus, what has ever been meant to be? What has ever worked out? You're ready to walk away from the woman you love to avoid marrying her."

His uncle was quiet for a few moments. *Dammit*, Boone thought. *Why did you say that? You're being an insensitive jerk. You're not the only one who has a complicated situation.*

"Jeez, Boone, I'm not used to you being the cynical one," Angus said. "You're the one usually trying to make me see the other side."

Boone inwardly sighed. "Right? I don't know what's with me? My head's all messed up."

"Mine too. I'm not sure if that means we're thinking or if we're *not* thinking."

Boone chuckled. "Yeah. I'm not sure either. Anyway, I'm off to go pay Will's bar tabs. At least I'll be able to cross those off the list. That'll lift me up a little."

"Take care, Boone. And give yourself a break. That's what you'd tell me to do."

Would he at this point? Boone didn't want his uncle to give himself a break; he thought Angus would be happier if he and Ingrid were together. But Boone was hardly one to talk or give advice. Not that he was using complicated as an excuse. His and Sarah's situation did have to be treated with kid gloves.

Yeah, but maybe you're jumping on that so you can feel good about backing away.

Like you always do.

Like father, like uncle, like brother. His father had married three times—left all three wives. The first two with young children. The third when she'd wanted her mother to move in with them. He'd moved on then, not marrying again and sticking around within an hour of Boone's and Will's hometowns. In the end, undiagnosed heart issues had taken him. The three Riley men had been teary at the funeral that Angus had arranged, all of them noting they hadn't seen Cal Riley in over a year at that point. Some things just left a person unsettled to the point they tried not to think about it, and Boone's dad—and his loss—was among them.

But Angus had actually made the ultimate commitment—he *had* gotten married, even if "permanent companion" didn't seem like the most romantic of reasons to say *I do*. He'd been a faithful husband, home every night except for fishing trips a few times a year with his buddies from the sheriff's department. Boone knew this because he'd once run into Angus's ex-wife not long after she'd left him, and she'd told Boone that it had been hard to leave a solid husband, a faithful, good man who helped around the house and even did the grocery shopping. *But all those years of me trying to get him to talk, to share something in his head, to make me feel like I wasn't alone... You think you can change a person for the better, especially if you're getting married because you have that base and forever. But that didn't turn out to be the case...*

Boone had left that interaction feeling rattled; he'd had to sit in his truck for a full five minutes to try to shake it off and hadn't been able to for a few days. He'd felt for her; he'd felt for Angus. Now here Boone was, trying to get his uncle to change his spots when his wife of thirty years hadn't been able to.

Maybe Boone should mind his own business.

But like Boone himself had said, Angus and Ingrid were not Angus and Christy. Different relationship. Different time. Different life experiences guiding his uncle now.

He felt a little more hopeful as he and Angus disconnected. Boone started his truck, eager for the distraction that the twenty-minute drive to Darlington and his business at McDeedles and Drink Up would provide.

Boone was familiar with the two bars. McDeedles was a pub and served Will's favorite burger in town, so he was a regular there. Boone had been there with him a few times over the years. Drink Up was more a dive bar where Will had spent countless hours shooting pool and playing darts. Both establishments were across the street from each other on the main drag in Darlington.

Boone's head was on a little straighter as he pulled into the small parking lot for McDeedles. They opened at 11:30, and it was just past. Good timing. Inside he went to the long bar. A tall, muscular guy in his forties in a Western shirt and bolo tie was stacking glasses behind the bar. Boone took a seat at the bar and grabbed a menu between the ketchup bottle and napkin dispenser.

"Steakhouse burger with the works is today's special," the guy said. "Comes with a draft beer and a side of fries or onion rings for ten bucks."

"Say no more. And I'll take the fries."

The guy nodded and typed in the order, then poured Boone's beer.

"My brother used to come here and ran up a tab, apparently," Boone told the bartender. "He, uh, passed away, and I'd like to pay off his debt."

The man paused. "You must be talking about Will. I

heard he died in a dirt bike stunt a couple of weeks ago." He shook his head. "He was full of life, that one. Up for anything." He eyed Boone. "Sorry for your loss. I have a brother, and I can't even imagine what that would be like."

Boone gnawed his lip for a second. "It's rough, and we weren't even as close as I always wished we could be. We were working on it, though. Or I was anyway." He winced at how personal he was getting; this guy just wanted to do his job, and here Boone was, telling him his sob story. "Sorry. Just fresh."

"Hey, it's part of a good bartender's job." He gave Boone a rueful smile.

"Will left a to-do list that I found on his bedside table. Paying back McDeedles was on it. That's why I came."

The bartender looked surprised. "That's nice to know…that he gave a damn about his debts. This is a small business, family-owned for decades. But forget the tab. I own the place now, and Will was a good customer—never got too rowdy like some could. And he did pay up when he could. He was only in for…" He typed something into the iPad on the bar, then looked back up at Boone. "Fifty-four bucks. So no worries." He tapped at the iPad again. "Wiped clean."

Huh. This was unexpected. And did a lot of good for Boone's head—and heart. "If you're sure. Thank you. Very kind of you."

"I'm sure. Besides, Will was volunteering at the local cancer center. My grandfather died from prostate cancer, so that really stuck with me."

Boone froze. *What?* Will was volunteering at a cancer center? "You saw him there?"

The bartender shook his head. "Nah, my grandfather died years ago. I overheard him telling a buddy he had to take off because he had a shift at the cancer center and had to pick someone up. Apparently that was his volunteer job—he gave people rides there and back."

Boone gaped at the man. What the heck? His brother was doing this, and Boone had no idea? Why wouldn't Will have said anything? Especially about something so nice.

"I was clearing their plates," the man said, "and I remarked how that was a really terrific thing and asked if he'd lost someone to cancer, and he said no but his brother did." He stared at Boone. "Oh hey, he must have been talking about you."

"My mother," he said in what sounded to him like a strange voice; he was unable to process what he'd just heard. Will was volunteering at a cancer center in Boone's mother's memory? His felt tears sting his eyes and blinked them back hard.

"Good guy," the bartender said, then nodded and went to greet the two women who'd come in and sat at the end of the bar.

Good guy. He'd never heard those words said about Will Riley.

If the bartender hadn't told him that Will specifically said *my brother did*, he'd have assumed that Will volunteering had to do with someone else he'd been close to.

But it had been for Boone's sake. Will had come to his mother's funeral, surprising Boone and their uncle. He hadn't stayed for the gathering afterward at a friend of his mother's home, but he'd been there at the service and graveside. That had meant a lot to Boone. He'd known there was a good heart in there and maybe with more time, he'd have grown into the person Boone knew he could be.

Or maybe that was unfair of Boone. Will had been who he'd been, and Boone shouldn't be judging.

He pictured Will in his beater, picking up a cancer patient who might not have family or friends to take them to their appointments. Will chatting away as he could sometimes, about the rodeo or sports. Will checking his phone for the time to go back and pick the person up from the clinic. With a bag of doughnuts or a coffee.

He smiled, those tears threatening again. He thought he'd known his brother pretty well, but clearly he hadn't.

That people could have good secrets was a surprise.

The bartender served his burger, which was excellent, then refused his money. Boone was deeply touched and shook his hand. He walked away from McDeedles with the kind of good shock he'd felt at discovering he had a nephew.

He couldn't wait to share all this with Sarah. And Angus. And one day, Cody.

Boone crossed the street and headed into Drink Up, which had just opened at noon. There were a bunch of people already inside too—a middle-aged couple at the bar and a few men at a table with a pitcher.

Boone wondered what he might learn about his brother here. But when he told the bartender, a tall, thin man in his fifties and wearing a Stetson, why he'd come, the guy frowned.

He tapped at the iPad on the bar. "He owed one hundred forty-seven dollars. Fifty-seven for his bar tab, and the rest for the mirror he broke that used to hang on that wall," he added pointing with a scowl. "Got into a fight with a guy whose girlfriend he tried to pick up right in front of him. Real character." He shook his head.

"Yeah," Boone said, except now not much could dim the admiration he felt for Will at the moment.

"Sorry," the guy added as though he remembered he was talking about the dead.

Boone nodded and handed over one fifty in cash; he'd taken out a wad of money from an ATM before leaving Darlington when he'd known he'd be paying people back. There was one more name on the list—Eli Charlton.

"I appreciate this," the bartender said. "My dad owns this place and is too much of a softy when people can't pay. He never cuts them off, which is why I started working more hours. How we're still in business…"

Boone nodded and got the hell out of there. At least one of the bar experiences had been easy on him. He mentally checked off those two bars from the list. Back in his truck, he typed Eli Charlson's name into the search engine. Apparently he was a rancher in town who owned a breeding operation. Boone had had enough of Darlington and surprises for one day, though. He'd go see Eli Charlson another time.

Right now, he had to get his head together. Between everything he was learning and thinking about, and the situation with Sarah, he needed a breather. He knew just where to get that too. The Dawson Family Guest Ranch, his new place of employment, where he could familiarize himself with the grounds by taking a good long walk around the property. The land, the mountains, the stables and grounds, the riverbank, all that beautiful summer air…he'd get his equilibrium back.

And he'd *feel* Sarah and Cody steeped into each step of the namesake ranch, reminding him that ignoring his feelings for Sarah was the right thing to do.

By the time he arrived at ranch's gates, he was already feeling more himself.

Chapter Twelve

Sarah had spent the morning on housekeeping. Laundry, a deep clean on the kitchen and bathroom, which had been a great distraction from her thoughts, an unnecessary organizing of her cabinets, and then checking in with her matchmaking clients. Lindy was going on a first date tomorrow night to Manelli's and was "warily excited," which made Sarah smile. She knew all about that feeling. Though right now, Sarah was all about the wary. And Deanna had texted to apologize for "being too inside" her head and said she was going to call Jeremy about getting together. Sarah was so glad for the both of them.

The distractions had worked. And at least her small apartment was spotless and smelled nice, her row of spices in alphabetical order. But the moment there wasn't a single thing left to do in her apartment other than feed her baby son, her brain went right back to the kiss.

It's just a crush on a handsome, nice guy, she told herself. *A guy who's important in your son's life. Special.*

She could tell herself that was all she wanted, but her burgeoning feelings for Boone could hardly be called a crush. He was the man—in heart, mind, and soul—

who she wished she could find for those who sought her matchmaking services.

When Cody had finished his bottle, Sarah knew she needed solid advice and arranged to meet the Cartwells at the Dawson Family Guest Ranch cafeteria. Cody would sleep through it for his afternoon nap. She needed Annie's positivity and Doreen to play devil's advocate.

An hour later, she was getting exactly that. The three of them had barely taken one bite out of their sandwiches in a back booth at the café before she blurted out that she'd kissed Boone.

"I knew there would be a kiss sooner than later!" Annie said, her hazel eyes twinkling.

"Was it just so-so?" Doreen asked, narrowing her eyes. "No sparks?"

Sarah grinned. This was exactly what she needed from Doreen—the naysayer, the negativity, the real questions. "Actually, I felt it in my *toes*," Sarah admitted.

"Oh boy," Annie said, her expression getting even more dreamy. "Toe-curling kiss."

Doreen reached across the table for Sarah's hand. Which meant she was about to get very serious. "Honey, I give up. I like everything you've told me about this man."

Sarah waited. And waited. But Doreen seemed to be finished. She patted Sarah's hand and then picked up her BLT and took a bite.

"Wait, you're saying you think the kiss was a good thing? Despite the problems getting involved with him could cause?"

"Look, there are times to be cautious," Doreen said. "Like with a guy you barely know. A smooth talker. A love bomber. But Boone seems to be a really great guy.

The way he is with Cody—I've only heard secondhand, and I'm swooning over what an amazing uncle he is. He took you and Cody to meet his uncle—*and* to get you and the baby away from the paint fumes. He bought you a new nursery—and then put everything together. He got a job here to be closer to Cody. And you, clearly."

Sarah felt goose bumps—the good kind—race along her spine. Boone was everything she'd always hoped she'd find. No red flags. No yellow flags, even. Except when it came to how a breakup could affect them all. She brought that up. "That *is* a real issue, though," she said.

Annie took another bite of her chicken-salad wrap. "Think of it this way, Sarah. Ten years from now, you and Boone have been happily married for almost a decade, have two more kids, and you have everything you've ever wanted. You're gonna let 'but what if…' stand in the way of that?"

"You're getting way ahead of yourself, Annie," Sarah said, her gaze briefly stopping on her friend's twinkling diamond engagement ring. "We're not even dating. In fact, we agreed *not* to date. To be platonic. Friends."

Doreen waved her free hand in the air. "Eh, that was this morning. I think you two need a new agreement."

Sarah smiled. "And that is?"

"To follow your hearts—and yes, to pay attention to your worries too. That means both of you insisting on transparency, honesty, and realizing that if it doesn't work out, Cody needs to come first, not your egos or pride. If one of you gets hurt, you have to agree that it can't affect his relationship with his nephew."

"Okay, now *I'm* playing devil's advocate," Annie said. "Isn't that easier said than done? I mean, right now, all's great. They have the serious hots for each other. What if Boone does disappoint Sarah—she's human, flesh and blood. Of course being hurt and upset will have an impact on wanting to be around him." She frowned as if realizing she'd turned into her mother, who'd turned into *her*.

Sarah bit her lip. "So what do I do?"

Annie and her mother looked at each other, then both turned to Sarah. "I think you just have to go with how you feel," Annie said. "Right, Mom?"

Doreen nodded. "You know who you are, Sarah. And Boone has shown himself to be of solid character. I'll put my trust in you two to navigate this like grown-ups."

"Grown-ups can be very childish," Sarah pointed out.

"I'll amend, then," Doreen said. "I'll trust you two to act like the good, compassionate people you are."

Annie raised her iced coffee. "I say we clink on that so she can go tell Boone the good news. That there's more where that kiss came from." She puckered up, and Doreen laughed.

Sarah felt more goose bumps slide up her arms and across her neck. The people she trusted most were giving her permission to follow her heart—if not her head, which was still saying *Noooo*. But there was a blinking yellow sign reading *Proceed with caution*. She'd do that.

"And after you two are done making out, see if he can meet us in the park this weekend," Doreen said. "It's high time we met this man."

Sarah grinned. She liked the idea of a long kissing session with Boone. "I'll definitely set something up."

Only when she was settling Cody in his stroller for the walk back to her car did it occur to her that Boone

Riley might still be a *no* on the idea of seeing where their attraction took them. Maybe she'd give the whole thing a bit more thought.

Hey, it's Sarah. Can we talk? I've been thinking...

Boone's heart leapt at the text from Sarah that night. It was just past 8:00. Still early enough that he could go over to her place.

He'd missed her all day. He'd missed his nephew, the bursts of laughter, the big blue eyes locked on his face, the sturdy little weight of him in his arms. He'd spent a few hours at the Dawson Family Guest Ranch, the ranch logo constantly reminding him of his two favorite Dawsons. He'd met his new coworkers, gotten to ride the horse he'd be assigned, walked for miles along the Bear Ridge River, and stopped into all the buildings, from the barns to the lodge to the cafeteria, where he'd had excellent chili. Once he'd thought he'd spotted Sarah pushing Cody in his stroller with two women, but they were a good quarter mile away and turned onto a path and he wasn't sure it had been her at all.

He'd been well aware that his heart had leapt then too. At just the possible sighting of her. On the drive back to his B and B he'd split his time thinking about how he was going to tamp down his feelings for Sarah and where he was going to live. He noticed a realtor's shingle a few doors down from the B and B, so he'd stopped in and gotten a solid education on the market in Bear Ridge. He could afford a small cattle ranch, and there were three for sale in town, all about fifteen minutes from downtown and just five or so minutes, in different directions, from his new job. He was meeting the Realtor tomorrow to see the properties. He'd be going from a small rented cabin to his own home. Boone felt another swell of pride about that. He was changing before his own eyes.

I could come by tonight, he texted back. And found himself holding his breath.

Great. 8:30? Cody will be asleep, but we'll be able to talk.

He frowned. Not so much that he wouldn't be able to play with the baby, but that maybe she'd be doubling down on what they'd agreed on. No more kissing. No nothing. Friendship. Family.

Which was for the best. But it just didn't feel sustainable. He hadn't been able to deal with it even in his head for more than a couple of hours. How would he handle it when he was with Sarah in person?

He left his B and B and walked the five minutes to her apartment. When he arrived on the doorstep he texted her to avoid ringing the doorbell and possibly waking up Cody.

When the door opened, he once again found himself holding his breath, overwhelmed at the sight of her. She wore faded jeans and a long-sleeved Wyoming Wildcats T-shirt. Even her feet—bare—were sexy.

"I missed you today," he blurted out before he could stop himself.

She smiled, a tentative smile, which worried him. She was going to double down on just being friends.

But then why call him over? They'd left things on exactly that—friendship.

"I missed you too," she said. "More than I wanted to. More than is good for me. Or us."

"Exactly the same here, Sarah."

She looked at him and bit her lip. He opened his arms, hoping… And she walked right into them. He wrapped her in an embrace, and she melted against him, he arms around his neck, her head against his chest.

Sarah… For a second he froze—he felt too much, way too much. But as she pulled her face away and looked at him, that was it. It was like his head and heart had joined forces.

"We'll take it slow," he said.

She nodded. "Very slow."

"Anticipation," he whispered, feeling every muscle in his body stiffen.

She took his hand and led him over to the sofa, where they sat—close.

He leaned toward her, a hand to her cheek, just taking in how beautiful she was. He could stare into her driftwood-brown eyes all night. Run his hands along her silky long blond hair forever. Breathe in the scent of vanilla and jasmine until he couldn't see straight, which was fine with him. *Go slow, go slow, go slow*, he mentally chanted.

Which meant just being together, giving both of them a chance to digest that they were giving up on platonic. They didn't have to start making out or rip each other's clothes off. Even if he was longing to do exactly that.

"Can I get a peek at my nephew?" he asked. "I know you said he'd be sleeping, but I missed him all day."

She smiled and reached a hand to his cheek. "Of course." She got up, and he followed her into the nursery. His heart pinged at the knowledge that Cody was sleeping in the crib he'd put together. He touched a finger to his lips and then gently pressed it to Cody's head the way he'd seen Sarah do a few times.

She smiled at him. "I could watch him sleep, watch his chest rise and fall, and never get bored."

"Same here. Especially in those bulldog pj's."

Sarah laughed and took his hand, and they left the nursery, closing the door.

As they sat back down on the sofa, he said, "I have an appointment with a realtor tomorrow to look at small ranches around town."

Her eyes lit up in surprise. "Buying your own place? That's putting down roots."

He nodded. "I'm serious about being there for my nephew. Really being there. For the both of you, Sarah."

She looked at him, something flickering in her eyes that he couldn't quite pinpoint. She seemed pleased by the news, though.

"I spent a good part of the day at the Dawson Family Guest Ranch," he added. "Got the lay of the land, did some riding, met my new coworkers. I start the day after tomorrow. And soon enough I can sneak over to find you on my breaks, steal a kiss."

She frowned, her entire expression and bearing changing. What had he said? She got up and walked over to the windows, peering out.

"Sarah? What did I say? What's wrong?"

Suddenly he felt like the confused Jeremy, who'd talked about the Maine mountains and unwittingly ruined what had been building between him and Deanna on their second date. Boone wanted to go to Sarah, to wrap her in his arms, but he stayed put on the sofa, instinctively knowing he should give her some space with whatever was bothering her.

She turned, then moved over to the console table where she had framed photos of Cody. She picked one up and stared at it. "Next week I go back to work. I guess what you said about finding me at the ranch on breaks reminded me of that—my maternity leave will be over."

Ah. He gave her a compassionate nod. "It'll be hard being separated from him after three months."

"In the abstract, it sounded doable" she said. "Like I mentioned when we first met, the ranch has a wonderful daycare for staff and guests. The people who run it are great—so warm and wonderful with kids of all ages. I know Cody will be in good hands. I just…"

"Don't want to be away from him for all those hours, even with breaks and your lunch hour to go see him."

She nodded. "Exactly that. I love my job. But I'm wondering how I'll concentrate when I'll be thinking about him and missing him." She put the photo down with a long sigh. "I guess I'll get used to it. Motherhood itself was a big change. Going back to work will be too. I'll figure it out."

He stood and walked over to her and held out his arms again. She stepped into him, and he just held her. "The good news is that he'll have both of us coming to see him during the day."

"That does make me feel better," she said. "And Annie will pop by to see him too. Speaking of, Annie and her mom are very eager to meet you. Up for that this weekend? We could all take Cody to the duck pond."

"Sounds good. I'm eager to meet people close to you."

She looked up at him and smiled, and he could see the trust on her face. The nervousness too. But trust.

He would not mess this up. He couldn't, for Cody's sake. Suddenly that seemed like a check on him, a guiding rule, instead of something to worry about.

He *wouldn't* mess up. He had strong feelings for this woman. And he adored his baby nephew. Everything would be okay.

"I learned something amazing today," he said, taking her hand and leading her back to the sofa. He told her about stopping at the bars, starting with Drink Up and that not-so-great conversation so that he could save everything he'd heard from the owner of McDeedles for last. About Will volunteering at the cancer center in Brewer in honor of Boone's mother's memory.

"Wow," she said, surprise lighting her face. "Was he close to your mom?"

"Never gave her the time of day. Not as a kid when my parents were still married and he'd be dropped off for a visit a couple times a month. And certainly not after they divorced and my dad was onto the next girlfriend. But he did come to the funeral—to support me, which meant a lot. I just had no idea I meant enough to him for him to actually volunteer at a cancer center. I was floored."

"I'm so glad you found this out," she said. "What a beautiful, poignant thing to learn about the brother you're getting to know even though he's gone."

A warmth spread in his chest, and he squeezed Sarah's hand.

"I found something else out too," he said. "The other woman on Will's list—Jennifer Parkalini. Turns out she's in her *sixties*. I got her number from a simple online search, but her voicemail said she was out of town for a couple weeks."

"In her sixties—interesting. I wonder what the apology is about."

"I spent a good half hour speculating. Could be anything. I'm very curious, though."

"Me too," she said.

He held her gaze, gently sliding a swatch of hair behind her ear. "It means a lot that I can talk to you about all this. About Will. My family."

"It means a lot to me too. Remember, I barely knew him. And yet Cody's asleep in the next room. I love that my son will know his father through you."

He squeezed her hand again, those worries suddenly back.

And for the first time, it occurred to him that *he* was the one who might be a novelty. Maybe the fact that he was a conduit to her baby's father was the driving force, the real source of her feelings, and she didn't realize it. Maybe she wasn't really falling for him so much as she was enthralled by the family connection.

When it's not so new, maybe she won't like the constant presence of Uncle Boone. Maybe she'll find it overwhelming. Overbearing. Maybe she'll matchmake herself with...that faceless guy at the end of the altar...

Stop, he told himself. *You two are just starting out. Exploring how you feel. Going with what's undeniable. Don't get ahead of yourself. Don't look for trouble.*

He turned off his mind and kissed her.

Chapter Thirteen

The next morning, Sarah woke up with Boone on her mind. And last night's kiss—long and passionate. He'd left soon after that since they'd agreed to take this very slowly. So slowly that their third kiss would have to wait till today.

Sarah had savored the thought all night.

He'd also invited her to tour three small ranches that a local real estate agent had arranged for him to see this morning. He'd only ever lived in room-and-board cabins on ranches as an adult, and he was afraid his standards might be low, which she found very touching. He also wanted to make sure he'd end up with a home that would suit having a pint-sized nephew over. So maybe nothing with steep stairs or on a busy road. Things he might not consider but that she would.

The man managed to deeply move her several times a day. She felt like they were in a discovery phase, learning about each other, taking it all in, giving each other time to process their feelings.

When the bell rang, she and Cody were ready to go. Boone had the addresses, and first up was a property fifteen minutes out from downtown Bear Ridge and minutes from the Dawson Family Guest Ranch, so the location was perfect. When they headed up the paved drive, she gasped at how beautiful the property was.

"What do you think, Cody?" Boone asked, looking in the rearview mirror even though the baby's car seat was rear-facing and he couldn't see his face. "Like the place?"

"*I* sure do," Sarah said, looking around, her heart actually thumping at the lovely white farmhouse with its classic black door and the small red barn. The place was wild and rustic, yet there was something manicured about it as if the owners had taken great care of it. The long driveway was a good quarter mile from the service road, which wasn't busy, a plus for having a little nephew over. And the house was an actual ranch, so no stairs at all. A hand-carved white wooden plaque was bolted onto the side of the front door: *Winding River Ranch, established 1959, with love.*

"That sign," she said, touching a hand to her chest. "How absolutely lovely. And look at that porch. So inviting. I love the swing and all the flowers."

"It's very nice," Boone agreed, staring at the house for a minute before getting Cody from the back seat. He expertly put on the chest carrier, then slid the baby inside with a kiss on the head.

The Realtor, who happened to also be a Dawson by marriage, came out of the front door with a smile. Her name was Danica Dawson, and she was married to Ford Dawson, a police detective on the Bear Ridge force. Sarah had met Ford and Danica a few times, more through town functions than through family events. He was a cousin of the Dawsons who owned the guest ranch but a third cousin of her branch.

They greeted each other, Danica making a fuss over Cody.

"I'm saving the best for first," Danica said as she led the way up the three porch steps. "This property has everything you asked for, Boone. One level, family porch, a barn, fifty acres of land that abut the woods, which has additional riding and hiking trails. And the house and barn are turnkey. It's higher priced than the other two I'll show you, but those need some tender loving care. This one, just move right in."

"I like the sound of that," Boone said.

Danica opened the door, and Sarah gasped for the second time in five minutes at how lovely the interior was. From the woodwork and moldings to the large windows and airy quality to the open concept kitchen and living room, the home was inviting and cozy. A stone fireplace dominated one wall, and Sarah could already envision the photos of Cody that Boone would set there.

There were three bedrooms, a primary and two smaller rooms, all decently sized with good closets. Two and a half bathrooms, all updated. The kitchen had been updated as well.

"Seems perfect," Boone said as they stood outside on the deck overlooking the huge yard, the land stretching forever. The mountains were visible in the distance.

"It is perfect," she said. "It has such a homey quality. It's funny how a place I've never been before can give me that feeling."

Boone nodded. "I can just see us sitting out here after work, Cody toddling around the yard."

She got more goose bumps that he'd included her in that imagery. Sarah could absolutely see herself here.

She froze for a second at how ahead of herself she was getting—they were barely at the kissing stage—but then let herself have the fantasy. Waking up every morning to her handsome cowboy. Listening to him sing that "Home on the Range" song while making pancakes for them, sitting outside on the beautiful deck, Cody in his bouncer. Evenings in the cozy living room, watching movies while curled up together on the sofa. Then him carrying her into their bedroom…

She felt a dreamy smile come over her face and quickly replaced it with a neutral expression. Nothing wrong with a little daydreaming. The places a really good kiss could take her mind was something else.

Ten minutes later, they were back in the car and then pulling up to another property, this one a bit run-down but still nice, the barn needing some work and a good paint job. There was no porch at all, but the house was in good condition—and a good thirty thousand less than the first property. Boone didn't like that it wasn't one level and wasn't sure he even wanted to see it, but Danica convinced him to at least take a look so he could make the best possible decision. Turned out the three bedrooms were all great sizes and there was even an office that Boone thought would make a great playroom for Cody. Sarah agreed it just wasn't special like the first house.

The third property was a ranch style, almost turnkey, but it was on a main service road even though the front yard was a good quarter mile away. The barn had a great wrought-iron weather vane and a horseshoe for good luck above the doors. Sarah could tell that Boone liked the place; there was something masculine about it, and she wasn't surprised that a confirmed bachelor rancher had lived here, raising chickens.

"Which is your favorite?" he asked Sarah. "I think I already know. The first one. It's a family house."

"It's very special. Just something about it. I can rattle off everything I love about it, but it's also the feeling I got while we drove up, when we walked up the porch steps, when we toured the house."

He nodded. "I know what you mean. I got that from the third place too, though. The loner-rancher's home. My Uncle Angus would love visiting me at that place." He turned to Danica. "Well, I'm ready to put in an offer."

"Clyde Minnow will be thrilled," she said, turning to look over the well-kept chicken coops they could see from the side yard where they stood. "Let's settle on the offer, and then I'll submit—"

"Oh, not *this* place," Boone said. "The *first* house. Winding River Ranch. The family house. I trust Sarah's gut reaction to it—she loved it like I did. And I need the house I buy to suit this little guy." He gently ran a hand over Cody's hair. "For decades to come."

A burst of warmth lit Sarah's chest and belly. "That house is perfect," she said.

Danica beamed. Then she and Boone talked about the offer, and moments later, with a promise to call the moment she heard from the seller's agent, she was driving off.

"Me, a homeowner," Boone said, shaking his head with wonder in his expression. "If anyone had told me two weeks ago how my life would change, I wouldn't have believed it."

"I'm very impressed," Sarah told him honestly. "And

very happy for Cody. It's like he'll always have another home when he visits Uncle Boone."

"He always will," Boone said. For a moment she had the sense he was about to add something, say more, but then he didn't.

"Let's go celebrate with lunch in town," she said. "My treat."

Boone smiled. "*My* treat. For helping me choose. And for all the help I'll need in picking furniture and décor. I don't know the first thing about decorating a house."

"I'd love to help." Although she'd likely get lost in fantasies again, about the Winding River Ranch being her home too.

"You really did it," she said as they got back inside his pickup. "You're buying a house here in Bear Ridge."

She felt her guard loosening and lowering. Something about him putting down roots, the permanence. Neither had anything to do with the two of them working out, but the man was serious. And that was everything along the road to trusting him.

After lunch at the diner, with Cody fast asleep in his stroller, they went back to Sarah's apartment, Boone easily transferring the baby to his crib.

"I'm getting pretty good at this," he said, his gaze soft on his nephew.

"You really are. You know, if you ever want to take Cody out, just you two guys, that would be fine with me."

He turned to her, the look on his face as if he'd just won a million dollars in the lottery. "Really? You'd trust me with him on my own?"

"Absolutely. You're, like, uncle of the year, Boone."

"I honestly think that's the nicest thing anyone's ever said to me."

Sarah smiled, the warmth in her chest spreading. She was falling for this man. And the feeling was so good that she wasn't letting any doubts creep in to scare her. She was just going with it. Letting the time they'd spent together and this present moment speak for themselves.

They tiptoed out of the nursery, Boone stopping just outside the door. He took her face gently with his hands and leaned down to kiss her.

She leaned up, meeting his lips with all the warmth and passion she felt.

But thcn a wail camc from thc nurscry, startling thcm both.

Boone smiled. "Wasn't he fast asleep a second ago? I was planning on that kiss lasting at least ten minutes."

"Fifteen minutes," she said with a grin.

Cody was fussing and crying, so they headed back in the nursery, Sarah lifting the baby out and rubbing his back. She could tell from his face that he wouldn't be continuing his nap. She continued to rub his back, a burp coming out despite the fact that he'd let out a monster burp after his bottle an hour ago.

"I'll give him a bath since that always makes him happy," she said. "You could spend the time making a list of what you'll need for the house. Room by room."

"If I even get the house," he said. But Sarah had a good feeling. He'd been preapproved by the main bank in town, and being Dawson-connected meant something in this town. Unless someone swooped in with a much higher offer that he couldn't counter, she knew the house would be his by day's end.

She told him as much, and he crossed his fingers, then kissed Cody on the head and went into the living room with his phone.

A half hour later, Cody sparkling clean and wrapped in her favorite baby towel with the bear ears, she came out of the bathroom and tripped on something—and almost went flying, a scream coming from her mouth. She landed against Boone's chest, his arms grabbing her to steady her, since he'd happened to be heading toward her from the living room.

She clutched Cody to her, breathing hard from how fast her heart was beating. She looked up at Boone, feeling tears sting her eyes. If he hadn't been two feet away to catch her, she would have landed hard—and Cody's head would have hit the floor or the hallway wall.

"Are you okay?" Boone asked, worry clouding his blue eyes. He looked her over almost frantically, touching Cody's face.

She was catching her breath. "I'm fine. We're fine. But God, that was scary." She turned to see what she'd tripped on.

Boone hurried over to the bathroom doorway, staring down. A piece of the flooring had come up, a loose nail exposed. "You could have stepped on this," he said angrily, shaking his head. "This place is a danger zone."

She nodded on a sigh. She was more shaken than she wanted to admit. The rent was just about affordable, and a nicer place was impossible on her salary, especially with no savings to fall back on. "Just needs some upkeep. Things come up, and I deal with them. I'll deal with this. A few minutes with a hammer and it'll be fine. I have my own cowgirl toolkit in the kitchen."

He shook his head. “You two could have gotten hurt.”

They could have. Usually what needing fixing around the apartment was limited to squeaky hinges and screens needing repairing. But Cody’s head *could* have hit the floor or wall. She shivered at the dark thought.

Boone looked troubled. He paced, then went into the living room and paced some more. He disappeared into the kitchen. Sarah put Cody into a portable playpen with the giraffe rattle Ingrid had given him, then went to find him. He was now pacing the small kitchen.

“Boone? It’s okay, really. We’re fine. We can tend to it now, and I’ll call the landlord and have him make sure he replaces the floorboards by the bathroom.”

“It’s not okay. The thought of something happening to you and Cody—over a preventable stupid floorboard…” He shook his head again. He paced again. Then he made a pot of coffee, though he’d just had coffee at the diner.

He poured her a cup, and she could use the caffeine boost. They sat at the table, sipping their coffee, Boone deep in thought. “I have a suggestion,” he said.

She tilted her head.

“I think you and Cody should move into the new house with me. You’ll take the primary. I’ll take one of the smaller rooms, and we’ll make a nursery for Cody in the third bedroom.”

She gaped at him. “What? Live together? Boone, we’re limited to kissing. We’re taking it slow. Very slow. We can’t move in together. That’s a hard no.”

Fantasy was one thing. Sped-up reality—quite another. They weren’t ready for that. It was just too much, too soon.

Boone sipped his coffee, then got up and paced some

more. He sat back down, looking at her intently. "Okay, then I have another suggestion. You two move into the house. I'll move in here—to your apartment. Let's see where we are in a few months. You and me, I mean. When it feels right, *if* it feels right, I can move in. Maybe that's in six months. Maybe it's in two years."

She bit her lip, feeling funny about this. "Move into your new house in six months? Two years? Boone. That doesn't sit right with me. That's *your* place. It's the start of your new life." But at the same time, she was also focused on how sure he seemed to be of them. That they'd still be together in six months. In *two years*.

He shook his head. "All of this is my new life. Right now—you and me and Cody. The ranch, great as it is, can wait for me. All I care about is that you and Cody have a safe place to live. We'll babyproof it. I want you two there, Sarah."

She stared at him, seeing on his handsome face how much he meant what he was saying.

"And listen," he added, "I've lived in a two-hundred-square-foot cabin with wonky plumbing for the last three years. Your apartment will be a huge step up. Stupid floorboards included. I can easily fix that. I'll make a deal with your landlord to be my own handyman, and I'm sure he'll have no trouble swapping tenants."

"Boone, I—"

"This is what I want, Sarah. You two are very important to me."

She had no doubt of that now. She was so moved that she could only sit there, speechless. Had anyone besides her parents ever cared about her this much? She knew the Cartwells did, of course. But had a man ever made her feel so special? Never.

She felt that guardrail loosening and lowering even more.

Chapter Fourteen

Just over a week later, Boone had the keys to the Winding River Ranch, a name he'd keep for the place. He liked the wooden plaque announcing it as such on the side of the front door. He also liked the significance of the name—winding like his life. The ebb and flow of a river.

And handing the place over to Sarah and Cody felt best of all. That he could do this for them filled him with a pride he'd never felt. And that he wanted to do such a thing in the first place let him know just how serious he was about being there for his nephew—for life. He was fully committed. When he'd shared the plan in a video call with his uncle, Angus had been floored. Boone had even seen tears come to his uncle's eyes as Angus had said how proud his mother would be of the man he'd become.

Once you cross off the two names left on Will's list, Angus had said, *you'll be fully ready to let the past go and focus on the future. That's good for you, Boone.*

He wholeheartedly agreed. Boone believed a certain peace would come over him when he finally took care of paying back Eli Charlton and delivering Will's apology to Jennifer Parkalini. He'd been so busy that he hadn't gotten in touch yet with Charlton, but he'd plan on that in the coming days. A few days ago, when he'd expected Jennifer to be back, he'd called her again but gotten her voicemail, which was unchanged. Perhaps she'd extended her trip or simply had forgotten to change her outgoing message. He'd keep trying every couple of days until he got ahold of her.

He'd been focused on his new job, the ranch, and the Dawsons. Every day after work at the Dawson Family Guest Ranch—Boone's hours were 7:00 a.m. to 3:00 p.m. with two breaks and forty-five minutes for lunch, kindly subsidized at the cafeteria—he'd helped Sarah pack up what she wanted to move from her apartment to the ranch. There wasn't much aside from personal things and Cody's belongings. She'd told him that she'd grown up in a few rental houses in Bear Ridge, her parents never quite able to swing buying a home, particularly after her mom died. When she'd moved out after high school graduation and had shared a bunkhouse with a couple of other cowgirls, she hadn't needed furniture. Until she'd gotten pregnant last year and needed a place of her own.

When she'd shared even more of her history with him, he was doubly glad she was moving into ranch. He'd really felt for her as she'd told him that her dad had insisted she take what she needed from his rental house, but it was bare bones as it was and she'd done pretty well at thrift shops. And after her father's death, she'd needed to sell most of the furniture to help with his medical bills. She'd taken a few special items, the way Boone had when he'd lost his mother and brother.

She'd never had much, and it meant a lot to him to be able to provide for her and Cody. He also could tell she was struggling with accepting his help, so he'd remind her that it was all for his nephew.

But it was for her too. He wanted to give Sarah Dawson everything. Everything she'd never had, everything she dreamed of for her baby. For her future. This past week, the moments his chest would tighten with worry that he'd mess things up with Sarah were fewer and further between. Maybe because they were taking things so slow. All they'd done was kiss. Hello, goodbye, a few times during the day in reaction to something. Nothing too crazy, nothing too passionate. Baby steps.

That he'd insisted she and Cody move to the ranch had caught them both by surprise—what it meant, how much he cared about the Dawson duo, that they'd been a little shy around each other the first couple of days after they'd agreed on the plan. That electric air all around them had calmed down into something a little sweeter, a little more tentative, both clearly a bit nervous that Boone was all in. And he was.

These last several days, he might have used taking apart the crib and doing some measuring of the apartment since he'd be taking over the place as an excuse to come over, but Sarah always sounded pleased and then happy to see him. He'd either bring over dinner or they'd cook together. Then they'd share in the bedtime routine for Cody, Boone telling his nephew how much he loved being a cowboy at the Dawson Family Guest Ranch, that he'd already made a solid buddy and had a lot of respect for his new boss.

They'd get Cody ready for bed, laughing over the way his hair formed peaks with the shampoo and how Cody loved—strangely—water being poured over his head.

Huge baby laughter. Once he was dried and changed into his new pj's, Boone would nestle Cody in his arms in the new glider chair he'd insisted on ordering, telling his nephew a made-up story about farm animals, then singing him a song. Boone had mastered putting a sleepy, droopy-eyed Cody into his new crib, and then he and Sarah would spend a couple of hours together, just enjoying each other's company.

They'd learned little things about each other. That her middle name was Joy. That he'd never loved pizza like most people. That they were both really good spellers, enjoyed superhero movies and taking Cody for long walks in the stroller after dinner. He'd finally met her good friends, the Cartwells—Annie, who was also a cowgirl at the ranch, and her mother, Doreen. They were warm and friendly and definitely had grilled him a bit, but he'd seemed to have passed their tests with flying colors.

Today he and Sarah would be heading to Brewer to do some furniture shopping for the house. A sofa, a soft area rug for Cody to crawl on in a few months, a TV stand. They'd also need to furnish the two bedrooms and buy all the stuff for the kitchen, like dishes and pots and pans and cooking utensils. He was looking forward to the trip.

Suddenly he was Mr. Domestic. Like he'd thought before—changing right before his eyes. And he liked it.

That night, in the new house that she still couldn't believe she was calling home, Sarah put her new soft sheets on her bed in the primary, then settled her new quilt on top. The room was done in blues and white, with warm wood tones. It had a coastal vibe that she loved. Cody was in his new bouncer by the window, watching her intently. He'd let out a big baby laugh when she tossed each of the four pillows at the head of the bed, so she'd done it again to hear that beautiful sound.

A few hours ago, Boone and a few cowboy buddies had moved over the heavy stuff, like the crib, nursery dresser, and Sarah's dresser, which had been her mother's. For now, when Cody would visit with Boone at the apartment, he'd nap in his bassinet, and she'd left behind the portable changing table with a pad with shelves for the basics like diapers and ointments.

During the shopping trip, they'd been able to get immediate delivery on the two beds. Sarah had focused the rest of their day on buying essentials for the kitchen and bathrooms. She loved her inexpensive coffee maker, which made a perfect cup of coffee in her opinion, and wanted to bring it over to the ranch, so Boone had gotten himself a new one for the apartment.

Over the next weeks, once she felt completely comfortable with this major turn of events, she'd turn the ranch into a home. But there was certainly no rush.

Now it was time to get into the kitchen. Boone was coming over for a dinner at 7:30 p.m., and it was now 7:00. Steaks, roast potatoes, and asparagus. A solid cowboy/cowgirl dinner.

She settled Cody into the portable playpen at the far end of the kitchen by the window, then got busy at the stove. "You'll have a little time with Uncle Boone before it's your bedtime, honeybuns," she said, cutting up the potatoes and brushing them with olive oil before sprinkling them with rosemary-parmesan seasoning.

She bit her lip as she laid the steaks on the grill pan. The day after tomorrow she'd be going back to work. She must have gotten used to the idea because she was feeling better about it. That was likely due to Boone coming into their lives. She just didn't feel so alone anymore; the workday separation wouldn't feel so...dire the way it had. It wasn't just her and Cody; it was the three of them. Someone else to care about Cody, to be dying to go see him at the daycare, to talk about the minutia of a baby's day.

And it wasn't their budding romance that made her feel that way. It was the family bonds she'd noted when they'd visited with Angus. Boone felt like *family.* And that had made all the difference in her life.

She'd have to adapt to not seeing Cody all day long the way she had the past three months, but that was life. About changes. Adapting.

Think about it the day after tomorrow, then. Not now, she ordered herself. Tonight was about celebration—the new house, their new relationship. The two of them were moving so slowly that she had time to think, space to breathe, and every day they spent together she'd felt more comfortable with the idea of them as a couple. It seemed to be the same for Boone. There was an ease to him these days, from his smile to his body language to the way he kissed her when he'd first come over to when he'd leave. Warm and soft and meaningful with just enough desire to let her know he wanted more. All these baby steps had her thinking a lot about taking a big one—into bed. But there was no rush for that either.

She heard Boone's truck coming up the drive, and goose bumps ran up and down her arms. She couldn't wait to see him. After work he'd gone to meet a rancher about buying a horse, so she hadn't seen him since yesterday.

With the steak and potatoes cooking and the asparagus ready for the oven, she went out to the porch to greet him. As always, the sight of him—his tall, muscular frame, the dark hair peeking out from under his Stetson, his Western shirt and jeans and cowboy boots—made her heart leap and her mouth water.

His sexy smile as he walked up the steps and wrapped her in a hug almost took her breath. As did his hello kiss. "How have things been with the house? Settling in okay?"

"Everything's great. It's like a dream I keep expecting to wake up from."

He smiled again. "I feel that same way. Let's not jinx anything."

"Definitely not," she said. She took his hand and led him inside, closing the door behind him and heading back into the kitchen.

"Mmm, I smell something delicious," he said as he followed her. "Steaks and something else. Or could it be my adorable little nephew who smells so good?" he asked, beelining for Cody in his bouncer. He kneeled down and unbuckled the harness, scooping him out.

"Roast potatoes with a sprinkle of rosemary-parmesan seasoning. But Cody did have a bath not too long ago, so he's smelling pretty sweet."

Boone shifted Cody to one arm, then came up behind her and pressed a kiss to the top of her head. "Can I help?"

"No, Superman. You've done enough for me, trust

me. I've got this. And you've got Cody, so you're already doing me another favor."

"Not a favor when it's my nephew," he said, tipping his hat, which he then took off and set on the windowsill. "I wish I could take tomorrow off, but that's the problem with a new job. I do get off at three, though. We can spend the late afternoon in the park, maybe a picnic by the duck pond. Unless you want him all to yourself the whole day, which I completely understand."

There went her heart leaping again. "I'd love for the three of us to spend the second part of the day together. That would be perfect. I'll have the whole morning and half the afternoon, just me and my little dude."

He smiled. "It's a date, then."

"You know, I've been feeling better about going back to work. And that's because of you. You make me feel so supported." She flipped the steaks and then put the asparagus, brushed with olive oil and salt, into the oven.

"That makes me very happy, Sarah. And the way you've talked about being a cowgirl, I get the sense you really love the job."

She turned to him and smiled. "I really do." She leaned down to check the asparagus and give them a poke. Another couple of minutes. "I never wanted to be anything but a cowgirl. My mom was a cowgirl and so was my grandmother. It's how she met my grandfather."

"A long line of cowgirls. Maybe someday you'll keep the legacy going and have a cowgirl of your own." He paused and seemed to freeze for a second as if he realized what he'd said.

They were dating, after all.

And he was talking about babies. A little cowgirl of her own.

Because he wasn't thinking about them one day getting married and growing their family? Or because he *was*?

Don't read into every little—or big—thing, she told herself. *You're just having a conversation. You said something and he said something that naturally followed. That's all it was.*

She cleared her throat, staring at the seasoned potatoes. "I'm blessed to have Cody, but I'd love to have a little girl. Who knows what the future will bring?"

"Who knows?" he repeated, giving the baby a kiss on the cheek. "I can just tell you'd make an excellent big brother, Cody," he added quickly, then paused as if lost in thought. What was going on in this man's head? "I've been thinking lately about why it was so hard for Will to be a big brother. I think I should have cut him some slack."

Ah. Sarah turned off the burners. She plated the steaks and potatoes, then got out the asparagus. "What do you mean? Why do you think so?" Will had been pretty hard on Boone. When they very young, fine. But as Will got older, Sarah wished he'd been more protective of his little brother. Then again she shouldn't be judging.

Boone put Cody back into his bouncer, then rooted around in the fridge for the pitcher of iced tea. He opened cabinets until he found glasses and flatware and set the table. "He was reacting to how our dad made him feel. And I was the symbol of it. Always was. Our dad left his mom for my mom."

Sarah brought over the plates, and they sat. "You

were just an innocent little boy, though. To take it out on you…"

"He was just an innocent little boy too, though."

"That's very true," she said, softening toward Will and the boy, the teenager, the young man he'd been. He might have been four years older, but Will had clearly been hurting himself. "You're a compassionate soul, Boone." She smiled gently at him, reaching a hand to his forearm. "But you have to cut yourself some slack too… You *both* acted and reacted the only way you knew how at the time."

He seemed to be thinking that over, and from his expression loosening a bit, her words had helped. "My stomach is growling," he said, digging in and immediately changing the subject to the mare he'd seen, a beauty that he was pretty sure he was going to buy. She could tell that the subject of his brother and father were weighing on him, though. Will's loss was still recent, and the grief would claw at Boone when he least expected it. He was no stranger to loss, so he likely knew that just as she did.

"This is our first dinner at the ranch," she said, knowing he didn't want to continue the previous conversation. About baby sisters or his brother.

He lifted his glass, and she did the same. "To many more." He leaned over then and kissed her, holding her gaze.

"To many more," she repeated, her heart full.

Boone's phone rang. He frowned, holding up the phone so she could read the name running across. Ingrid. "She asked if we could exchange numbers months ago when it was clear she and Angus were serious, 'just in case.' I sure hope this isn't one of those times. She's never called me before."

He clicked Accept Call. "Ingrid? Everything okay?"

"Honestly, I'm not sure," Sarah could hear her respond. "He took off after an argument, and that was over an hour ago. He won't answer my calls. Could you call him? Make sure he's all right?"

Sarah looked at Boone. He seemed more relaxed that his uncle was likely just upset and stalking off a bad frame of mind rather than injured.

"Ingrid, I'll call him and then I'll call you back."

"Thanks, Boone. Sorry to trouble you."

"No trouble at all," he said, disconnected, and then pressed in Angus's contact button.

He got up and paced a bit. "Voicemail," he said. He tried that two more times.

He sighed hard and tried calling again. He froze, holding the phone closer to his ear. "Angus? You okay? Ingrid called me worried about you." He sat back down beside Sarah.

"I answered so you'd quit calling." Once again, Sarah could just make out what he was saying.

"Where are you?" Boone asked. "Mayfield's?" He glanced at Sarah and mouthed, *Favorite bar and grill.*

"I'm walking on the trail behind my house. I've gone miles in a loop. Maybe I should just go live out in the woods or something. Off the grid. That's where I seem to belong."

"Angus, you like televised sports and Guinness a little too much for that," Boone said, probably hoping a little levity would help things.

"What does it matter anyway?" Angus bellowed. "I

like the land. I'm walking the woods now behind my house. Just me and the mosquitos."

"Angus, I'm on my way. Sounds like you could use a nephew."

Boone frowned. He looked at Sarah. "He hung up on me."

"Go," she said. "Try to keep me informed so I don't worry, okay?"

"Will do." He kissed her, then walked to the playpen and dropped a kiss onto Cody's head. He left, and she could hear his truck starting up.

Her heart went out to Angus. The subject of marriage must have come up, the ultimatum, and poor Angus was having a rough time with it. Walking in the loop in the woods with the mosquitos nipping at him?

That Angus Riley would rather do that than try to reach a compromise—if not outright propose—to the woman he loved…

Given Boone's frame of mind a little while ago, when he'd been talking about his brother, helping Angus right now might end up helping him too.

Or take him in a totally different direction. Sarah shivered a bit, despite the nice breeze coming through the kitchen's bay window. She scooped up a very sleepy Cody and held him against her, resting her head gently on his.

Instant comfort. If only everything in life could be as simple and sweet as this feeling right now.

Chapter Fifteen

Boone parked in his uncle's driveway, sprayed himself with insect repellent, switched on the flashlight app on his phone, and set off on the trail his uncle had said he'd taken. When he'd called Ingrid back to let him know he'd gotten through to Angus, he'd let her know he was on his way and that he'd text her when he found Angus and she should go home and get some rest. She hadn't been sitting on the stoop when he'd arrived, so he hoped the poor woman was home and not fretting too badly.

He sighed and made his way down the trail, about two feet wide and surrounded by dense brush in some places, open grassy areas in others. He saw a few woodland creatures and hoped he didn't make any of them nervous enough to dart out and bite his ankles. So far, so good.

He'd walked his loop with Angus a bunch of times, so he was familiar, helpful in the dark. With only his phone's flashlight and the moon guiding his path, he didn't see much up ahead. Certainly not a six-foot-tall man who was likely wearing his trademark light tan Stetson or a similarly colored fishing hat, which would make him easier to spot.

He walked a good twenty minutes before he saw a glint of what was probably the silver trim of Angus's

Stetson. Relief washed over him as he saw his uncle coming toward him on the loop. He quickly texted Ingrid that he'd found Angus and not to worry.

Somehow Angus looked annoyed and glad to see him at the same time. He had a feeling his uncle was all talked out yet still needed someone to talk to, a typical combination for the man.

"You sounded pretty down on the phone," Boone called out as they were about to meet on the path.

Angus waved his hand dismissively, another of his uncle's trademarks. "I just want Ingrid to see things my way. But she doesn't."

Boone bit back his smile. "That's kind of how relationships are, though, Angus. We can't always get our way. There's another person in the mix with thoughts and feelings of their own."

"And when those thoughts and feelings are in opposition?" he said with a scowl.

"Were you two talking about compromising?" Boone asked, curious what had led to the argument.

"I invited her over to talk because I missed her so much," he said, his expression softening. "And she told me that she thought we both needed to compromise. If I could give her a reasonable time frame where she could expect a marriage proposal, she could move ahead with that. But if I couldn't, then she needed to move on."

"That sounds reasonable, though, Angus."

"No, it does not," he snapped, quickening his pace. "If you really love someone, you don't let them go." His face was stony, and Boone suddenly realized that this might be the core of the issue for Angus. He didn't want to have to get married to keep Ingrid, but he didn't like that she *could* walk away.

"But aren't you doing the same thing by not proposing?" he asked. "You're letting her go by not asking her to marry you."

Angus stopped walking, seeming to consider that, then frowned. "It's not the same."

"I think it is."

"Then where's your marriage proposal?" Angus said. "If ever two people should get married, it's you and Sarah. You're in love. You have that grandnephew of mine to raise. She needs you. And you definitely need her."

Boone stared at his uncle. "We're not talking about me and Sarah, though. This is about you and Ingrid."

Angus's blue eyes flashed. "Well, put your money where your mouth is and then tell me what to do."

Boone had said his uncle was a toughie, and he might have actually gotten tougher. But just as Boone had been changing in front of his own eyes these past weeks, so had Angus. And change wasn't easy. Without even realizing it, most likely, his uncle was working through all the pain, all the issues, that kept him from proposing. And Boone did believe he'd come out the other end ready to pop the question. It might take another month or two, but he'd get there. That was why the man was so darn cranky.

"Sarah and I have an agreement to take things very slowly," he reminded his uncle. "We want to do this right."

Angus stopped suddenly and hung his head, his shoulders heavy, his expression…equally heavy. He glanced up at Boone. "I know things will work out for you two. Me, I'm not too sure. I'm too set in my ways."

"Can you imagine a life without Ingrid?" Boone asked.

"No. But I want to spend my life with her without having to make a big fuss about it."

Boone sighed. "You've said that a hundred times, Angus. It's not gonna work for Ingrid. So you have to compromise. She's willing by asking for a time frame. A few months. Six months. Can't you see yourself easing up on your aversion to marriage in six months? With the woman you love by your side? The two of you could be walking this trail right now, holding hands and making plans for the rest of summer. Instead, you're being your own worst enemy."

Now it was Angus's turn to sigh. He gave a big shrug. "I want to go home." He waved away at some little insects. "The bugs are getting to me."

You're *getting to you*, Boone thought but kept the biting thought to himself, hiding his smile at his own pun.

Talking was good. At least Angus was doing that. He wasn't refusing to discuss how he was feeling. That was a good thing.

They finally popped out of the woods back onto the residential area. Boone walked Angus to his door. "Can you at least text Ingrid and let her know you're home, that you've got some thinking to do and you'll call her soon?"

Angus sighed again. "I guess."

Boone mentally shook his head. It was all a start. And all hopefully leading somewhere good for him and Ingrid.

All Boone knew for sure was that he wanted to be at the ranch with Sarah. Telling her all about this. Sharing.

Kissing her until he forgot everything jumbled up in his brain.

Sarah was rearranging framed photos on the mantle in the living room when her phone pinged with a text. Boone. Love to see you for a bit if you're up for it. I'm almost at the apartment but could easily drive past it.

Come on over, she typed back, those excited goose bumps racing along her spine. She loved that he wanted to bypass his place and come to hers. She still wasn't used to that—that they'd switched homes. It lent a *what's mine is yours* quality to their relationship, even if it was unspoken. She herself didn't have much to give Boone, but she could already hear him correct her as she thought the words. *You gave me my nephew. And that is everything. Not to mention priceless.*

He sent back the smiley-face-wearing-a-cowboy-hat emoji.

She glanced down at herself. She wore a silky lavender robe, not quite to the knees, and cotton undies. She told herself to change. It would take Boone fifteen minutes to get here. She could easily throw on a T-shirt and yoga pants to remain as comfy as she was right now. But after cleaning up the kitchen and then getting spit up on by Cody, who'd woken an hour after she'd put him to bed and fussed for a while before falling back asleep, she'd taken a shower. And put on her robe.

She headed to her bedroom but caught a glimpse of herself in the antique floor mirror she'd brought from the apartment.

She looked…sexy. She liked the changes to her body since giving birth three months ago. She was curvier when she'd always had a more boyish figure, and she had the feeling her new body was here to stay

Greeting Boone at 10:15 p.m. in a nightie-robe is not exactly taking it slow, she pointed out to herself. But it wasn't like she was showing even a hint of cleavage.

She stared at herself in the mirror. She wasn't changing. It *was* late and she *was* comfortable. And maybe she was ready to move on from kissing. All the way to the bed? She wasn't sure. She'd know in the moment.

What she did know now was that all he'd have to do was lift a finger under the "knot" on her robe's tie and it would fall open, revealing her in just white cotton underwear.

She left the bedroom and resumed rearranging photos on the mantle, including the one she'd taken of Boone and Cody the day she'd met him. Yesterday she'd wanted to get some hard copies of her zillions of photos of Cody, and when she'd been selecting her favorites to order online, she'd come across the one of uncle and nephew.

She traced a finger across Boone's face. So handsome.

She heard the tap on the door and set the photo in its seashell frame back on the mantel. She looked down at herself and sucked in a breath. Then she went to the door.

When she opened it, he stared at her, hard, taking in the robe. Usually Boone wouldn't be that obvious, but maybe he couldn't help it, which absolutely thrilled her.

His gaze traveled up to her face, then down again, then back up. "I won't stay long," he said—and was he swallowing? She was sure he *was*. "Looks like you're getting ready for bed."

Oh, maybe I am, she wanted to say. *But not alone.*

"I'm not tired at all. Despite the big day I had. So tell me what happened with Angus." She took his hand and led him over the sofa, then sat with her legs curled behind her.

He sat down right next to her and took her hand again, holding on to it. "It wasn't great. He's having a really rough time." He told her about their conversation, how Ingrid had asked him for a time frame as her way of compromising. "I'm not sure if Angus really believes what he says about how she can't really love him if she could walk away or if that's just an excuse he's using in his head."

She thought about that. "Probably a little of both. He's got some real tender, raw spots on that subject from his marriage."

Boone nodded. "Every muscle in my body is knotted up from the conversation I had with him on the trail. I just wish I could get through to him. I love the guy. I want him to be happy."

"I know. And he knows it too." She leaned closer to him, putting a hand on his arm. "Hey, turn away a bit," she said, shifting onto her knees. "I'll work on your shoulders."

"I wasn't fishing for a massage, but man, could I use one."

More goose bumps ran up her arms and her spine. "Coming right up." She pressed her hands firmly into his shoulders, kneading, squeezing, rubbing and fully enjoying his low moans of appreciation.

"That feels so good," he said, his voice low. "Just what I need."

She continued massaging, thinking about going into

the bathroom to get an oil or lotion, but she couldn't imagine moving or taking her hands off his body. She kissed the back of his neck, and she felt him practically vibrate.

He turned around, and suddenly he was kissing her, his hands in her hair. He pulled her closer, and she found herself straddling him, little between them at this point besides her underwear and his jeans. He let out a groan and opened his eyes, looking at her so intently, with such desire in his eyes that she felt herself letting go, her inhibitions slipping away.

He reached for the tie of her robe, and she kept her gaze on him, wordlessly telling him to pull. He did. The sides of the robe parted, and he sucked in a breath, his hands going to her waist and then up her sides and to her breasts. He ran his hands over them, then kissed her again, breathy moans escaping her lips.

"You are so beautiful, Sarah," he whispered.

"You too," she whispered back.

He smiled so sweetly and cupped her face with his hands, leaning in for another kiss. She slid her hands under his shirt, and he sucked in another breath, then she slowly undid the buttons and pushed the shirt off. The sight of his bare chest had her licking her lips. He was magnificent.

Suddenly he picked her up and carried her into her bedroom, laying her on the bed. He stretched himself over her, kissing her neck, her shoulder blades, her breasts, suckling her nipples until she arched her back and let out a moan. She was vaguely aware of his jeans coming off. Then her robe slipping from her shoulders until it fell in a silky heap to the floor right on his jeans.

Now they were both in just their underwear, and when he started inching hers down, slowly, looking right at her, the anticipation was too much.

And suddenly they were naked, exploring each other's bodies with their hands and lips, Sarah barely able to contain herself.

As she kissed her way back up toward his mouth, Boone let out a groan, reached for his jeans and his wallet, and placed a condom on the bedside table. "It's been in there a *long* time," he said. "Not *expired*-long, though."

"I'm just glad it's there," she whispered.

He smiled and ripped open the foil packet. Then he kissed her, long, deep, and passionately. The next thing she knew, she and Boone were one, and she was lost to the sensations, the absolute pleasure.

They exploded together, Boone dropping down on top of her, kissing her neck, holding her hand. She had her other hand in his thick hair.

"That was everything I fantasized it would be," he said.

"I was thinking the same thing."

He squeezed her hand and dropped a kiss on her shoulder. "I could go if it's too much."

"No way," she said. "I want you to stay."

He wrapped his arms around her, and she felt herself drift off to sleep. She could get used to this.

Chapter Sixteen

Sarah had fallen asleep with Boone spooned against her, and she couldn't remember ever feeling so safe in a man's arms. That today was the last of maternity leave was still poking at her heart, but it gave her such comfort to know that Boone would be checking in on Cody during his workday too, that someone she trusted was there for him.

Boone had left early, and they'd shared a long, sweet kiss goodbye and made plans to meet at the park's footbridge at 3:30 for their picnic. She couldn't wait.

Now, as she tidied up the kitchen from breakfast—Boone had made them omelets and toast—she awaited the arrival of Deanna, who called an hour ago and asked if she could stop by. Sarah hoped Deanna had good news to share about her and Jeremy's relationship, if there had been a third date.

As Sarah finished loading the dishwasher and then wiping down the counters, she found herself smiling at how good this felt. All of it. Making love with Boone. Him checking on Cody, who'd been fast asleep. Their early-morning shower together, where they'd kissed constantly under the hot spray, all four ears peeled for the baby monitor on the vanity. They'd soaped each other up and shampooed each other's hair, giggling like teenagers. Boone at the stove, flipping their omelets, buttering their toast. Sarah making coffee. Boone cuddling her baby son against his chest with a kiss on his head before handing him over to Sarah. Then kissing her man goodbye at the door, wishing him a good day and a *See you later.*

A dream she hadn't even realized she'd so desperately wanted. She'd spent the past year thinking she was done with love—for a while anyway—and she'd buried that part of herself that longed to be in a committed, loving relationship with a man who'd love Cody like she did.

Against all odds, and the complications in her and Boone's situation, she had done just that.

Since Cody was having his mid-morning nap and Deanna wouldn't arrive for another twenty minutes, Sarah sat down on the sofa with her laptop and notebook. She'd gotten another two matchmaking inquiries yesterday but hadn't had a chance to respond. As she picked up her mug from the coffee table she'd picked out, sitting on the brown leather sofa Boone had chosen, and eyed the pretty throw blanket and pillows they'd decided on together, she felt so at home. The furnishings were still bare bones at this point, but everything was a combination of the two of them.

She opened her email. A part-time twenty-two-year-old ranch hand in online college for agricultural science was hoping to find a fun, spontaneous guy with a big heart. Pluses were loving the rodeo, horseback riding, and traveling. The other email was from the cafeteria's new lead cook, twenty-three and fresh out of culinary school. He was looking for a "fun gal who loved food, horses, dogs, and learning." Sarah's eyes widened and she smiled. Her newest hopefuls could be looking for *each other*. She took some notes in her journal about them and perused the five or six singles she knew about who were still looking for The One. She made some more notes and emailed both newbies back to set up in-person chats. She had a good feeling she'd be pairing them first.

The doorbell rang, and there was Deanna, looking tense. Uh-oh.

Deanna smiled, but it couldn't hide that something was bothering her. "Love your new place. It's so beautiful. I'll fess up that there's some happy, hot gossip about you and the new cowboy at the Dawson Family Guest Ranch—that you're living here together."

Sarah hoped she wasn't frowning. It wasn't so much the gossip, which was fine—people talked, especially about the ranch matchmaker making her own match with the new guy. But she didn't want to explain the intricacies of the situation—that Boone was Cody's uncle who hadn't known she and the baby had existed until recently. That they'd just started dating. That Boone had bought the Winding River Ranch and then swapped homes with her because he wanted her and Cody to know they had a safe home.

That they'd made love for the first time last night.

That she'd never felt like this before.

"It's still very new," Sarah said, then quickly offered Deanna coffee and a pastry she'd gotten from the bakery yesterday. Once they were in the kitchen, Sarah pouring coffee, she immediately turned the subject to Deanna herself.

"Have you been in touch with Jeremy?" Sarah asked, then took a bite of the delicious mixed-berry scone.

Deanna took a sip of her coffee, then shook her head. "I know I told you I would, but I picked up my phone to call or text a few times and I just couldn't. Every time, my heart just clenched up."

"Are you comfortable sharing why?" Sarah asked gently. "Might help to talk about it."

Deanna gnawed on her lip for a moment. "When I think about why I cut things short, I feel so wrong. But then I start thinking about it and I just seize up."

Sarah sipped her coffee, giving Deanna a little time.

"I liked Jeremy so much—and then he mentioned his dream of hiking some Maine mountains, and it brought back some terrible memories for me."

"Oh, Deanna, I'm so sorry. I thought it might be something like that. That what he'd said about Maine was like a trigger for you."

Deanna nodded. "That's exactly it." She took in a breath. "My grandfather, who I never had the chance to know, was an avid hiker. He used to take my mom out on hikes, starting when she was just a toddler. Easy, kid-friendly mountains. But when she was twelve, he slipped on a wet stick and fell and hit his head hard."

"I'm so sorry," Sarah said, touching a hand to Deanna's arm.

"His death completely destroyed my nana. She never got over it and turned inward. My mom felt so alone—and at a really formative age too. She was twelve, and suddenly her mother seemed not only uninterested in her but to *dislike* her. And made my mother feel so alone." She sighed hard and sipped her coffee, turning to look out the window.

A little red bird was on a branch, and Deanna kept

her gaze on it as if it offered some comfort. The cardinal flew away, and she turned back.

"As you can imagine, my mother was pretty affected by all that," Deanna said. "She married her first boyfriend when she was eighteen, and he ended up leaving her alone with a toddler—me—by age twenty. I've seen my dad maybe a handful of times in my life." She wrapped her hand around the mug. "I must sound so dumb, dumping a great guy because he said he wanted to hike Katadhin." She burst into tears, covering her face with her hands.

Sarah leapt up and kneeled in front of Deanna. "Honey, I completely get it. Sad, painful memories, whether deeply buried or right there on the surface, can be so easily brought back. And for a man you were very interested in to suddenly mention hiking a mountain where your mom lost her dad and seemed to set the family on a lonely path… I totally understand."

Deanna sniffled and nodded. "Exactly. And every time I think of his cute, sweet face and see the word *Katahdin* come out of his lips—that a moment ago I'd been dreaming of kissing—I just close up. Like a snail going back into its shell."

"Jeremy seemed to understand that—that he'd said something that had upset you."

"I know. I feel terrible about it."

"He's such a sweetheart," Sarah said. "Do you think you could open up about it with him? Honestly, Dee, I think he'll promise you that the word *Maine* will never come out of those lips again."

Deanna gave a tentative smile, then even chuckled a

bit. "Do you think so? What if I turned him off and he thinks I need a lot of therapy?"

"He'll understand," Sarah said. Of that, she had no doubt.

"But as a matchmaker, wouldn't you say it's a lot for a third date? Hearing all that? I'll probably cry. Ugly cry. And he'll be sitting there wishing he could bolt."

"Not a chance," Sarah said. "I believe that a hundred percent. In fact, I have a good feeling that you'll be leaving wherever you have that conversation holding hands and feeling very close to each other."

Deanna seemed to think that over, then brightened some. "You really think so?"

Sarah nodded. "I really do. No doubt." And she didn't. Or she wouldn't put Deanna in the position to be hurt or disappointed. "But no matter what, it's better that you know one way or the other."

The woman took that in, then nodded and popped up. "Thank you so much, Sarah. I have a call to make to a certain very cute, nice guy." She smiled and then was gone, leaving Sarah feeling very good about the situation.

Her phone pinged with a text, and she grabbed it, glad that Cody seemed to be a heavier sleeper lately than he'd been his first three months. It was Lindy McDonaugh.

Would love to meet guy 2, she wrote. No chemistry with Lawrence. Nice guy, though.

Huh. She'd been so sure they were a great match. But sometimes what worked on paper didn't work in person.

Sarah texted her back the guy's phone number, since he'd opted for that, and wished her luck. "Guy Two" was divorced with a toddler, and Lindy was open to dating a single father.

She'd just set her phone down when she heard Cody fussing in his nursery. She'd gotten him changed and was heading into the living room when her doorbell rang. Busy morning.

It was Doreen Cartwell, holding a bakery box. "I come bearing those raspberry cookies you like." She eyed Sarah, tilting her head. "I stopped by to see the new digs and to check in." She turned and looked all around. "Wow, this ranch is beautiful. I love the red barn. What a place for a toddler to run around!"

"I still can't quite believe we're living here. How it all happened. It's a dream, Doreen."

"That Boone is very generous—I'll give him that. He keeps adding wonderful adjectives to his good points checklist."

Sarah could even think of a few new ones from last night alone. She smiled to herself. She and Doreen were very close, but she'd keep her sex life to herself.

As they entered the house, Doreen gasped. "Wow, just lovely. And so nicely furnished already. A few plants, some art on the walls, and it'll be so cozy."

Sarah smiled, proud of the Winding River Ranch. "I'll give you the grand tour."

Doreen held up the bakery box. "And I'll trade you these cookies for this little guy."

Sarah smiled and handed Cody over, who happily went to "Auntie" Doreen. "Thanks for the cookies," she said, then set the box on the kitchen counter before taking Doreen on the tour.

"What an upgrade," Doreen said, shaking her head—in a good way—as they went into the primary bedroom with its en suite bathroom. "And Boone is really living in your place next to the feed store?"

"Yup. He said *that's* an upgrade over the tiny cabin he lived on at the ranch he used to work at." The final stop was the half bath off the hallway, then she led the way to the kitchen. The open box of scones were on the table. "We have our share of treats this morning. I met with a matchmaking client."

Doreen settled Cody into his bouncer, the baby mesmerized by the slow-twirling little stuffed animals on the attached mobile. "You could be making a small fortune," Doreen said. "Especially now that you'll be going back to work and won't have the same free time. You might think about that."

Sarah smiled. Doreen had been telling her to charge for her services for months now, but Sarah just didn't see it that way. She knew people because of the ranch, had a good sense of matching folks, and it was something that made her happy—particularly when it worked out.

"Tomorrow's the big day," Doreen said, pouring cream into her coffee.

Sarah was all coffee'd out. She opted for orange juice. "Yup. I'll visit Cody on my two breaks and can spend my whole lunch hour with him. Well, lunch forty-five-minutes. Plus Boone will visit him too. Double the love."

Doreen nodded. "That's so nice. My goodness, what a whirlwind."

Sarah tried not to frown, but was Doreen saying it was all too fast? She certainly hadn't planned to sleep with Boone last night—well, beyond not changing out of her slinky robe when he asked to come over. She'd known then it was a possibility. But before that moment, she'd expected to take it as slow as they'd decided on.

"All I know is that I feel good and safe and happy," Sarah said. "You know I'm not one to be impulsive."

"Well, sometimes you can be," Doreen said, eyeing her.

She'd told Doreen about Will Riley. And another guy a few years before that who'd ghosted her. She'd certainly been impulsive then. But she'd also certainly learned her lesson. She didn't leap without looking. And with Boone, she looked hard and deep.

"What's his endgame is what I'd like to know," Doreen said, wrapping her hands around her coffee.

"Endgame?" Sarah repeated, suddenly wishing Doreen would revert back to the pro-Boone stance she'd had the other day. But Sarah was pretty sure she understood where Doreen was coming from. That he'd bought a ranch and then handed it over to Sarah to live in with her son—that was serious stuff. Doreen likely wanted to know what it all meant.

"Have you two talked about commitment?" Doreen asked.

"Not as far as our relationship."

Doreen paused mid-bite into her scone. "Then as far as what?"

Nothing got past this woman. But Sarah knew she needed this. And, frankly, wanted it. If Sarah's mom were alive, she'd be sitting here over coffee, asking the same probing questions, making sure Sarah wasn't sticking her head in the sand. These kinds of conversations weren't always pleasant, but Sarah was almost grateful for them from Doreen.

"Well, as far as his relationship with his nephew," Sarah said, realizing that would not satisfy Doreen. That had always been the case. And Doreen had been talking about something else entirely.

"Honey, he's been all in on Cody from day one. Hour one. What about the two of you, though? You're romantically involved now, right?"

She bit her lip. "We definitely are," she said, and she could tell from Doreen's expression that she understood loud and clear what the *definitely* referred to.

"So no more taking it slow," Doreen said.

Sarah bit her lip. "I guess we just feel what we feel and we're going with it. But we know what's at stake. We're very clear on that."

"I'm not trying to rain on your parade, honey. You know how much I love you. I want him to be as committed to you as he is to his nephew."

Sarah realized at that moment that she did too. She was falling in love with Boone.

She froze, then kind of melted, those familiar goose bumps racing up and down her spine.

She loved Boone Riley.

Of course she did. It was why she'd opened the door to him in that robe.

Why she'd slept with him.

Of course she wanted him to be committed to her. But it was early for that. Rushing for a word, for a label to feel safe wasn't what she was after. It would only matter if Boone *felt* it like she was starting to.

"Am I making you crazy?" Doreen asked, squeezing Sarah's hand. "I am happy for you, Sarah. Very happy. Just being a worrywart."

"I appreciate you. It's been a long time since I had my mom's voice in my ear. And she'd be cautioning me just like you are. I'll heed your advice—trust me."

But her heart was already taken.

Chapter Seventeen

After their picnic on the side of the duck pond, which Cody had stayed awake for, Boone had suggested a drive along the mountain road. It provided one of his favorite views in Wyoming, and whenever he was in need of clearing his head, he'd take that route.

Today, though, he only wanted to show Sarah something that was special to him.

"Wow, it *is* something," she said, looking out the side window at how close parts of the mountain jutted out.

Sarah, however, had seemed to need to clear her mind. She'd struck him as a little distracted, which he'd chalked up to tomorrow being her first day back at work after her maternity leave. When he'd asked if she was okay, she'd told him that Deanna had come by and opened up about why she'd cut her date short with Jeremy. He'd been right—the mention of one of the Maine mountains had been a very emotional trigger, but he was glad to hear Deanna had been planning to call Jeremy to open up about it. Sarah had also shared that she'd gotten a match wrong; a client said she had no chemistry with a guy she'd been paired with, and Sarah seemed a little disappointed that she'd gotten that wrong.

"Maybe my picker is off," she said now—and clearly the subject was still very much on her mind.

"Well, then I guess you're also talking about me," he blurted out. Was she?

He glanced over at her just in time to see her cheeks pinken. "Sorry. I guess I just have a lot on my mind. And yes, you're on it. And my clients. And Cody. And tomorrow. Back to work."

"I hope I *ease* your mind, Sarah," he said, slowing down around a curve. He had precious cargo today and would drive just under the speed limit when it came to this road. "I never want to add to your stress."

She gave him a smile. "New relationships are exciting but scary. Can't be helped. Aren't you a little anxious?"

"Yeah, I suppose. I don't want to mess up."

She took his hand and held it, which eased *his* mind.

He noticed a sign announced Raccoon Valley town limits. "Hey, I'd never forget the name of that town. Someone on Will's list lives here. The last of the paybacks—Eli Charlton. Maybe I could give him a call and I can pay him back while we're here." He still had the cash to cover the fifty bucks—and more, if Eli wanted the interest that Will had noted on the list.

"Call him," Sarah said with a nod.

Boone took the next turn off and pulled over. He looked up the guy's number and then typed it in. It seemed to be a work number because Eli Charlton answered with his name.

"Hi, my name is Boone Riley. Your name was on a list my late brother left behind—seems he'd intended to pay you back fifty bucks…with interest?"

"Huh. Yeah, I lent him that money months ago. Never thought I'd see it."

"I'd like to take care of it for him," Boone said. "Could we meet?"

"I feel funny taking the money since he's gone," Eli said. "But you say I was on a list?"

"Yeah. You and a few others. Not a long list, so I think if you were on it, paying you back meant something to him. It's why I'd like to take care of it."

"Well, okay. Why don't you come to my office? Twenty-three Main in Raccoon Valley. Are you nearby?"

"Actually, I happen to be in town right now. It's why I figured I'd call."

"Come by now, then. There's a couple of picnic tables outside. I'll be waiting there."

Boone sucked in a breath and disconnected. He looked at Sarah. "I have no idea what we'll be walking into—who this man is, what the fifty dollars was for. He'll be waiting for us at a picnic table outside his office."

"Well, at least it's a business of some kind and not a dark alley," she said gently, touching his arm. "I kind of like the idea of joining in. Not so much for me, but for Cody. Something we can share with him when he's a teenager."

Boone liked that too. But then he frowned. "What if it's something bad, though? Like at Drink Up?"

"Then we'll be glad Cody's just a baby, and maybe we won't share this particular story with him."

Boone nodded and pulled back onto the road, heading for Main Street. And who knew what.

Five minutes later, Boone slowed as he neared the number *twenty-three.* "It's a rec center," Boone said, looking at the sign on the brick building. "The Raccoon Valley Community Center."

Boone parked and found a man in his thirties in a *Raccoon Valley CC* T-shirt and shorts sitting at the picnic table. "I wonder what Will did here. Maybe took a class or was on some kind of sports league."

Sarah got out of the truck and went to get Cody. Boone pulled the stroller from back, and Sarah settled the baby in. He was wide awake and curious-eyed. "Well, let's go find out. I'm very curious."

"Me too," Boone said as they headed up the sidewalk. As they approached, the guy looked up from the brochure he was looking at. "Eli Charlton?"

The man nodded and stood, extending his hand. They both shook, and he smiled at Cody. He gestured at the table, and they sat across from him, Sarah parking the stroller at her side.

"Like I said, I'm Will's brother, Boone. This is Sarah and Cody."

"Nice to meet you. Sure was surprised by your call."

Boone took out his wallet and two twenties and a ten and slid them across. "He wanted to pay interest too. I'm happy to cover that too."

"That's all right," he said. "The center could use this, so I appreciate it." He put the money in his pocket.

"I'd like to know what the money was for," Boone said. "And how you knew Will."

"I was his sponsor. Alcoholics Anonymous. Will wasn't sure he was an alcoholic, but the fact that he wasn't sure worried him. He felt he drank more than he should, that it got him into trouble, and he didn't like that he wasn't in control of himself."

Boone frowned, his stomach twisting. "There was a flask of whiskey in his jacket pocket when he died. Dirt bike accident."

"I'm real sorry to hear that. He was something. Big personality, full of life. Always had an interesting story." He seemed to be remembering something, then looked at Boone. "Oh right—the money. He asked if he could borrow fifty dollars to rent a garden plot."

Boone looked at Sarah, then back at Eli. "A garden plot?"

"He said there was a community garden in Bear Ridge—know it? There's that popular dude ranch there. Anyway, he said he'd passed a community garden where he could rent a patch of land and grow something. He wanted to on behalf of someone who made him want to stop drinking. He told me he'd met someone who was really special but he'd ghosted her, and that she made him want to be a better person. I'll never forget it—he said she reminded him of strawberries and wanted to try growing a strawberry plant in her name."

Bear Ridge. He glanced at Sarah, and she seemed on the verge of tears.

"Do you happen to remember her name?" Boone asked.

"I don't think he said. But he told me he'd planted the seeds on the edge of the plot and he wrote her name in pebbles embedded in the dirt." He looked at Boone. "I'm sorry for your loss."

"Thanks," Boone said. "And thanks for telling us all this."

The man smiled and nodded.

"Eli?" Sarah called out.

Eli turned.

"When was this? That he borrowed the money?"

Boone knew exactly when it was. Last May. Probably not long after Cody was conceived.

"Late May," Eli said. "I remember because I commented how late May is my favorite time of year, perfect weather. I can't remember the exact date."

Boone saw Sarah's face pale, and she nodded. "Thanks again."

Eli headed back inside. Boone and Sarah stayed put, Sarah as clearly moved as he was.

"Late May," Boone repeated.

"I'm floored," she said. "It's the strangest thing—how you can think you meant absolutely nothing to someone, when it turns out you left quite a mark on them."

He felt that in his chest, in his gut. "I have no doubt those pebbles spell out *Sarah*."

"I guess what I don't get," she said, "is that if I left such an impression on Will, if he thought I was so special, why not get back in touch with me?"

Boone looked at her intently, and he could see in her expression, in her eyes, hear in her voice, that she'd moved on emotionally from that question. She might've wanted answers, but she wasn't hurt over it anymore. He could've been wrong, of course, and might've been flattering himself, but he'd gotten to know Sarah Dawson pretty well in a short period of time, and she wore her feelings on her pretty face. She wasn't asking to fill a hole, salve a wound. She wanted to know for closure, to put it to rest.

I know all this because I know you, Sarah, he thought in a kind of wonder. He'd never experienced anything like this before.

"I think it's the same thing that kept him from me and Uncle Angus," he said. "He never felt like he was enough. It means a lot to me to know he was trying the last year of his life. Acknowledging he had a drinking problem. Wanting to do right by the people he knew he'd hurt or let down."

Sarah nodded, putting her hand on top of his. "I certainly didn't know him like you did, but that sounds right to me. It's meaningful for Cody."

"Do you want to go to the Bear Ridge Community Garden and see his plot?" Boone asked. He could use a mental break from his brother, which struck him as sad, but revelations always took some processing. He'd change his mindset and gladly go, though, if Sarah felt pulled to.

She shook her head. "Not today. Another day, for sure. But not now."

He pulled her into a hug, not surprised they were left with the same reaction. "Yeah, I feel the same way. We'll go when we're ready."

She nodded and lifted up her face to kiss him. "Big day tomorrow. Back to work."

"I'll get you two home," he said.

Boone could see the relief on her face. Home was exactly what she wanted and needed right now. Tomorrow *would* be a big day, and today had been a doozy, full of those unexpected revelations. She'd already seemed distracted when they'd met at the duck pond. She could likely use a quiet night to herself.

"I'm sure I'll run into you at dude ranch tomorrow or just see you from afar," he said. "That'll be nice."

Her warm smile lit up his heart. "Very nice." She leaned toward him and kissed him, and right now, Boone felt like all was all right in his world.

Chapter Eighteen

Sarah had been assigned the stables for the week at the Dawson Family Guest Ranch, checking over the horses as they came in from guest rides or work. She could not have asked for a better placement her first week back. Some of her cowgirl duties could be strenuous or have her out in the hot sun chasing down a runaway goat, but here she was, slipping Catalina—a beautiful white-and-brown mare—a piece of apple in climate-controlled comfort. Plus, the lodge was just a few minutes' walk down the path, and that was where the daycare was housed. She'd gone to visit Cody on her fifteen-minute morning break, and just getting to hold him for five minutes and kiss his sweet little cheek had done wonders for her frame of mind. The director, Maisey, who was married to a Dawson, had let her know that Boone had visited Cody on his own morning break. She'd known he would, but it had warmed her heart nonetheless. Sarah had added Boone's name to the short list of people who could visit her baby son or sign him out—Annie and Doreen were the other ones.

Plus she'd gotten a warm welcome back, two new matchmaking clients who'd heard people sing her praises, and she'd seen Boone twice, from a distance, his long, muscular form and dark brown Stetson unmistakable. She'd run into her fellow cowgirl and friend, Deanna, who'd happily reported that she and Jeremy had talked—Deanna had opened up and he'd been wonderful and they were going out again tonight. Not a bad first day back from maternity leave.

Now she did her final check of two quarter horses who'd been returned to the stables from guests, then glanced at her phone. Time for lunch. She'd brown-bagged it so that she could eat in the lodge with Cody in his stroller. Right outside the lodge was a very long and wide hallway with huge arched windows overlooking the mountains and many upholstered chairs and padded benches.

When she arrived at the lodge, none other than Boone was sitting on one of those benches, her baby son cuddled against his chest. Her hand flew to her heart.

She'd already acknowledged that she loved Boone Riley.

But now that love was spilling over, bursting from her heart.

He must have felt someone staring at him because he glanced down the hall, and when he saw her, he smiled, his handsome face lighting up, and stood, walking toward her. He whispered something to Cody and turned the baby so he could see her.

And once again, her heart exploded with love. Her little boy and the man she loved.

As they approached, he leaned toward her and kissed her cheek. "How's your day been going? I hear you're in the stables. I couldn't get down there to say hi without being late."

"Today's been great so far. I thought it would hurt far more than it has to be away from this little darling," she said, holding out her arms to pluck Cody from him. She snuggled him against her, kissing the top of her head. She told him about her favorite horses and getting the good news that Deanna and Jeremy were going on their third date. And that she'd heard Cody had had a special visitor besides her this morning. "Thanks for going to see him."

"He was napping away," Boone said, "but I whisper-sang to him. I could only stay a few minutes between getting here and then back to the pasture. But it was worth the short time."

Her heart really would explode any second. This was all she'd ever wanted—someone to feel about Cody the way she did. And now here he was. Her handsome, wonderful cowboy. She leaned close and kissed him—a few beats longer than she normally would in public—on the lips. She just couldn't help herself.

"Aww, you guys are the poster family for getting married and having a baby," a female voice said, and they both practically jumped and turned. Coming up the hall toward them with a big smile was the new female ranch hand who Sarah had been introduced to this morning. Tina, she was pretty sure. Sarah had met several new staffers today, most seasonal employees for the summer. "Don't tell my boyfriend I said that," she added on a chuckle. "He'd run for the hills since we've only been dating a month."

Sarah felt her cheeks pinken at the assumption, especially with Boone standing right beside her, her supposed husband. But inwardly, a secret thrill sent tingles up and down her spine. She loved the idea of someone thinking the three of them were a family. Wife, husband, baby.

She glanced at Boone just then. He was smiling—awkwardly. She knew him enough to plainly see he wouldn't mind if the floor opened up and he could drop down in a chute that would carry him away from this conversation. And that he'd been mistaken for a husband. A father.

Back at the baby store, she'd thought he'd been slightly insulted that he'd been rightly pegged as the uncle. Not the dad. But he didn't seem to like being taken for Daddy either.

"Honestly, I already know he's the one," Tina said, "but a month is way too soon to be thinking that way!"

Got you beat by a couple of weeks, Sarah thought, a funny feeling landing in her gut.

"We're, uh, not married," Boone said, then his own cheeks flushed.

"Cody's my son," Sarah added, wishing she didn't always feel the need to explain herself. Some people were so good at just smiling and nodding and moving on. Sarah continually found herself saying too much and feeling exposed.

Like Boone just now. If his still-awkward expression was anything to go by.

"Oh. It's funny how much the little dude looks like your boyfriend here," she said with a smile, glancing from Cody to Boone and back to Cody. "Well, I'll let you two get back to your kissing." She chuckled again and headed down the hall.

Sarah pursed her lips.

Boone's eyes widened, an eyebrow raised, and then

his whole demeanor relaxed. He smiled, shook his head, and started laughing. "Jeez."

"Right?" Sarah said, though she wasn't quite sure what he was thinking.

And as Boone kissed both of them goodbye, since he was only on his afternoon break whereas she had her forty-five-minute lunch period, and left, Sarah felt that funny feeling grow in her gut.

Boone didn't seem comfortable that he'd been taken for a family man. Someone's husband, someone's father.

And now everything—from her happiness to her great first day back at work—just felt a little…dimmed.

A few hours later, Boone said goodbye to the group he'd taken on an easy hike up Clover Mountain—a bunch of relatives at the ranch for a family reunion—and dropped down onto a bench in front of the lodge. It was just after three, and it had felt like a long day.

Because things had taken a weird turn. His fault. He'd had an odd reaction to the ranch hand assuming that he was Sarah's husband and Cody's dad.

You guys are the poster family for getting married and having a baby...

He'd immediately felt uncomfortable, like the collar of his Dawson Family Ranch staff polo shirt was suddenly too tight around his neck and arms.

Why? That was what he couldn't figure out. He was very attached to Sarah—in a romantic sense. In every sense.

Maybe it was someone thinking he was Cody's father? Why would that make him uneasy?

Boone recalled what his mom would advise when he

was troubled by something, when he couldn't figure out his own feelings.

Just let your mind go where it wants instead of trying to block what's eating away at you. You'll get to the bottom of it.

Okay. He'd do that. *What* was bothering him so hard?

Will Riley, in his black leather jacket, no helmet, grinning on the damned dirt bike he'd bought last year, floated into his mind. That easy smile. His slightly too long hair, always tousled. Will would go quiet for like fifteen minutes and seem lost in thought and then suddenly come out with a funny joke or start a debate about hot sauce varieties.

Boone's eyes started stinging as emotion welled up, and he tried to focus on something else—Sarah's pretty face. The way tiny Cody had such a big laugh.

Let your mind go where it wants, he heard his mother's voice say.

Will. Sarah. Cody.

He pictured Will holding his baby son, smiling proudly, hoisting him up. *That's my boy!* he imagined Will announcing. Now he saw Will teaching six-year-old Cody how to ride a two-wheeler. How to fish. How to use hair gel for the coolest look.

And then some thoughts slammed into his brain.

Cody has a dad. My dead brother. Who'll never know his own baby son. Never see him grow up. Never know what he could have had.

If Will hadn't been Will, he'd have never left Sarah in the middle of the night. He wouldn't have given her a phony telephone number. They'd have dated. The unplanned pregnancy would have scared Will, which was fine and expected, but maybe it would have changed him too. Deeply moved him. Made him want to be that better man he'd been working toward with the list.

If only Will had known he'd had a child out there in the world, just a few towns away, he'd never have been doing daredevil stunts on his dirt bike at midnight, taking swigs of whiskey from the flask, though granted, the flask had been full.

He let out a hard sigh at that. He and Angus had talked about the flask at the memorial on the boat they'd taken out to scatter Will's ashes. Angus thought the fact that the flask was full meant Will clearly hadn't drank a drop. Before a crazy stunt. The flask, filled to the brim with whiskey, was there as comfort only. Boone had liked that theory. He hadn't known Will had an AA sponsor, but now that he did, it sure did lend credence to what his uncle believed.

It all helped *Boone* believe that had Will known about Cody, he would have stepped up. He wasn't sure if Will would have done so with Sarah as a partner, no matter the impact she'd made on him, but he would have as a father.

You want to believe that, but you have nothing to base it on. The word *father* was loaded for Will Riley. Who knew how it would have affected him to be someone's daddy? To be in those shoes. Will had been so critical of his own father. Surely he'd have taken the opportunity to be the opposite of Cal Riley, be the dad he'd wished he had.

I don't know, Boone thought, gnawing his lip.

But he was sure that if Will knew he was a dad, he'd have sold the stupid dirt bike to have money in his pocket for diapers and pj's and pediatrician visits. He wouldn't have been doing stunts at midnight. He wouldn't be risking his life when he was someone's father. He wouldn't have died.

Boone sucked in a breath, blinking back tears.

Will felt like you took his dad away from him. And now you're taking his son.

Boone actually gasped as the truth hit him. It was convoluted and complicated, but he'd let his mind go where it would, and that was what was knocking around in there. Maybe there was some truth to it. Or a lot of truth. Something he'd need to deal with, work out. He could talk to Sarah about it, not that he wanted to. It was a heavy thought and not one she needed dumped on her.

Sarah. Now she came to mind—her beautiful face, the warm, kind driftwood-brown eyes and her blond hair waving down past her shoulders.

Or, he thought, a weight settling in his stomach, *you got awkward about being mistaken for Sarah's husband because you're a Riley, and Rileys don't commit. And the idea of it, of you being a husband—Sarah's husband—made you squirm.*

Boone wasn't sure of anything. He took a long slug of his water and stared up at the sky, beautiful blue, fluffy white clouds.

Enough thinking, he told himself. Things were good right now. He and Sarah had a great thing going. He had a baby nephew he adored. He had this new job he loved. He'd bought a small ranch and turned it over to the woman who'd been raising Cody all alone.

He was blessed right now and should remember that.

And he'd taken care of Will's list, except for number

five. Jennifer Parklalini and whatever apology Will had in mind for her.

Try her again, he told himself. He pulled out his phone, found her number, and pressed it in. Boone waited as the line rang, and instead of getting the usual outdated voicemail, a woman answered. He bolted up, surprised.

"Jennifer Parkalini?" he asked, his heart speeding up.

"Yes. Who's this?"

"My name is Boone Riley. I'm—"

"Boone Riley," she interrupted, a slow lilt to her voice. Then she said, "Ah, I know who you are. You're Will Riley's brother. Cal Riley's son."

Huh. She knew his dad? "That's right." He cleared his throat. Who was she? What was her connection to Will—and their father?

He explained about the list. That she was on it, owed an apology. "I don't know what about or anything like that. The list just said 'Apologize to Jennifer Parkalini.' So I'd like to pass that along."

"Well, you just did," she said kind of gruffly.

"I'm hoping we can meet. To be honest, I'm trying to make peace with losing Will. I'd really like to know what he was apologizing for. And you knew my father?"

She didn't respond. Finally, she said, "I accept Will's apology. Thank you for sharing it. Toodles."

The call disconnected.

"Wait," he said stupidly, since she'd ended the call.

What the heck?

Chapter Nineteen

That night, Sarah was putting away the box of children's books that Annie had dropped off earlier. Annie and her fiancé had been antiquing and found a treasure trove of children's classics in hardcover and immediately bought them. Sweet friend. And thanks to Boone, Cody already had his own bookcase under the window in the nursery, one of the many housewarming gifts he'd insisted on buying. "One day I'll be reading you *Winnie-the-Pooh* and you'll turn the pages," she whispered to the sleeping baby as she slid the book next to the collected fairy tales of Hans Christian Andersen.

She was glad to have something to do since she was all moved in and was trying not to think too hard about Boone and how uncomfortable he'd seemed in the lodge when he'd been mistaken for her husband and Cody's father. He'd texted since, asking how she was, if the second part of her first day had been as good as the first—the answer was yes—but otherwise, radio silence.

Let him be, she thought, not that she'd call him to try to probe. *And let* yourself *be. You two will have ups and downs, and you don't have to analyze every little thing, every little expression, every blip along the way. He's given you plenty of reasons to have faith in him. And the two of you as a couple.*

Her phone chimed with a text: Up for a visit? I miss you. Smiley face in the cowboy hat.

Her heart leapt. *See, stop ruminating. Just be.*

Miss you too. And yes. Come on over.

Fifteen minutes later, he was on the porch, and the sight of him actually made her weak in the knees—and heart. He opened up his arms, and she stepped right into them, resting her head on his chest. He tightened his hold.

"I could stay like this all night," she said, the evening June breeze wafting through her hair. It was just past nine and too early for the stars to be out in summertime, otherwise she'd make a wish. That this would all work out.

"Me too." He rested his head on top of hers for a moment. "I wanted to apologize for acting weird in the lodge—when that woman thought I was Cody's dad. I've been doing a lot of thinking today—" He paused, something coming over his expression that she couldn't quite read. "I didn't even realize what it was that unsettled me until right now." He stepped out of the embrace and took her hand, leading her inside the house to the living room, where they sat on the sofa.

Sarah wrapped her arms around her knees, a little nervous for what he was about to say.

"She said, 'He looks just like you.' That landed hard."

Sarah tilted her head. "He does look like you—the coloring, for one. The Riley eyes. But why did that affect you the way it did?"

He took in a breath and let it out. "I realized today

that a lot of what's all jumbled up in my head when it comes to Will is how he always resented me for taking our dad away from him. Away from his mother and him. I guess after I heard that woman say what she did, I was thinking how here *I* am now, taking Will's son. A baby boy who looks enough like me that I could easily pass for his dad."

She took that all in. To a degree, she understood what he was saying. "Taking his son? Is that how it seems to you?"

"Here I am," he said. "In deep when it comes to Cody."

It was sinking in—Will had always made him feel guilty, like a thief, an interloper, the younger brother who'd stolen his father's attention from him—and from his life. It was part of the reason—aside from plain old loving his big brother—why he'd chased Will all his life. Now Boone, trying so hard to make peace with the loss, worried his brother was looking down from heaven and feeling that way all over again—and this time, it was his baby *son* Boone was taking. The son who Will hadn't even had the chance to know.

She took his hand and held it. This was complex and deep-rooted—she hoped she'd find the right words. "Let me ask you something, Boone. Let's say you and Will had a great relationship. No resentment. No emotional distance. Let's say you were super close. Could you see yourself doing anything differently than you have since that first day when you rang the doorbell with the list in your pocket?"

He was quiet for a moment. "No. Don't see why I would. If anything, I'd be even more uncle-y."

"I don't think that's possible," she said, giving him

a gentle smile. "But I think what I'm trying to say is that you simply discovered you had a nephew you didn't know about. I don't think your relationship with Will has anything to do with how you treat Cody. It's all *you*, Boone. It's like all you needed to know was that he's your nephew, and you loved him instantly. You certainly didn't take your dad away from Will—Cal Riley did that. And you're not taking Cody away from his dad. You're just being you—you're just being a wonderful uncle."

He seemed to be letting that all sink in, his gaze going to the photographs on the mantel. She was pretty sure it had stopped on the one of him and Cody. "Except this time I struck someone as more like the *dad*."

"That's about the depth of your feelings for Cody. How much you care. We were in that baby store on what—day one, day two after we met? Since then you've spent a lot of time with Cody. You moved to his town. You got a job here. You gave him your new *ranch* so he'd have a safe home."

He looked over at the photo of him and Cody again, his entire body seeming to relax, to soften.

"You're not taking anything, Boone Riley. You're *giving*."

He looked at her then and seemed so touched, so moved by what she'd said that she knew to stop talking, to let him have a moment.

"I don't know what I'd do without you, Sarah."

"Don't find out, okay?" She smiled, reaching a hand to his face.

He held his own hand against hers for a moment, then pulled her into an embrace. "Thank you."

She pulled back a bit, just enough to tilt up her face

for a kiss. He leaned down, the warm, soft feel of his lips on hers making her knees go weak again. Then he tightened his hold on her, and she laid her head on his chest.

"Oh—and there's something else," he said. "After work today, I finally got through to the only outstanding name on Will's list. Jennifer Parkalini."

She felt her eyes widen. "Really? What happened?"

"It was strange. The minute I introduced myself, she interrupted me and said she knew who I was, that I was Will Riley's brother and Cal Riley's son. I told her about the list, that she was on it and I didn't know why but would like to meet to pass it along. She said apology accepted, then hung up with a *Toodles*."

"There's a lot to unpack there," she said, sitting up and looking at him. "She knew your dad?"

"That was my immediate question—to myself. I didn't have a chance to ask her anything. My dad died when I was thirteen—a long time ago. He'd recently gotten divorced from his third wife, and it had been contentious. Same kind of relationship he'd had with his other ex-wives. He had nothing to his name at that point. He was working as a ranch hand and living in a bunk house with other hands. No personal effects, except a wallet with a long-expired driver's license and seven bucks in cash."

"Nothing else? Nothing from his life?"

He shook his head. "That was hard to find out. For both Will and me. I remember Will snapping at me, 'What did you expect? That he'd hang on to your old report cards or arts and crafts?'" He let out a breath. "And of course not. I knew what my father was like. But not even a damned photo of his sons?"

Sarah squeezed his hand. "I guess Will wasn't much

comfort? Thirteen is such a tough age for a complicated loss like that. You always think there's a chance you'll reconnect, get close, and then the person dies."

"Just like Will," he said numbly, and she wrapped him in a hug.

Oh, Boone, she thought, tears misting her eyes.

He held on to her, and they were quiet for a few minutes.

"My uncle arranged the funeral. It was just the three of us and a couple of cowboy friends at the gravesite."

"I'm glad to hear that Will was there," she said. "Maybe he wasn't a huge comfort to you and offering hugs and assurances of any kind, but he was there."

"Yeah. That's how I've always thought of it. Times I'd be furious at him, I'd remember that—him standing beside me in that cemetery in his black cowboy hat." He let out another breath. "I really needed him then, and he was there. He often went off about my dad, but not that day."

She rested her head on his shoulder for a few seconds, then straightened and took his hand again. "The way it's been in your family—that's all over, Boone. You've started a new tradition, and you're building a legacy. And your Uncle Angus is part of it too."

He nodded, seeming to feel better. "I'll try Jennifer again tomorrow. I want to know how she knew my dad. I'm more curious about that than what the apology was over."

"Maybe with a little time, a night to sleep on it, she'll be more open to talking. You probably just caught her off guard."

He nodded again and pulled her close.

"You're doing good, hard work, Boone," she said. "It's

not easy stuff to deal with. You don't have to know how you feel about everything and anything. Things take time."

"They do. And no, it's not easy. Which is why I'm extra glad you're in my life." He tilted up her chin and looked intently into her eyes.

I love you, she thought. *So much.*

She wanted to say the words, but now was not the time. Instead, she kissed him again, and they just sat in silence for a while.

In the back of her mind, where she did all her worrying, she wondered if all this would make him pull away instead of lean in. If it would just be too much. Especially with whatever Jennifer Parkalini had to share. But he was being so open, so vulnerable, and that was a good sign.

She'd have to take her own advice. She couldn't know everything and would just have to trust in how she felt—and the two of them.

And when he looked at her with such emotion on his handsome face, then kissed her, softly first and then more passionately, her knees got all weak again. He took her hand and began to stand, his eyes still on hers. She stood with him. He took her hand and led her into her bedroom, and there was nowhere else she wanted to be right now.

The next morning, Boone had woken up with a smile, his body and mind both rejuvenated after quite a night in Sarah's bed. She'd taken charge, which had been just what he'd needed. Had he ever had better sex in his life? Never. Had he ever felt so much during sex? Never.

He was falling for her. And instead of getting any kind of itchy feeling, he just wanted to be closer to her.

Now, having spent the last hour fixing an area of fence in a far pasture, he was ready for his afternoon break. He intended to go see Cody at the daycare just down the path. He wished his breaks were longer than twenty minutes, but at least he'd get to lay eyes on his little nephew. He'd given Cody his bottle this morning, the baby's eyes so focused on his face the entire time.

One more *never had I ever*: how connected he felt to the tiny human. And he believed it was the same for Cody. They had a bond.

He hurried into the barn where he had his locker and pulled out his backpack, taking a swig of the sweet tea in his water bottle and grabbing the oatmeal-chocolate-chip granola bar Sarah had nicely tucked into his shirt pocket as he was saying goodbye at the front door at the early hour of 6:50 a.m. Because his workday started at 7:00, his lunch period was at 11:30, and despite the big bowl of chili and hunk of corn bread he'd had, the physical work since had him hungry again.

"Boone Riley?"

He turned, surprised to see an unfamiliar person peering at him with a strange expression. A woman. Middle-aged. She wore a straw sun hat atop her long, thick, graying blond hair in a loose braid over one shoulder, and faded overalls over a tank top with daisies all over it. Hunter-green Crocs. She wasn't a staffer, far as he knew. Maybe a guest.

"I asked for you and was told you'd been seen going into this barn," she added, lifting her chin. She seemed wary and uncomfortable. "Hope I'm not interrupting. But I wanted to get this over with."

He immediately knew he had to be looking at none

other than Jennifer Parkalini. He'd called her again this morning at 9:00, figuring he'd get her voicemail, and he had. He'd left a message saying he was sorry for intruding on her, catching her off guard, but that it would mean a lot if they could talk. He'd said he'd welcome a call back or she could find him in person whenever it was convenient for her, either at the Dawson Family Guest Ranch from 7:00 a.m. till 3:00 p.m. or otherwise at the Winding River Ranch in Bear Ridge.

He was surprised she'd opted to come see him in person. But glad she had. There was so much more he could learn and glean in person than he could over the phone.

"I'm Jennifer Parkalini," she said, tossing the braid behind her shoulder.

He extended his hand. "Boone Riley. I appreciate that you came to see me. Thank you."

She accepted the handshake and nodded, tilting her head as she studied him. "Will looked more like your dad than you do. Even though he has the blond curly hair."

He almost gasped, not expecting such a personal comment, but then again, she was on Will's list for a reason and she'd clearly known their father too. "I suppose that's true," he found himself saying. "I have the same eyes and coloring as my dad and Will, but I take more after my mother."

She continued to study him, then looked off to the side as if lost in a memory, and he had no doubt she was. Of his father? Will?

"How did you know Will?" he asked, hoping she'd be forthcoming. She was here, so he assumed she'd tell him the story.

"I wouldn't say I knew him. I *met* him—completely by

chance. I was at my bank, waiting for the teller to finish processing my deposits, when I overheard the guy at the teller to my left say he was sure he had more money in his account and could the teller double-check. Then he said, 'Maybe you're looking in the wrong account. Will Riley?' And something about the name—Riley—and his face made me realize he must be related to Cal Riley."

Ah. Interesting. It was his father she'd known. Not Will.

"He looked so much like Cal," she continued. "I wanted to chat with him, and since I was done at the teller's window I hung around to wait for him. He gave up on thinking he had more money in his account and was stalking to the door, not in a good mood, obviously. I said to him, 'Are you related to Cal Riley, by any chance? You look so much like him,' and he snapped back at me, 'Why do you want to know?'"

Everything she said sounded so much like his brother that he got a lump in his throat. For a moment, Will was alive and in a bank, doing basic errands. That his brother had no money in his account and thought it was the bank's issue also sounded like Will.

"I told him I once knew Cal," Jennifer added. "And he said, 'Girlfriend? Ex-wife number ten?' That took me aback, but I said, 'Ex-girlfriend from ages ago. Back in high school.'"

High school? Maybe she'd known Angus too.

Jennifer eyed the hay bale a couple of feet away and went over and sat down on the edge. "I asked if he was Cal's son, and he said, 'Barely. And he's been dead for years.'"

Yes, that definitely sounded like Will.

"He didn't elaborate or seem particularly interested in talking to me," she added. "He started to leave, and I trailed him out. He had a motorcycle of some kind parked out front. I hovered while he was getting on."

Boone could just see Will straddling the dirt bike, getting impatient that this woman was talking to him—and having zero interest in anything she was saying despite the fact that she could share a treasure trove of information about their dad. Fill them in on things they'd always wanted to know, details Angus, his own brother, didn't have because he'd been five years older and never attended the same schools at the same time, never ran in the same social circles back then. A girlfriend could reveal so much about the teenager their father had been. But Will had been too stubborn to realize all that. Or just plain uninterested. Boone wasn't sure which.

"I told him I was sorry Cal had passed on," Jennifer said, "and that I'd always wondered about him, what became of him, that I always felt bad for breaking his heart."

She'd broken his heart? He'd never heard her name come up. If Angus had known about a heartbreak of his brother's, he'd never mentioned it. And Boone used to ask his uncle plenty about his father when they were younger.

"Will finally looked up at me then," she said. "Oh, the glare he gave me—I actually stepped back. He said, 'So it's all *your* fault. Thanks. He was a crap father because of you. Could never commit because of you. Great job.' He revved the bike, and I said, 'Wait, please. Let's talk.' But he sped off. I wish he would have let me explain. I was only seventeen when I dated Cal. I wasn't ready to run away with anyone. And we'd only been a couple for, like, three months."

"Run away?" Boone repeated. "He wanted to elope?"

She nodded. "Cal was such a romantic—in an intense way. I liked him a lot, but for some reason, he really took to me. He used to tell me how beautiful I was. That I looked like Michelle Pfeiffer. Trust me, I *never* looked like her. And he'd say, 'I can tell you anything, Jenni Cole'—that was my name then. When I got married right after graduation, I thought Jennifer sounded more grown up and nicer with Parkalini."

Jenni Cole. He'd ask Angus if he remembered that name.

"I felt so terrible for days after that interaction," she said, moving her long blond-gray braid back over her shoulder and playing with the ends. "My poor husband tried to tell me to let it go, that Cal's son clearly had issues with his dad and I was just a reminder." She peered up at him. "*Was* Cal a bad father?"

Boone felt his heart seize up. If *he* was having trouble with this conversation, he could imagine how Will, always raring for an argument concerning Cal Riley, had felt. Bulldozed, likely. Suddenly, for Will, there had been a *reason*, a poignant one, for their father's behavior that didn't stem from Boone and his mother stealing him away.

That must have really struck Will, stayed with him days, weeks after, made him think.

And maybe that was why he'd tried to be a better person. *Do better by Boone...*

Do better, period.

And Will had put Jennifer on the list, which meant

he was sorry for how he'd treated her and had intended to tell her so. That was progress.

Both chills and hot flashes ran up and down Boone's spine. He was unsettled to say the least.

"Our dad had trouble committing," he said, finally answering Jennifer's question. "Not just to wives but to his sons. He was a rolling stone."

"Ah, I'm sorry to hear that. Like I said, we'd only been a couple for three months before I ended things. For all I know, a few months later, he might have dumped me." She brightened a bit at the thought, as if she could finally shake off Will Riley yelling at her, blaming her for his dad's entire personality.

And who knew? Maybe Jennifer was right. Maybe Cal would have left her like he ended up leaving everyone else.

"We certainly have our answer about why Will wanted to apologize," Boone said gently. "That sounds like it was a rough interaction. Heck, *I'm* sorry."

She gave him something of a smile. "I guess you never know the effect you have on people. I knew Cal had big feelings for me, but like I said, we were so young."

Boone nodded. He himself had had "big feelings" for a girl at seventeen and he'd had his heart broken too. A few years later, he'd fallen for someone else, like he'd told Sarah. And he'd gotten hurt all over again. Twice burned, long-time shy, he figured. But he'd never been like his dad—marrying women he'd only known a few months, cheating, walking away, repeat, repeat.

Boone had always been more like Angus. Once his uncle had committed decades ago, he'd *committed.* Angus had been faithful. He might not have been the husband his ex-wife had wanted in the end, but he hadn't been the one to leave.

Boone knew he was more like that. If he committed, he'd *commit*. Will, though, had always taken after their dad. Maybe that was part of his ire, the older he got. That he was so much like a man he'd been so angry at.

"Jennifer, when did this happen—that you ran into Will at the bank?"

"Two months ago. It was early March."

Timing seemed about right for that run-in to have had a big impact on Will—after the fact. He'd sat down and written up the *Stuff To Do* list.

"I'm glad you came and shared all that," Boone said. "It's a big help to me in a lot of ways."

"Good," she said. "I was nervous to talk to you—afraid you'd yell at me like Will did." Her expression softened. "And I'm sorry about your brother." She stood, put a hand on his arm, then left the barn.

It wasn't until a couple of cowboys came in that he realized he'd been standing there staring into space and thinking for a few minutes. And that he'd missed the chance to go see Cody. He would after work.

The talk with Jennifer left him uneasy and there was some stuff to think about, but he didn't want it knocking around his brain anymore. It was time to get back to work. His feet weren't cooperating, though. Something kept poking at him, at his gut.

Just a minute ago, Boone had been thinking he was more like Angus than his dad. And wasn't his uncle done with love, really? The forever kind? The man was stuck. Unable to move forward.

Maybe you're the same. Stuck and don't know it. Able

to commit to a baby, sure. Your relative, your family. But what about Sarah?

Another chill ran up his spine.

That got him moving. He'd finish out his day, then clock out and go see Cody in the daycare. A little time with his favorite baby would help turn his head around.

Chapter Twenty

After work, Boone did go see Cody, which had done wonders for his mood. Since Jennifer had left, he'd been unable to stop thinking about all she'd said, but the minute he'd set eyes on Cody, wearing his pj's with the little Siamese cats all over them, he'd focused solely on his nephew. He'd signed the baby out, leaving a notation in the little box beside the time that he'd be outside on the balcony with Cody if anyone was looking for them. Sarah's afternoon break had come and gone, so he was sure it was just the two of them, and it had been. Just what he needed.

Unfortunately, the minute he'd returned Cody to the daycare a half hour later, planting a big kiss on the baby's head, the walk he'd taken along the river had brought back the entire conversation with Jennifer Parkalini.

Boone's mom had saved a photo album with their wedding pictures and others of the young couple, some with their son through age five, when his dad left. Cal Riley had been a handsome guy. He could easily envision his dad at seventeen. Harder was seeing his father heartbroken and sobbing into his pillow, if he'd done that.

* * *

Now, on his way back from the two miles he'd gone, he stopped at a big rock on the path with a nice view of both the river and the woods across, where he could see a beaver pulling twigs. He sat on the rock and pulled out his phone, then pressed Angus's name in Contacts.

"Hey, Boone, how are things?" his uncle asked. Did Angus sound a bit off, distracted?

"Okay," he said, not entirely truthfully. "How about you? Talk to Ingrid?"

"Did you call to ask about that?" Angus asked, Boone easily imagining the man's scowl.

Okay, then. He'd talk about the reason he'd called. He explained about leaving a voicemail for Jennifer and how she'd actually shown up at the dude ranch to see him. Boone told his uncle everything she'd said.

"I didn't know Dad had his heart broken in high school. Same as me."

"Can't say I knew either. I was in the army by then and didn't get home often. And Cal hadn't been one to reach out."

"Do you think the breakup made him the way he was? Turned him off love and commitment?"

Angus was quiet for a moment. "Well, he fell in love pretty easily. He loved Will's mom. He loved your mom. He loved the wife after. He stopped introducing his girlfriends after that. I guess he figured they wouldn't last so what was the point."

"Touching," Boone said on an inward sigh.

"Yeah, well, I don't know if there's really a reason we turned out how we did. Our parents were married till

Gram died from cancer. Will was six, so you were just two years old at that point."

His paternal grandparents had died when he was so little that he barely thought of them and hadn't thought to consider their impact on his dad and Angus.

"What was your dad like after your mother passed?" Boone asked.

"I guess he turned pretty inward. He certainly didn't marry again. Or date. Unless he did on the down-low."

Boone could see his lonely, grieving grandpa having a profound effect on his sons, Cal and Angus. *Love and look what happens? You lose the person and your happiness. You become a shell of a person.*

Boone felt those chills return, racing up and down his spine. He would not let this happen to his family. Not let loss, whether through death or someone walking away, turn the relatives he loved into shells.

Like you have control over how Angus feels? The man hasn't listened to a word you've said since Ingrid left him with that ultimatum.

"We can't be like that, Angus," Boone said. "We have to fight against our own nature."

"Well, that's stupid. And impossible."

Maybe so. "*Nature* might have been the wrong word," Boone amended. "We were more *conditioned* to be noncommittal. It's no one's nature to choose to be alone at heart." That seemed to describe Angus at least. Willing to be part of a couple to a degree, but alone at heart, keeping an emotional distance. "I'm just saying we have to break the cycle. And guess what you get—the woman you're in love with."

Angus didn't respond for a good fifteen seconds. His

uncle was either going to agree with a *You know what, Boone, you're right. I'm calling Ingrid now and asking for those three months to get completely behind a marriage proposal* or he'd tell Boone to go to hell. Boone honestly had no idea what was coming.

"It's *over* over," Angus snapped. "I told her there won't ever be a marriage proposal and I didn't want to waste any more of her time."

Boone's heart sank. "She must have been so upset."

A few seconds ticked by. "She said no time spent with me would ever be a waste," Angus said, his voice cracking a bit. "And then she said goodbye, and that was that."

Dammit. *Can't you hear how upset you are? This is what you want, Uncle Angus?*

Obviously yes. Get it through your thick skull, Boone. Angus is a grown man. He's in his sixties. He knows his own mind, his own capabilities. Leave him alone already.

Boone felt kind of sick, though, acid churning in his gut. He was who he was. Just like all the men in your family. *Just like you*, he thought, feeling something close off inside him. Shutter.

"Angus, I—"

He was about to say that he finally got it. He understood. In the end, Angus just couldn't commit to real love.

"Stop, Boone," his uncle interrupted, anger lacing his voice. Angus had clearly expected Boone to keep poking, keep contradicting how he felt. "You're no different. I don't see a ring on Sarah's finger."

Boone froze. Everything in him went cold. Why? Did the thought of proposing to Sarah not feel…right because they'd known each other such a short time or because he really was a Riley through and through?

He didn't know. "Let's table this conversation for now, Uncle Angus."

"For now? Try for good." And he disconnected.

Leaving Boone sitting on that rock, the chills snaking up and down his spine.

That night, Sarah sat across from Boone at the kitchen table and nabbed another slice of the excellent pepperoni pizza he'd ordered for delivery. It was so good she felt guilty that toothless Cody couldn't have any. In due time, she thought with a smile, looking over at her son in his bouncer in the corner. At the moment he was gazing up at his gently spinning mobile, enjoying the soft-playing songs.

If Boone, however, was enjoying anything, she couldn't tell. He was definitely distracted. That wasn't a surprise given all that had been on his mind last night. As she'd clocked out at the dude ranch at 5:00, he'd texted her that he'd stuck around the ranch after he'd gotten off work, walking by the river to sort through some things, and if she was free, maybe the three of them could head to the ranch and they could order in a pizza. She'd been relieved that he didn't want to retreat, take some time to himself; instead he was reaching out. Wanting to be with her and Cody.

But in the hour they'd been home, he was miles away.

"Boone," she said, reaching a hand to his arm. "Something happen?"

He took a long swig of the iced tea she'd made. "Yeah, something did. I was waiting on telling you until I wrapped my head around everything, but I guess that's not going to happen anyway."

Uh-oh.

He explained about leaving another message for Jennifer and her surprising him with a visit at the dude ranch. All she'd said about breaking his dad's heart when they were in high school. Will yelling at her that she was to blame for his dad being unable to commit to anything.

And then the heavy conversation with his uncle on the phone by the river. Angus telling Ingrid he'd never propose. Boone insisting Angus break the cycle. Angus getting angry.

"There's more, though," Boone said, staring at his half-eaten slice.

She'd been right about the *uh-oh.* But she could tell it was about to apply to whatever he was going to say.

"I've always been honest and open, straightforward with you," he said. He looked at her, then away, then back at her, his expression serious. He was conflicted.

Her heart started speeding up, and she tried to brace herself. "Yes, you have." *But stop now, she wanted to say. Just don't say anything. I have a bad feeling about this.*

She'd wondered, anxiously, last night if he was going to pull away or lean in. When he'd texted earlier about getting together, ordering pizza, she'd thought he was definitely leaning in. But now she noticed his expression, the set of his jaw, how tense his shoulders were.

Shoulders she'd kissed every inch of last night. Raked her nails on as they'd made love.

No, no, no, Boone. Whatever's got you all torn up inside, we can work it through. And when he would finally tell her, that was what she'd tell him. They'd get through it together. That was what couples did, partners.

"When I was telling my uncle that we had to break the cycle of Riley men, he said something that made me realize—" He stopped talking and glanced at Cody, his eyes troubled.

No, no, no. Hands over ears—don't say it. Don't destroy this beautiful thing we have.

Her chest started to ache now.

"What did he say?" she asked in a low voice she barely recognized, high and tight. Nervous.

"He said, 'I don't see a ring on Sarah's finger.'"

Sarah felt her eyes widen, the ache in her chest intensify. "Boone, I hope you reminded him that we're brand new. That we're both dealing with a lot, and—"

The look on his face, as she stared right at her, stopped her. There was a finality in his eyes, resignation.

Well, she wasn't going to let him go so easily.

"It's true, though. You and I are not Angus and Ingrid. We haven't been together for two years."

"Which is why maybe we should call things off now," Boone said. "Before we do get any further. I am a Riley, Sarah. I've followed the same pattern as every man in my family. I haven't been able to commit. And when Angus mentioned a ring—I froze. Then seized up."

"But you just said you told Angus to break the cycle. That you all were conditioned to be lone wolves. You can fight to join a pack. That's much more natural."

He didn't respond. He just stared out the window as if he was already completely lost to her.

"Boone, your uncle got in your head. You just need some time and space to work this through. To think about what you really want. And I think it's me. Me and Cody. As your family. The three of us—a family."

"For your sake, Sarah, I think we need to cut things off. Go back to being platonic."

"For my sake? I think it's more for your sake," she said, hating the anger in her voice, but she couldn't help it. She *was* angry.

"Of course I'm doing this for you. For you and Cody. So that two years from now, when I'm still not able to propose, you're not like Ingrid, upset and alone. So that I don't cause issues in my ability to be a great uncle to Cody."

Okay, now she was spitting mad and felt like steam had to be coming out of her ears. "Boone, I *love* you. I'm madly in love with you. And I feel so connected to you that I believe, in my heart, that you feel the same way. So you can't end this. We can't be friends. We belong together, end of story."

He reached his hand to her face, and for a moment she thought she'd made enough sense that he'd take it all back. Tell her she was right. That he loved her too. But instead he pulled his hand away and looked sorry. Like he was about to smash the heart he was breaking into smithereens.

"I'm going to put the deed to this ranch in your name but keep the mortgage in mine," he said, and the flatness in his voice, the resignation, stabbed at her heart. "I'll take care of you and Cody financially. I'll always be there for you in that regard and as a friend you can count on. You have my word."

She stared at him, a lump forming in her throat. *Do not cry*, she ordered herself. She sucked in a breath, trying to get ahold of herself. "So you're just giving up. Just like Angus. That's what you want to teach Cody? To give up? To follow in the Riley men's footsteps? To be alone? Not to be in charge of his own destiny, make his own choices based on his own heart and mind. *This* is the path you want for him?"

Boone's face contorted. The narrowed eyes, the frown…suddenly he looked horrified. And like he was about to be sick.

"I'm sorry, Sarah. But I have to go." He got up and walked to the front door, grabbed his Stetson off the peg on the wall, and left.

And Sarah's heart split in two.

Chapter Twenty-One

Sarah, Annie, and Doreen sat in the living room at the Winding River Ranch, a box of tissues and three mugs full of soothing chamomile tea on the coffee table. Half of the tissues had to be gone already. Sarah had done a lot of crying, a lot of dabbing at her eyes.

The moment Boone had left, Sarah had grabbed her phone and called Annie, and instead of being able to form words, she'd cried. Annie had said to hang on tight—she and Doreen would be right over. And they'd come immediately, Annie bringing the tissues and Doreen a quart of coffee-chip ice cream from her freezer. They'd grabbed her into a hug and let her sob—huge wracking sobs, her shoulders shaking, her knees barely supporting her.

She'd been glad Cody wasn't awake to see her fall apart completely. She'd been crying earlier but had tried to hold it together for his sake. The way she'd paced the house with him in her arms, cuddling him close like a lifeline as she'd waited for the Cartwells to arrive had soothed him to sleep early.

She'd told Annie and Doreen everything, and they'd been sitting in stunned silence for the past few minutes. Every time Doreen would open her mouth to speak, she'd shut it and walk over to the French doors to the deck and stare out. The sun wouldn't set for a couple of hours, but it was overcast now, matching Sarah's mood.

"I'm just shocked," Doreen finally said, turning around. "Nothing I've heard about this man makes this make sense." She walked back over to the upholstered chair across from the sofa and dropped down with a shake of her head, picking up her mug.

"Right?" Annie offered. "And after everything he said to his uncle about breaking the cycle, about love? Then Boone turns around and does the same thing to Sarah? Chooses the past? Chooses to be alone? He has to be thinking out loud, Sarah. Working through all this stuff. This isn't Boone."

But maybe it was. Maybe she just didn't know this part of him. After all, they *hadn't* been a couple for two years like Angus and Ingrid. They *were* brand new. Maybe this *was* Boone Riley. Like all the men in his family.

No. She shook her head and sat up straight. She refused to buy that.

But then she recalled the way he'd left, just walked out with an *I'm sorry*.

"I was so sure I'd broken through when I asked him if this was what he wanted to teach Cody. To be the kind of Riley who couldn't commit—or wouldn't. The kind who would rather be alone than risk the possibility that they could get hurt."

"I can imagine," Annie said. "That's powerful stuff. You were exactly right to say that. It's the hard truth."

Sarah felt a sob rising up in her throat. "You should have seen the look on his face. *Stricken*." The tears did come, and she closed her eyes, her chest aching.

She felt Annie covering her hand with her own. "Maybe that means you did get through."

Sarah sucked in a breath and opened her eyes. She shrugged. "I don't know. Maybe I did because he just walked out after that. Or maybe he left because it was just upsetting to hear. I really don't know."

"I do," Doreen said. "The way you said he apologized and hurried out—*that's* a man in serious turmoil. Not someone sure of his decision. Had he been sure, he would have stayed, calmly making his points. But what you said got to him, went to the heart of things, and he had to bolt. He couldn't take it."

Annie nodded. "Right now, I have no doubt he's somewhere thinking long and hard about everything."

Sarah wrapped her hands around the mug, comforting in its warmth and the scent of chamomile. She took a sip. "And what if he's not coming back? For me, I mean. I know he'll be back for Cody. It'll be awkward, but he'll never stop seeing Cody. Even if it's just at the ranch during his lunch and after work."

Her phone pinged with a text, and Sarah's heart leapt. She grabbed it off the table. *Please be Boone asking if we can talk.*

It wasn't. It was Deanna Wooley with five heart emojis. Just wanted to let you know that Jeremy and I are going away this weekend—to Jackson! We owe you!

Sarah couldn't even muster a smile. She was very happy for both of them. The mention of the Maine mountains and all it had brought up in Deanna hadn't been able to keep her from a man she had feelings for, even new feelings. Deanna was well aware that she and Jeremy had something special; it had been obvious on their first date alone. And she'd spent some time working it through and then was able to come back to Jeremy.

Maybe Boone just needed that time. The situations weren't the same, of course, but the inner angst, all that raw stuff churning deep inside, *was* the same no matter what the issue was.

She eyed the heart emojis preceding Deanna's text, longing for one from Boone right now. An *I'm coming back to talk—sorry for walking out. I love you too.*

Right. *That* wasn't coming.

Annie picked up her coffee mug just then, Sarah's gaze beelining to the twinkling diamond engagement ring on her finger.

She'd meant what she'd said to Boone—that they were brand new and a marriage proposal was far in the future. But she already knew, without a doubt, that she wanted to marry Boone Riley. That if he asked her tomorrow, she'd say yes without hesitation because she was that sure of him, of *them*.

And Boone was sure of himself as a man who couldn't get there that he was walking away early, at the start. To do the least amount of damage. She knew that was how he saw it.

"I told him I love him," Sarah said. "That I was madly in love with him. If he felt the same way, he couldn't walk away from our relationship. That kind of love would keep him here. I should just focus on that—he *doesn't* love me. I have to accept it, face facts, and somehow get through the heartache I'll be dealing with for a long time." She let out a breath, tears stinging her eyes.

Doreen leaned forward on the chair. "Let me tell you something, Sarah Dawson. Based on everything you've told me, everything I've thought over, I believe this: that man loves you so much he can't handle it at the moment. That's all this is. It's the same problem his uncle is having, but his uncle is set in his ways. Boone's not. Boone's had his whole life turned upside down—losing his brother, gaining a baby nephew, falling for you. You got through to him with that comment about Cody and what Boone will be teaching him by walking away from you. Trust me, he'll be back."

Sarah felt herself brighten some. A spark of hope. Doreen was usually right about pretty much everything.

"I agree with my mom one hundred percent," Annie said. "He'll be back. If not tomorrow, in a few days. He just needs some time."

Sarah wanted to hold on to that. But the Cartwells hadn't seen his face, heard his voice as he was telling her it was over and why. He was done.

Please let me be wrong and Doreen and Annie be right.

Had Boone ever been this miserable? Even when he'd found out his ex-girlfriend had betrayed him, when he'd been furious and hurt, he hadn't felt like this. Like his heart had been ripped out of his chest, a gaping wound being constantly rubbed raw.

He'd left the Winding River Ranch hours ago, walked out on Sarah and the pain in her eyes, all over her beautiful face, and had been lying on his bed in the feed-store apartment, feeling Sarah all around him everywhere he looked.

He'd seen her for the first time on the doorstep to this apartment. Discovered he had a baby nephew while sitting in the kitchen. Learned how to hold and feed that nephew in the living room.

He'd kissed Sarah for the first time within these four walls, which at the moment were closing in on him.

He needed to get the hell out of here, if just for the night until he could calm down, get his head together. But where would he go? Angus wasn't talking to him. He was too new to his friends at work to just show up at someone's cabin or home with a story about a breakup he didn't want to talk about. And he was all walked out from earlier this afternoon.

Go see Angus, he told himself sitting up. *Go fix things there. You can't handle losing Angus and Sarah in the same day.* Granted, his uncle wouldn't be lost to him just because they'd had words. They'd make up like they always did. And he and Sarah would always be in each other's lives because of Cody. Just not the same way. But to be so disconnected from both of them was too much.

He grabbed his keys and wallet and headed out, looking up at the stars as he approached his truck. Will's image came to him, stopping him in his tracks, his brother on the dirt bike, the easy grin, the tousled dark blond hair.

"You watching all this, Will?" he asked skyward. "I'm a mess. Send help."

He could have sworn he saw one of the stars twinkle just then, but maybe Boone just needed something to hang onto. He was aware that he no longer felt the weight of Will's lifelong resentment, that had seemed to dissipate with all Jennifer Parkalini had told Will. His brother had, just as wrongly, shifted the blame onto *her.* And Will had known he was wrong about casting blame on either of them. And he'd intended to do better by Boone and apologize to Jennifer.

At least I have that, he thought. *A huge weight lifted.*

He tried to focus on the star that had twinkled, but now he wasn't sure which one it was. *I love you, Will*, he silently said. *And I know you know it.*

And I know you love me.

He stood there for a moment, staring up at the white stars in the night sky. Feeling a bit more settled in his head, if not the region of his heart, which felt like it was being stabbed with hot pokers, he got in this truck. For the half-hour ride to Culpepper, he turned up the volume on his favorite rock station, trying to mute his thoughts. Didn't quite work.

When he arrived, the pale blue Cape Cod was dark but Boone could see a light was on somewhere inside. It was late, close to midnight, but his uncle was a night owl and he doubted the man would get to sleep before 3:00 a.m. anyway because of their argument.

Not to mention that he'd broken things off for good with Ingrid. He must've been as miserable as Boone was.

He walked up to the front door and rang the doorbell, noting another light popping on. The door opened, and there was Angus, looking like hell. He wore navy sweats and a gray Wyoming Wildcats T-shirt, his hair mussed, five o'clock shadow on his jaw and the start of dark circles under his eyes.

His uncle sighed. "I should have known you'd come." Could he look more disappointed? "If you're here to make your case for me and Ingrid, save it. I'm done talking about."

"I'm not," Boone said. "In fact, I'm here to tell you

I *get* it. It's why I broke up with Sarah today. What you said was the cold hard truth, and I wasn't ready to hear it. But you *won't* see a ring on Sarah's finger because I can't commit either. I can't even imagine proposing. I thought it was because we were so new, but it's not that. It's *me*. I'm a Riley."

Angus was staring at him, slightly slack-jawed. His uncle looked even more upset than he had when he'd opened the door. Boone couldn't imagine why. He'd just said he'd finally gotten it, he understood. Love, marriage, forever was for other people. Not Riley men.

But suddenly Cody's face popped into his head. That sweet baby, the big blue eyes, the wispy blond curls. The huge baby laughter out of that little body.

He loved that baby. So much.

This is what you want to teach him? To be alone?

Suddenly Boone's gut twisted and his chest ached all over again.

He closed his eyes, feeling like he might fall over.

"Boone?" Angus asked, concern etched on the lines in face. "What is it? You okay?"

"No. I'm not."

Angus took his arm and led him inside, then shut the door. Boone paced the living room, thankfully just illuminated by a table lamp. A bright light would be too much for him right now. He told Angus the whole conversation he'd had with Sarah earlier. And what she'd said about Cody. About teaching him to be alone.

Angus had the same expression on his face that Boone knew he'd had at Sarah's when he'd heard those words. "Oh God, Boone," he said.

"I know. I feel like I'm right about all that I said to

her—that I'm walking away from the relationship for her sake because I know I won't be able to commit, same as always. But then I get to that part—about Cody. How do I reconcile *that*?"

Angus, with a deep frown, dropped down onto the sofa. "In all our talks about this, I never thought of that. Cody's a baby. But Sarah's *right*."

Boone nodded. "We're the Rileys keeping the tradition going. Of walking away. Of not committing. And his last name might be Dawson, but that's only because Will ghosted Sarah and gave her a phony number, so he had no idea his baby son existed. Cody's a Riley, though. And we're gonna make him one." Boone felt a raw ache in his heart and walked to the window.

"Boone, I was hard on you earlier because I was mad. I shouldn't have said any of that about you and Sarah."

Boone turned and stared at his uncle. "I deserved it."

Angus shook his head. "No. You didn't. You were never like any of us. You were the *glue*. *You*. You held this family together. It should have been me, your uncle, your elder. But I was too… I don't know what. Scared, I guess. Stubborn. Broken."

"I couldn't have gotten through anything without you, Angus," Boone said. "You've been there for me."

"Not lately. You've been trying to tell me something important, and I wouldn't listen. I *did* let the woman I love go because I'm a scared idiot. I am scared of marriage. I'm scared of divorce. I'm scared of getting blindsided. I'm scared of feeling torn in two. But I don't want to teach my grandnephew to be like that."

Boone could hardly believe what he was hearing. His

Uncle Angus—changing before his eyes. Or maybe the change had been coming for a long time.

"Me either," Boone said, then paused. "I was talking to Will just before. Looking up at a star in the sky. I think maybe he's good with me taking carc of Cody on his behalf. I thought he'd be upset that I was taking his son away like I took his father. But I don't feel like that anymore. Dealing with the list, my relationship with Sarah, loving that baby to pieces, the talks you and I have had… Things are *different* now. Everything is different."

"I know what you mean. And good—you were in your own way before over that. But no matter what happens between you and Sarah, you'll be very important in that boy's life. The connection to the father he never got the chance to know. You might be his uncle, but you'll never just be one thing to Cody."

Boone felt that straight in his heart. He was so touched he could only nod.

And suddenly Sarah's words from last night came back to him. *The way it's been in your family—that's all over, Boone. You've started a new tradition, and you're building a legacy.*

He thought about all the changes he'd made. The move to Bear Ridge. The job at the Dawson Family Guest Ranch. His romance with Sarah. Which he'd blown a hole through tonight.

He walked to the sliding glass doors and stepped out onto the patio, looking up at the stars again. "I'm going to do right by you, Will," he whispered. "I thought taking care of your to-do list would take care of that. But it's not just about that. I know that now. It's about being the man I want to be, the man I can be."

He closed his eyes for a second, feeling his promise snake its way inside, deep in his heart. He came back in, closing the door behind him.

“I heard that,” Angus said, his eyes misty. He walked over to Boone and pulled him into a hug. “Good for you.”

Boone tightened his hold on his uncle, then stepped back, feeling his own eyes get misty. “I want to teach Cody how to be a man. The man Will would want him to be if he’d known he’d had a son. A loving, kind, generous man. A man who doesn’t walk away from those he loves.”

Angus put a hand on Boone’s shoulder. “I want to teach him that also. It’s part of my job as his great-uncle.”

Boone smiled, relief flooding through his entire body. “Then we have to let go of old stuff, Angus. Fight against what feels scary as hell. Like really loving someone.”

Angus frowned and turned away, but whereas there was always annoyance in his expression before, now it was more despair. “I think it’s too late. I really hurt that woman. She’s gotta be done with me.”

“Not if you show up at her house with a diamond ring,” Boone said, wondering how his uncle would respond to that. If he’d bite Boone’s head off. “And a certain *question*,” he dared to add.

Angus moved to the sliding glass doors and stared out at the inky night. Then he turned to Boone and said, “I will if you will.”

Now it was Boone’s turn to stare slack-jawed at his uncle.

Chapter Twenty-Two

Sarah didn't hear from Boone that night, not that she expected to—but a little hope had been burning bright. She'd tossed and turned till close to 2:00 a.m., alternating between crying, taking care of Cody when he'd woken up twice, then heading back to bed and looking a few times at that sweet photo of nephew and uncle on her phone. All that had done was make her more upset, but she'd been so drawn to the picture.

In the morning, she'd made a strong cup of coffee and filled her travel mug, determined to get through the day like the professional cowgirl she was. She'd actually been glad to learn she'd been moved from the stables to the petting zoo stalls, on muck duty. Raking out the goats' and lambs' straw bedding was the kind of solid physical labor she'd needed. Plus, even in her state of mind, the goats had managed to make her smile.

And she hadn't spotted Boone once all day. Another good thing. Because she would have burst into tears. Not a good look at work.

Sweet Annie had met her in the café for lunch, but Sarah had barely been able to eat her BLT. She'd run into a very happy Deanna, who'd been talking a mile a minute about how excited she was for her weekend away with Jeremy. She'd hugged Sarah and flitted off, leaving Sarah feeling a little brighter that she'd brought those two together. And while she'd been mucking out the lambs' stall in the petting zoo barn, she'd spotted a moony-eyed Lindy McDonaugh, who was smitten with the single dad Sarah had paired her with and his little boy. Lindy, who worked in the cafeteria, was mapping out a day of fun for her new man and his young son, who loved the petting zoo. Love was in the air at the Dawson Family Ranch… except in her case. Nothing new, except for a little while there, she'd thought wistfully. A wonderful little while.

Five o'clock had taken its time coming. She grabbed her backpack from her locker in the barn, eager to get to the daycare in the lodge and pick up Cody. The sight of her precious baby boy, the feel of him in her arms, would set her straight, remind her of her blessings.

Fine, that was true, but the ache in her heart was not going away any time soon.

Now, as she headed to the lodge, her breath caught in her throat as she spotted Boone pulling open the side door and going in. Was he on his way to see Cody? That was odd. It was 5:00, and his workday ended at 3:00. He certainly wouldn't be going to see his nephew when he knew she would be there to collect him.

She sucked in a breath and headed up the steps to the main entrance. Inside, she peered down the hall where the daycare was located. She didn't see Boone. But the door he went in was right by the daycare's entrance. Maybe he was already in there. Or perhaps he was visiting the ranch library on the main floor or the social room, which had a large-screen TV and a movie projector if large groups wanted to get together for a screening. He could also be on one of the many chaises on the upper balcony, which had a beautiful view of the mountains.

She pulled open the door to the daycare, greeting the young woman who sat at the front desk. She signed herself in, then headed through the large space to the baby room. She peered through the window on the door and again, her breath caught. Boone was indeed inside. He was settling Cody, wide awake with a happy expression, in his stroller.

Sarah opened the door and went inside. Larissa, one of the baby room regular nannies, was sitting in the corner by the window, feeding a baby girl, Delilah, who didn't get picked up till closing time. Larissa smiled at Sarah, then turned her attention back to her little charge.

She walked over to Boone. "I'm surprised to see you," she whispered.

Boone whirled around, his expression not quite readable but nothing like it had been the last time she saw him. "Can we talk in private?" he asked.

Did he have to look so handsome? He wasn't wearing his Stetson, and the sun lit up his chestnut-colored hair and his blue eyes.

"Sure," she said, wondering what this about.

They left the baby room and both signed out at the front desk. Boone led the way to one of the small balconies, which she was relieved to see was empty. The balconies usually had at least one couple taking selfies with the mountain behind him.

"I thought for sure you'd want to avoid me," she said, "but there you were, in the daycare at five p.m. when you knew I'd be coming to pick up Cody."

"Because I wanted to make sure I ran into you," he

said. "I didn't want to leave anything to chance. Like that if I called, you wouldn't be ready to talk. Or if I rang the bell at Winding River, maybe you wouldn't answer. I just mean that I wanted to make sure we could talk. I hope that's okay."

Hope surged in her heart. "Of course it's okay. But honestly, Boone, you don't have to explain anymore. I heard you loud and clear. You feel how you feel. I don't think I can bear listening to you tell me you don't love me all over again. It'll make me want to fight for you."

"I never said I don't love you," he pointed out. "And you *did* fight for us. By telling me you love me. By telling me that Cody deserves better than an uncle who'd teach him that love hurts. That love led to loss. That love isn't the most important thing in the world. Because it *is*."

She stared at him, almost unable to believe what she was hearing. "Boone?"

He gently caressed Cody's hair, then stepped closer to her. "I love you too. So much, Sarah. And I already know, right now, that I want to spend the rest of my life with you. I want to marry you. I don't need another minute, another year or two to know that. I know it *now*. I know I want to be a father figure for Cody. Whether I'm Daddy or Uncle Boone. We can talk about that, and how you feel is how it'll be."

She touched her hand to her heart, so moved, so happy. She threw her arms around him, then leaned up to kiss him.

He kissed her back, warm, soft, full of everything he felt. "I love you, Sarah. I love Cody. I want us to be a family. I have so much to tell you about the incredible talk Angus and I had last night. Guess who bought an engagement ring for Ingrid today? Guess who's proposing as we speak?"

She gasped. "Oh, Boone—I'm so happy to hear that I could cry. Wow."

"The ring is a real beauty. I know because I was there, helping him pick it out. I had today off."

"Ah, that's why I didn't run into you. I was half hoping I would, just to lay eyes on you. But I knew it would kill me to see you."

He touched a hand to her face. "I'm so sorry I put you through that, Sarah. I understand myself—and my family—a lot better than I did yesterday. I mean, I've been changing all along, but I finally came full circle last night and today."

"I could not be happier," she said, kissing him again.

"Oh, maybe you could," he said, getting onto one knee.

Her hand flew to her mouth, tears misting her eyes.

Boone pulled a small velvet box from his inside jacket pocket. "Angus wasn't the only one who bought an engagement ring today." He looked up at her, love shining in his eyes. "Sarah Joy Dawson, will you make me the happiest guy on earth and marry me?"

"Yes, I will!" she whispered, barely able to speak, her heart thudding.

He stood and slid the beautiful round diamond ring, set in a gold band, on her finger. They both looked at the ring, then he kissed her and wrapped her in a hug.

A few seconds later, he leaned down to get Cody from his stroller and cuddled him against his chest. Sarah cuddled close herself, and he put his free arm around her. "We're a family."

"We're a family," she repeated with a smile. "I can't wait to tell Annie and Doreen that they were right about you. They were sure you'd be back. And boy, *were* you. And I love that it all went down in the daycare." She chuckled.

He smiled too and shifted Cody in his arm. "I appreciate their faith in me. And speaking of daycare, you'll never have to drop off Cody and pick him up ever again. If you'd prefer to be a stay-at-home mom."

Her heart just might burst. "Let me think on that. I do like the idea of working part-time."

"Whatever makes you happy makes me happy," Boone said, leaning over for a quick kiss. "Let's go home. If you'll have me at the ranch."

"Oh, I'll have you. For *life*."

As they turned to head back into the lodge, Sarah marveled at how she and Boone were once unaware that the other existed. And now they were a family, united by love and a baby who'd changed everything.

* * * * *